WYATT

ALSO BY GARRY DISHER

The Dragon Man

Kittyhawk Down

Snapshot

Chain of Evidence

Blood Moon

WYATT

GARRY DISHER

SOHO
CRIME

Published by
Soho Press, Inc.
853 Broadway
New York, NY 10003

Library of Congress Cataloging-in-Publication Data

Disher, Garry.
Wyatt / Garry Disher.
p. cm.
ISBN 978-1-56947-962-9
eISBN 978-1-56947-963-6
1. Jewel thieves—Fiction. I. Title.
PR9619.3.D56W93 2011
823'.8—dc22
2011013484

Printed in the United States of America

10 9 8 7 6 5 4 3 2 1

To Scott Phillips

1

Wyatt was waiting to rob a man of $75,000.

It was a Friday afternoon in spring, and he was parked near a split-level house in Mount Eliza, forty-five minutes around the bay from the city. The house belonged to a harbourmaster for the Port of Melbourne and offered water views but was an architectural nightmare—not that Wyatt cared, he'd always known that wealth and crassness went together. He was only interested in the money.

So far, he was down $500, the brokerage fee he'd paid Eddie Oberin for the harbourmaster tip. The way Eddie explained it, the waterside unions were powerful, but so was this harbourmaster. It was in everyone's best interests for ships to moor, unload, load and depart as swiftly as possible, but some delays were unavoidable—a Filipino sailor breaking his neck in a fall, for example; a customs raid, or a strike. And some delays were of the harbourmaster's own making: three or four times a year he would quarantine a ship.

The guy's salary was pretty good, but he had expenses—gambling debts, child support and the cost of running two dwellings. An apartment near the docks, where he lived five days a week, and this split-level monstrosity in Mount Eliza. He'd paid a lot for his view of the bay, the repayments were killing him, and so from time to time he quarantined ships. Another term for it was extortion: give me seventy-five grand, Mr Ship Owner, and I'll give your ship a clean bill of health.

Time passed, Wyatt waited, and he thought about Eddie Oberin. Eddie had been a useful gunman and wheelman—a couple of credit union robberies, a payroll hit—but now he was mostly a fence and the kind of man who hears whispers and then sells or trades the things he hears. Five hundred bucks for a whisper in the right ear, thought Wyatt.

Just then a Lexus nosed out of the harbourmaster's steep driveway, a smooth, silvery car quite unlike the man himself, who was pale, sweaty and beer-fed, with small features crammed together at the centre of a large, balding head. Wyatt knew all that from having shadowed him for several days, and everything said the harbourmaster would be no threat. Unless he'd brought a hard man with him this afternoon, riding shotgun.

He hadn't. Wyatt turned the key in the ignition of a battered Holden utility with 'Pete the Painter' logoed on both doors and tailed the Lexus out of the street. Eddie Oberin had rented him the vehicle. There really was a painter named Pete, currently serving two years for burglary and unable to enjoy what Wyatt was enjoying: the bay waters smooth and shiny as ice, the distant towers of Melbourne like a dreamscape in the haze, the sun beating from the windshields of the vehicles toiling around the dips and folds of Mount Eliza, the opportunity to steal $75,000.

Soon the harbourmaster was heading down Oliver's Hill to where Frankston lay flat and disappointed beside the bay. Frankston was testament to the notion that you couldn't have too much commerce, but it was cheap, noisy, exhausted commerce, for this was an area of high unemployment and social distress. Wasted-looking junkies lurked around the station, overweight shoppers crowded the footpaths and sixteen-year-old mothers slopped along, snatching mouthfuls of cigarette smoke and urging their kids to drink Coke laced with downers to keep them docile. The fast-food joints did a roaring trade and little girls paid too much for plastic jewellery in the specialty shops.

And so Wyatt was surprised when the harbourmaster turned off the Nepean Highway into the shopping precinct. Perhaps he wanted a haircut or had run out of bread and milk, and wasn't here to collect an envelope containing $75,000.

The Lexus turned and turned again, eventually pulling into an undercover car park beneath a cinema complex. Wyatt considered his unbending first rule: always have an escape route. He didn't want to drive into the car park. He didn't want to be boxed in by concrete pillars, people pushing shopping carts, delays at the boom gates. He parked Pete's utility in a fifteen-minute zone, wiped his prints off the wheel, gear knob and door handles, and entered the car park on foot.

He found the Lexus in a far corner. The harbourmaster was locking the doors with a remote before pausing to glance around uncertainly. He was carrying a cheap vinyl briefcase. Was this the drop-off point? Wyatt hung back beside a pillar, where the weak light from outside and from a handful of overhead fluorescents barely penetrated. The air smelt of urine and trapped exhaust fumes. There was something sticky on the underside of his shoe. His hands felt grimy.

He waited. Waiting was a condition of Wyatt's life. He didn't fidget or get impatient but stayed composed and alert. He knew that nothing might come of the waiting. He continued to watch the harbourmaster, ready for a sound or a smell or a shift in the quality of the air that meant he'd better run or fight. In particular, he was watching for certain signs in the people nearby: the way a man carried himself if he was armed, listening to an earpiece or staking out the car park; the clothing that didn't look right for the conditions or the season but was intended to conceal.

Suddenly the harbourmaster was on the move again. Wyatt held back as he tailed the man out of the car park and through heavy glass doors that led to the cinema foyer. The harbourmaster led him across the vast space and out onto the footpath. Here Frankston's extremes were most apparent: the glittery new multiplex on one side, a strip of miserable two-dollar shops, a butcher, a camera store and a chemist on the other. The harbourmaster crossed the road and went down into a short mall, where a busker tuned his guitar, racks of cheap dresses crowded the pavement, and exhausted shoppers sat hunched over coffee at a few outside tables.

Soon Wyatt knew how the payment would go down. Seated at an otherwise empty table was a man wearing a suit, an identical vinyl briefcase at his feet. He was young, disgusted-looking, and Wyatt guessed that he worked for the shipping company. The suit knew why he was there. He watched sourly as the harbourmaster nodded hello, put down his briefcase and pulled out an adjacent chair. No talking: the young man drained his coffee, grabbed the harbourmaster's briefcase and walked away.

That's when Wyatt moved. He was counting on swiftness and surprise. He wore a faded blue towelling hat, sunglasses, jeans and a roomy Hawaiian shirt worn over a white T-shirt. Clothing that distracted attention from his face. His features were attractive on the rare occasions he smiled or was lifted by some emotion; otherwise repressive, unimpressed, as if he understood everything. Knowing this, he always hid his face.

He slipped into the vacated chair and his slender fingers clamped over the harbourmaster's wrist.

The harbourmaster recoiled. 'Who the fuck are you?'

Wyatt murmured, 'Look at my belt.'

The man did and went white.

'It's real,' Wyatt said, and it was. A little .32 automatic.

'What do you want?'

'You know exactly what I want,' Wyatt said, increasing the pressure and leaning down for the briefcase. 'I want you to sit here quietly for five minutes and then go home.'

His voice was mild, soft, calming. That was the way he worked. Most situations demanded it. In most situations it was failsafe. He didn't want a panic, a scuffle.

The harbourmaster took in the hardness and long muscles of Wyatt's shoulders, arms and legs. 'Are you from the shipping company? I'll just detain your next ship, you stupid prick.'

'I'll be there to intercept that ransom, too,' Wyatt said expressionlessly.

The harbourmaster adjusted his impression of the man who was robbing him, seeing behind the dark glasses a relaxed, immobile face, the face of a man who might have been sitting alone in a room. He swallowed and said, 'Go your hardest, pal.'

'A wise decision,' Wyatt said.

He got to his feet, mildly irritated for saying too much, playing this out for too long. The little mall was thronging with the lunchtime crowd and he began to edge into it when a voice shouted, 'Police! On the ground! Both of you! Now!'

There were three of them, two hyped-up young guys in suits, and the busker. Uniformed police were probably guarding each end of the mall. Wyatt ran at the detectives, windmilling with the briefcase, which struck an umbrella stanchion and flew open, tumbling a large, crammed envelope into the air. Wyatt caught it neatly, a small part of him wondering if in fact it held only paper scraps, the main part telling him to escape or die.

People were screaming or struck dumb, seeing the detectives with drawn .38s, the broken crockery and now racks of cheap clothing rolling along the footpath and into the street. A stoned-looking bikie whooped as Wyatt tipped over tables and chairs and ducked into a narrow space between racks of dresses and T-shirts in the adjoining shop.

It was dim inside, cramped, the air percussive. Wyatt didn't recognise the music. It wasn't music. It was loud, that's all, and supposed to attract customers. There were no customers, only one shop assistant avidly watching out of the main window and another snapping gum behind the cash register in the rear.

'Can I help you with anything?' she asked. She didn't think she could help the man, who was tall and prohibitive and gave off waves of coiled energy, but it was her job to ask. He passed her unhurriedly and her jaws continued to chomp.

Wyatt found himself in a short corridor, with a staff washroom on one side and a storeroom on the other. Peeling floor tiles, a broken-wheeled clothing rack, a bin of coat hangers and a wad of thick plastic shopping bags, deep purple, bearing the store logo. He crammed the harbourmaster's ransom money into one of the shopping bags and kept going, out into the alley.

2

The alley was empty, but Wyatt took no comfort from that. He didn't want to shoot it out with the Frankston cops, or be arrested carrying the .32, so he wiped it down and tossed it up onto the roof of the clothing store. He heard it clatter to stillness on the galvanised iron. Then he tore off the brightly coloured shirt and the towelling hat and crammed both into a rusty downpipe further along the alley. That left the sunglasses. He wiped them too, smashed the lenses under his heel and tossed them into a dump bin. Now he no longer resembled the man who had hijacked the harbourmaster's ransom money.

But he needed to get out of Frankston. Forget about a train, bus or taxi. Forget about waiting around for the heat to die down, too. The police would soon be at saturation strength on the streets and in and around the station and the bus stops.

Still carrying the harbourmaster's cash in the purple bag, Wyatt headed away from the warren of lanes and turned in to the Aussie Disposals on Beach Street. He bought combat pants, purple mirrored sunglasses, a black T-shirt, an Army forage cap and a daypack, reflecting that women had it easier in this game. Small alterations—a ribbon, a scarf, hair up or swinging free—could be an entire makeover. The kid who served him was incurious: she had seen it all before, homeless guys who'd come into a few dollars, students trying out a new image. Wyatt in his jeans and T-shirt was just another guy.

Bundling his old clothes and the purple bag into the pack, Wyatt thumbed the ugly sunglasses onto his nose and headed down side streets toward the waters of the bay, a block southwest of the Nepean Highway. As soon as he reached the sand he intended to stroll away from danger, bearing north towards the city for five or ten kilometres, which would bring him to the beachside suburbs of Seaford, Carrum and Chelsea. He could risk catching a train or bus from there. But then, as he was crossing the Nepean, he saw the service station.

It was like every fuel stop on every highway: fill the tank, check your tyre pressure, buy a pack of cigarettes or a stale donut, use the restroom.

At this one you could also book your car in for an oil change and tune. You dropped your car off in the morning, went to work, and collected it that afternoon. The mechanics were busy: if all you wanted was a simple service, they'd do it quickly to free up the hoists for more demanding jobs. They'd park your car outside, next to the rental trailers and the barbecue gas. Sometimes they'd lock your car and hang the keys on a hook in the office. If they knew you they might leave your car unlocked, keys in the footwell.

That's what Wyatt was counting on, and it got him a well-cared-for Toyota Cressida. He checked behind the rear seats because he always did, and was gone before anyone noticed. As he drove, Wyatt visualised the owner, a man of precise habits. A man like himself in fact, but older and from the other side of the fence.

Wyatt kept to the Nepean Highway as far as Mentone, where he took Warrigal Road and then Centre Road into Bentleigh, an endless tract of small brick veneer houses and modest, easily dashed expectations. The people of these suburbs were the backbone of governments that taxed them dry and sent their sons to die in foreign wars. Wyatt found Lithgow Street, looking for a particular house. Especially the granny flat in the backyard, where six years ago he'd secreted a .38 Smith & Wesson, $5000 in cash and papers in the name of Tierney.

The house no longer existed. In its place was a block of flats in a carpet of concrete. He turned around and drove out of there, wondering if they'd found his stash. Maybe it was buried in a landfill somewhere.

He headed across the city to Footscray and another house, weatherboard this time. The house was still there. It hadn't been altered. The street hadn't been altered. But the residents had. There were two police cars out the front, another in the driveway, lights flashing, and surging around them were a dozen Somali teenagers, abusing the cops who were arresting their friends. Wyatt drove by.

Battling heavy traffic, he pulled into the car park at the rear of a Sydney Road pub, where he checked the harbourmaster's pay-off. He'd been partly right about the contents of the envelope. There were eight tight wads of cash in it, green-toned hundred-dollar bills showing top and bottom, so that at a glance the harbourmaster would have counted seven bundles of ten grand each and one of five, buying the police time to move in and arrest him. But between the genuine bills it was all scrap paper. So Wyatt was wealthier by only $1600 and poorer by one handgun.

The gun mattered. It was an essential tool in his line of work. Ditching the car, Wyatt caught a tram back into the city. It was almost 5 p.m. He didn't want to miss Ma.

If she was still alive.

If she was still in the game.

3

At that moment it was 8 a.m. in London and a Frenchman known for his blade work was tailing a nondescript man out of Blackfriars underground station and along Queen Victoria Street towards Bishopsgate. Alain Le Page kept well back, but not so far that he lost the man, who wore a dark suit, a vivid white shirt, a vaguely old-school tie and glossy black shoes. An overcoat to ward off the crisp autumn stillness.

When the target looked both ways at a pedestrian crossing, Le Page saw the plain glasses, skin that hadn't seen the sun in a while, short, tidy, windproof hair, plain leather briefcase. Young, but like many young men in the City, middle-aged looking. Expressionless face, average height, erect bearing. There was no immediate way of telling if his background was Oxbridge or redbrick polytechnic, Eton/Harrow or distressed council-estate comprehensive, London or the provinces, or if he was a banker or a mail clerk.

There was nothing about him to suggest that he was worth killing.

Unless you knew what Le Page knew.

When word came through that the target was putting out feelers, Le Page had done a quick background check. It seemed the man was no more than a messenger boy. He looked like a City gent because the banks, law firms and insurance companies liked their messengers to be suitably kitted out. No bicycle couriers in red Lycra and purple hair. No barrow-boy accents. No perspiration odour or gum-snapping jaws in lifts and foyers. No backpacks or plastic document wallets. The City firms wanted their contracts, cheques, prospectuses and wills delivered in leather briefcases.

Except that this guy worked for Gwynn's, a small private bank, and had claimed he sometimes carried bearer bonds and Bank of England treasury bills, so Le Page dug deeper.

First, the bank. Gwynn's had been in business since 1785, according to the discreet wall plaque next to the main entrance. By Royal Appointment to various monarchs. Slow to adapt to the modern world. Run by fogies, young and old. A gentleman's word is his bond, kind of thing. There might be sharks in the world of finance, men and women who would break a contract, embezzle funds or engage in insider trading, but one did not do business with them. As for rapists, murderers and pickpockets, this was the City, not some awful high street.

Gwynn's had never been robbed, so the firm didn't bother with security vans and armed guards. In fact, one of the senior partners had argued that the presence of vans and guards was bound to *attract* the attention of thieves.

Besides, think of the cost, the vulgar display.

And so they used a messenger who looked like a banker. And the messenger was selling them out.

Next, Le Page did a deep background on the man, learning he'd been a messenger for two years and hired because he was an ex-soldier. Not a bonehead but someone who could look after himself and pass muster in a suit, overcoat and briefcase. The work was easy; the pay poorish, but his nerves were too badly shot for anything more demanding. He'd been in Iraq and seen men die in terrible ways and had believed that he'd be next. He'd survived but hadn't come back a hero. He hadn't even gone there a hero. Only the Prime Minister of the time had thought that.

Le Page put it together. For two years the messenger had endured shitty pay and the condescension of soft, plump men. One day, seeing with perfect clarity that he was going nowhere, he'd put out feelers. When the Russian, Aleksandr, got wind of it, he sent Le Page.

That was a week ago. Le Page reported back, got the go-ahead from Aleksandr, and made contact. The Gwynn's courier didn't want to know who, didn't want to know the details. All he knew was, his end would be £25,000 and maybe a few cuts and bruises, to make it look good to the cops.

Le Page intended to make it look very good to the cops.

He idled next to a newspaper kiosk and watched the target enter Gwynn's. He waited, indifferent to the miserable clacking of office workers on their way to work. Then the messenger reappeared, his body taut, anticipating the handover. It was a crisp morning in autumn and Le Page knifed him and left him to die among the rubbish sacks behind a Waterstones with get-rich-quick books in its windows.

4

Ma Gadd sold guns to men like Wyatt.

She operated out of a flower stall at Victoria Market. Hers wasn't one of the many makeshift stalls in the market's huge open area, where vendors displayed their fruit, vegetables, boxes of socks, cheap jewellery or T-shirts on trestle tables, and kept their supplies stocked in the rear of a Toyota van. Too open, too dangerous. Ma was an old-timer, one of the lucky ones with an indoor stall, a tiny sealed room among similar stalls along a narrow corridor. On her left was a man who sold second-hand books; on her right a woman who sold pet rabbits, kittens and budgerigars. If people wanted Ma Gadd's flowers, they fronted up to her fold-down counter and pointed to the blooms crammed in the buckets at their feet or in the space behind Ma. If they wanted a handgun and ammunition, they came to the door at the back. If she didn't know you, or you didn't know the right people or say the right thing, that was as far as you got.

It wasn't Ma who answered Wyatt's knock but a guy of about thirty, who looked lean, wiry and cunning rather than bright. His tattooed forearms tensed. 'Yeah?'

'Is Ma in?'

'Who wants to know?'

'Is Ma in?' Wyatt said.

The guy blinked. Wyatt read him in an instant: jail time— adult and probably juvenile—and now his natural habits were suspicion and belligerence. Wondering if Ma was under surveillance, Wyatt began to back away.

'I see you've met me nephew,' said a crone's voice. 'Don't let him put you off.'

A large shape materialised behind the nephew, whiskery, overalled and built like a storage tank. Ma wore a Collingwood Football Club scarf summer and winter, together with a general air of derision. Her breath wheezed around a bobbing cigarette and her eyes were like small cracked buttons above her ballooning cheeks. She looked as nasty and close to death as ever. Wyatt had bought from her only once, a Glock pistol, but that was twelve years ago and he had those years on him now. She'd had plenty of other customers in the meantime, and yet she knew him at once.

'Ma.'

'Heard you were back. Working with Eddie Oberin, right?'

Wyatt cursed inwardly. He didn't like anyone knowing anything about him. But in this game someone was always impressed or offended, couldn't keep his trap shut. Wyatt could never be entirely invisible. Not yet, anyway. All he wanted was to pull one big job and disappear again.

'You buying?' Ma asked.

Meanwhile the nephew was stepping from foot to foot, as if ready to punch somebody, an impression encouraged by hair that stood up in tufts and knots. Probably sculpted by a hairdresser, but looking to Wyatt as if he'd been trying to pull it out. 'Ty,' Ma said, 'look after the shop. I got business with Wyatt.'

Wyatt closed and opened his eyes, but it was too late. The man named Ty went on full alert, his jaw dropping. 'This is Wyatt?'

'Tyler,' said Ma, seeing Wyatt's face shut down.

'Yeah, yeah, whatever,' Ty said, trying for indifference now, not awe.

'Me nephew, what can you do?' said Ma.

Wyatt had no interest in Ma or her family or anyone else just then. 'What can you show me?'

'I'm just closing up.'

The whole market was closing. Spruikers were shouting out bargains, trying to offload their last tomatoes and cabbages. Metal shutters were clanging down. The throngs of shoppers— inner-city students, academics, yuppies, artists, young professionals and immigrants—were beginning to wander home. Wyatt said, 'I can go to a thousand.'

Ma gleamed and moved her bulk away from the door. 'Come in.'

Her storeroom was small and dark, a place of perfumed air and flowers bunched in buckets. 'Here,' she said, snapping off a rose head. Its petals were curling and Wyatt caught a whiff of decay.

Which could have come from Ma. There was a mess of other odours in that cramped space. 'Let's see,' she wheezed, shifting cardboard boxes and a stack of limp wrapping paper to reveal a metal trunk. Her vast upper body broke Wyatt's view as she fiddled with a combination lock and lifted the lid.

'Take your pick,' she said, stepping aside.

Tyler came in and there was no room to move. 'You locked up?' said Ma.

'Yep.'

'Emptied the till?'

'Yep.'

'You can go home now if you like, love.'

But Tyler was watching Wyatt. The nephew was unlovely, driven by impulses and grievances that he probably couldn't name but which Wyatt recognised: envy, rivalry, paranoia, hate. Low self-regard kicking against a huge, unwarranted ego.

'Not yet,' Tyler told his aunt.

'Suit yourself, love.'

Ma grunted as she retrieved a tray of pistols and revolvers. Wyatt watched her, wondering why on earth she'd let her nephew know about her sideline business. He put it down to the blindness of familial love. He'd never experienced it, but knew it existed.

'You're pulling a job,' said Tyler with a challenge, as if he'd heard of the legendary scores and wasn't impressed.

Wyatt ignored him and looked at the guns. Ma had kept them oiled and sealed in Glad bags: two .38 snub-nosed revolvers, a .357 Magnum, a .32 automatic like the one he'd abandoned in Frankston, and a sleek pistol that drew a second look.

Ma nodded. 'Nice,' she purred in her smoke-and-whisky voice. 'Good stopping power.'

Tyler was hopping from foot to foot again. 'What job? Bank? Armoured car? I know this credit union in Geelong, fuck all security, we could be in and out in two minutes, tops.'

'May I?' Wyatt asked Ma.

'Be my guest.'

There were many things to like about the pistol, a Steyr GB 9mm. Wyatt removed it from the bag and hefted it experimentally. Unloaded, it weighed little more than a kilogram, and the 18-round clip, plus one bullet in the chamber, would not add much to that. He peered at it, noting the magazine catch behind the trigger, the absence of wear.

'Never used,' Ma said.

Wyatt said nothing. He wasn't buying a car. He wasn't after a bargain. He knew and liked the Steyr, that's all. Other automatics lacked the Steyr's efficiency, were liable to misfire, jam or fail to cycle. You could also take a Steyr GB apart and reassemble it in less than twenty seconds, and Wyatt did that now.

'How much?' he said.

'Two thousand,' Tyler said.

'Shut up, Ty,' Ma said. 'One thousand.'

'Okay, a grand—including a box of shells,'

'Done.'

Tyler flicked his fingers. 'Dough.'

'Ty, love.'

'Well, I don't fucken trust him.'

Wyatt counted out notes from the harbourmaster's ransom. Ma placed the Steyr back in its Glad bag and then into a fat wedge of red tissue paper around a bunch of leafy rose stems. Wyatt walked away like a man going home to his sweetheart.

He left behind a fat old woman with a fat old purse and a wannabe gangster boiling with resentment.

Somewhere along Elizabeth Street he ducked into a McDonald's, dumped the roses in a restroom bin and tucked the Steyr into the waistband at his back, under his jacket. Then he went home. He needed to secure the pistol before he did anything else.

Wyatt lived on the Southbank side of the Yarra, in a region of newish apartment buildings behind the riverbank cafés, specialty shops and pedestrian tracks. Westlake Towers consisted of four blocks around a courtyard, walking distance to the river and the Melbourne CBD. Each block offered six apartments per floor, its own underground parking, a rooftop swimming pool, a basement gym and no view of the water at all. Wyatt owned two of the apartments. One was a bolthole, on the top floor. His day-to-day apartment was on the first floor, at the end of a dim corridor where no one but he had any reason to be. He went straight in and locked the Steyr in a floor safe.

A prickling sensation took him to the main window. He looked out. Sometime later, he walked back across the river, into the thick of Friday afternoon, glancing at reflective surfaces and putting the next stage together in his head. Tyler Gadd was a chancer, but would he come looking for a confrontation?

Elizabeth Street was hectic, crammed with shoppers, school kids and office workers hurrying to buses and trams, anxious to get home. Cars idled bumper to bumper, trams sounded warnings, horns tooted and toxins hung in the air. No one minded the little drama when, outside a crowded camera shop,

Wyatt whirled around and drew Gadd into a headlock. It might have been the roughhouse greeting of two old friends.

'Urrgh,' Gadd said.

Wyatt's forearm was squeezing the guy's life away. He released the pressure, squeezed again, released again. His eyes cold but his voice mild, he said, 'You followed me home.'

'Didn't know I was there, did you, hotshot?' said Gadd, gasping, rubbing his neck.

That was true. Wyatt didn't excuse it: he'd failed to spot the tail. But his senses hadn't let him down entirely, and he compressed Gadd's windpipe again. 'Stay away from me.'

'Look, I got ideas, good ideas.'

Wyatt turned away. 'Not interested.'

'How about I buy you a beer? Coffee?'

'I'm going. Don't follow,' Wyatt said.

'Wait!'

Wyatt walked. He didn't look back. He walked until his skin relaxed, then retraced his steps and veered right into Collins Street. Near the brow of the hill he turned left along a lane behind the headquarters of a bank, and finally down some piss-stained concrete steps to a watchmaker's grimy basement, where he paid rent on a locker. The same proprietor was there, looking a little older, more short-sighted and stooped, his glasses scratched and filmed with grease, his hands cobbled together from cuts, scratches, bones and leathery flesh. He remembered Wyatt, even though it had been years.

Wyatt walked away from there with his last $5000 in cash.

5

Le Page took the next available Paris train from Waterloo, carrying shopping bags from Harrods, the bonds inside a cardboard cylinder from the National Gallery gift shop. He hated the trip, hemmed in under the English Channel.

At noon that Friday he checked into a small pension near the Tuileries Garden. One of Aleksandr's goons came for the bonds. Grunted, 'He will see you tomorrow,' but in Aleksandr's kind of business the left hand doesn't know what the right is doing, so Le Page followed the goon and staked out Aleksandr's apartment. During the afternoon he watched a man and three women arrive and leave separately, carrying briefcases. Le Page tailed the last courier to the airport, all the way to the departure gate, and saw her board a flight to Toronto. He guessed the others had flown to destinations such as the United States, southern Africa, South or Latin America.

Le Page returned to his pension with time to kill. He fired up his laptop and checked for on-line news updates. One video clip showed a Gwynn's spokeswoman expressing well-oiled sorrow for the dead man—and bemusement, since the messenger had only been delivering mortgage papers. One of those unaccountable tragedies, she said, an opportunistic mugging that went terribly wrong.

The story might have fizzled out, remained a three-liner at the bottom of page five of the *Evening Standard*, except that the ex-soldier had been stealing kisses from an accountant in Gwynn's securities division and she knew when things were being swept under the rug. Outraged that her dead boyfriend was about to become a statistic, she leaked to the press that he'd been carrying £260 million in bearer bonds made up of certificates of deposit and Bank of England Treasury bills.

Gwynn's huffed and puffed and refused to confirm or deny. Le Page curled his lip. He knew how it would go. The firm would stay in business. Gwynn's dated from 1785, after all, and you don't kick a chap when he's down.

Aleksandr sent a car for him at ten the next morning. The Russian was glitteringly cold and urbane, his apartment hot and crammed with icons and samovars. Coffee, some bored conversation, and Aleksandr handed him a wad of bonds in a business envelope. 'Next week you will deliver these to my people in Mexico City.'

'Not now?'

'Go home. Rest. You deserve it.'

Le Page took a taxi to Charles de Gaulle and counted the bonds in the men's room. They amounted to £25 million, in denominations ranging from £100,000 to £5 million. A pittance, he assumed, compared to what the other couriers were carrying. Le Page thought about that as he flew out. Home was near Toulouse, a short hop to the south, but he got there via

Frankfurt. He collected his BMW and drove to the mountain village of Boussac, two hours southwest, where finally a winding road climbed through mountain shadows and drenching sunlight. This was a world of terraced fields, stone walls, hikers, the tinkling of sheep bells, village hens pecking at roadside verges.

And solitary houses like the converted eighteenth-century barn that was Le Page's home, situated on an elevated fold, with views across to all of the approach roads. A rutted track, barred by a steel gate with an intercom, led to the main building. He'd also fixed security cameras to the gate and at each corner of the house. Alarms and lights. Four handguns and a shotgun stowed away at crucial vantage points. Assuming a stranger or untrusted acquaintance made it that far: any visitor was obliged to pass through the village, itself part of Le Page's early-warning system. He'd paid good money to the taxi driver, the stationmaster, the gendarme, the mechanic, the postmaster and a handful of the kids who wheeled around the village on their bicycles and knew everyone's business.

Le Page parked his car, unpacked, mixed a drink and sat in the waning light, looking at the white-capped Pyrenees on the Spanish side of the border. The wall at his back was one metre thick and held the warmth of the sun. He closed his eyes and thought about Aleksandr.

It worked like this:

One of Aleksandr's legitimate occupations was dealer in high-end gemstones and jewellery, and Le Page was his legitimate international courier. Amsterdam diamonds, Swiss watches, Australian opals, Thai emeralds, French and Italian rings, brooches and necklaces. Given that a man carrying these items in a titanium case handcuffed to his wrist is liable to have his hand chopped off by a thief wielding a machete, Le Page always wore a corset with Velcroed compartments. He'd remove it while on the plane to New York, Quebec, Cape Town, Auckland or Melbourne, then strap it on again before walking through customs, waving the required paperwork.

He'd started life as a thief. Le Page grew up in the suburbs of Marseilles, the son of an accountant who was later jailed for embezzlement. Shame, penury and chaos forced Le Page and his mother and sisters to a tough part of the old port city, where the boy learned how to use a knife and climb a wall to a second-storey window. Thieve or die—or, to cut back on the melodrama, serve time in a lowly job somewhere.

Le Page would take his second-storey pickings to his local fence (an alleyway barber who sat the long hours in one of his chairs, reading and smoking), earning fifteen to twenty per cent of their value. A €500 gold Heuer Chronograph would net him around €100, depending on how generous the barber was feeling that day, and once, gloriously, he'd pocketed a €20,000 Rolex. But the suburbs in which he operated were generally modest and he hadn't the skills to rob a highly-secured chalet or mansion in one of the better locations.

Le Page had thought about this and decided that the answer lay in volume, not value. He knew people. Soon he had a network of burglars in place, committing the robberies for him in and around Marseilles. He moved rings, necklaces, a few Rolex Princes, a Queen Victoria Gothic crown, now and then a 1652 Philip IV eight-reales coin worth €1500. He paid 12.5 per cent; the barber paid him 15 per cent.

But some of his burglars were addicts. They got caught.

The old barber began to baulk at having to move so many items for Le Page. Householders and the police were more vigilant. So Le Page searched further, making contact with burglars, pawnbrokers, second-hand dealers and gym rats in nearby cities.

One day he walked into the back room of a jewellery store in Toulouse with an Omega Speedmaster, knowing the owner would want it for the deceased-estate section of his front window, and saw the jeweller had company. The stranger pointed a Glock automatic at Le Page and said, in a foreign accent, 'You are trespassing on my territory.'

The Russian mafia, Le Page thought, closing his eyes, expecting to die. When nothing happened, he opened them again. The jeweller smirked. 'Mr Davidoff has a—'

'Aleksandr,' the Russian said.

'Aleksandr has a proposition to make.'

Le Page waited, still trembling inwardly.

'Stealing an Omega Speedmaster in Nice and displaying it in a Toulouse shop window is stupid,' Aleksandr said.

Le Page tried not to pout. He was here to learn. 'Why?'

'The police in one city talk to the police in another. They talk to the insurance companies. This watch,' the Russian said, waving the Speedmaster at Le Page, 'appears on a database somewhere—its appearance and its serial number.'

'So?'

'So we will sell it in Berlin or Amsterdam or Melbourne or Cape Town,' Aleksandr said.

Aleksandr knew a lot about Le Page. 'I admire your abilities. You have nerve, intelligence.' He looked the lithe, fleshless thief up and down. 'You have presence.'

He trained Le Page as a courier. Most of the work was legitimate. Le Page would fly into a city like Chicago with a corsetful of rings, necklaces, chains and watches, and make prearranged deliveries to various jewellers and jewellery manufacturers. All above board, except that one of these jewellers might also take delivery of a stolen Tiffany brooch, another a Patek Philippe watch. The money was already taken care of; all Le Page had to do was fly in, deliver, fly out again. What would it matter if descriptions of the stolen goods were posted on police and insurance company databases? How likely was it that a Berlin detective, holidaying in San Francisco, would recognise a shopwindow Rolex as one stolen from a house in Kreuzberg? Or that a Melbourne detective would browse a Toulouse database?

Le Page made an extra €50,000 a year doing this, but he started to brood. On one trip he delivered a choker of graduated Broome pearls worth €200,000, and on another an 1847 Blue Mauritius stamp. He'd wondered, at the time, what was so special about the charmless little scrap of paper; when he discovered the stamp was worth a couple of million, he started to dream. Resentment set in, too. He felt cheated.

And so for the past eighteen months Le Page had been taking his *own* Omega Speedmasters and Rolex Oysters on these international trips, selling them to his *own* network of buyers, all carefully cultivated.

His cousins in Australia, for example.

Henri and Joseph Furneaux were children when they emigrated to Melbourne with their parents. Now aged in their forties, the brothers were manufacturing jewellers who owned a high-end store in the eastern suburbs and sold their designs to other jewellers. Each year they made sales trips to buyers in and around Melbourne itself and then out to towns to the east and the north, so it was a simple matter for them to arrange under-the-counter sales of Le Page's gold Heuer Chronographs and Queen Victoria Gothic crowns at the same time.

But still Le Page was dissatisfied. Henri and Joseph always found reasons why they couldn't pay him what he wanted. By the time he'd bought a Rolex Oyster from his pawnbroker contact in Lyon and sold it to his cousins on the other side of the world, his take was only a couple of hundred euros.

Now, as the sun settled, Le Page sipped his drink and brooded about the London job. He knew what the bonds were worth. His standard fee didn't begin to approach their value.

He could maybe remove one of the bonds, see if Henri could get him a good price for it. The face value of a £5 million bond was around $12 million Australian. If Henri found the right person, someone willing to pay twenty cents in the dollar…

Better still, sell all of the bonds. Cut Aleksandr out of the loop. Le Page had already taken measures to separate himself from the Russian. He'd been living in the shadow of the Pyrenees for the past year, but Aleksandr continued to believe he commuted from Marseilles. Ironically, Aleksandr's own protective measures helped Le Page: the Russian would only use e-mail, disposable cell phones and newspaper classifieds to make contact. He can't find me, Le Page realised, and if he's arrested, he can't point the police in my direction.

Sunday passed. Le Page gave all of his attention to two questions: Why did the Russian want him to sit still for a week, and why so few bonds?

This is Aleksandr's big score, he concluded. He intends to disappear, sacrificing a small percentage of the bonds and leaving behind a fall guy.

Le Page made a few phone calls. He packed the bonds with his laptop and a change of clothes and flew to the Canary Islands. He monitored the news.

On Monday, he smiled. According to reports from Rio, New Delhi, Cape Town and Los Angeles, Aleksandr's couriers had been arrested.

On Tuesday he grinned: Aleksandr was dead, shot by police in Paris.

A profound peace settled in Le Page. He felt wonderfully free. Still, he telephoned one of his neighbours, an old shepherd, who assured him, 'No strangers have been to your house, monsieur.'

Le Page didn't go home. Asking the shepherd to keep an eye on his cottage, he fired off an encrypted e-mail to a corner of the world that might not have heard about the bonds, the couriers or Aleksandr.

6

While Le Page schemed, Wyatt spent his days in stillness, thinking, walking and sitting.

He rarely spoke. A simple request to shop or café staff, a nod hello to a fellow tenant, that's all. Wyatt wasn't a typical Southbank resident, but nor was he unusual. There were some Asian students, and a handful of vigorous retirees aged in their sixties, but most of his neighbours were young, tertiary educated and interested in making a lot of money fast. They forked out to attend wealth creation and grow-your-own-money seminars, worked in brokerage firms, retail and IT companies, liked to go clubbing and cycling in designer clothes, and snorted cocaine, believing it gave them a dangerous edge. They were successful and felt entitled. They would move into a swanky apartment, stay for a while and go somewhere else. They didn't talk to one another. They didn't notice Wyatt. They were too self-absorbed to notice that he was older and didn't use the gym or drive a BMW. He was just some guy.

The week passed. Sometimes Wyatt cooked for himself, but mostly he walked to Southbank to eat. Then he'd stroll back to the apartment and sit, sometimes listening to jazz, concentrating on the rhythms of the music, his body and his life. He'd been away for a number of years, after things got too hot for him, and he hadn't known what to expect when he came back. What he found was that there was still money around, despite the recession, and most of his old acquaintances were dead or in jail.

Sometimes he'd pour a drink and stand at the window. A view of other apartment buildings, and beyond them, on the other side of the river, construction cranes stencilled against the sky. He wondered if he'd have to walk away from it all. He needed money. He needed anonymity. Both were in short supply, and he began to feel that he'd lost the swiftness and clarity of his life.

He didn't seek company. The women he liked to spend time with after a job didn't know who he was or what he did. He knew they'd find him emotionally invisible in the end; he stopped seeing them well before that happened. His was a life of few intimacies, with strangers.

As he thought about all of these things every day, he attended to the new pistol. He drew comfort from the routine of cleaning it. First breaking it down into its main components: barrel, frame, slide, slide stop, magazine, bushing, recoil spring plug, recoil spring and its guide. Then he swabbed the barrel with solvent, turning his head slightly away from the odour. He dipped a fresh cotton swab into the solvent and used it to clean the frame, repeating the action with the slide and the breech face, working it liberally over each surface and into every groove. He cleaned away the excess solvent and finished with the barrel interior, running a brass wire brush in each direction, followed by a final run through with a clean swab. When he was satisfied, Wyatt reassembled the pistol, a deep part of himself finding satisfaction in the hard efficiency of the weapon's design and action.

He thought about Eddie Oberin and the harbourmaster job. Clearly Eddie's intelligence had been good: it was too bad that one of the shipping companies had balked and gone to the police. Eddie hadn't said who'd told him about the harbourmaster and Wyatt hadn't asked. Eddie knew people, that's all, including lawyers who with one face carried out their duties as officers of the court and with another stockpiled information and passed it on for a flat fee or a percentage of the action. They got their tips from bank tellers, casino croupiers, taxi drivers, personal trainers, bent cops, pawnbrokers, street girls, private detectives, insurance assessors, real estate agents and the installers of alarm and surveillance systems—anyone at all who wanted a favour, cash, credit, a name dropped, a nod in the right direction.

No doubt a lot of it was worthless, pie in the sky. Some, like the harbourmaster's scam, was sweet.

Or like the accountant and her gambling stake. According to Eddie's intelligence, a city accountant liked to follow the country races with a $10,000 float in her car. Wyatt followed the accountant to the Balnarring races one day, watched her park, open the boot, fiddle near the spare tyre—an inbuilt safe, he guessed—and remove an envelope. She made her way to the bookies and began to bet. She was a cautious gambler. She won steadily. At three in the afternoon she returned to the car parked among the gumtrees, unlocked it by remote, and stowed her winnings. Wyatt waited until she was at her most vulnerable, sliding behind the wheel, before he slipped into the back seat and let her feel his pistol at the hinge of her jaw and hear the low, dangerous rasp of his voice.

He let her out on a nearby dirt road, vineyards on one side, alpacas on the other, and dumped the car in Frankston. There was $35,000 in the safe. Wyatt gave Eddie 5 per cent. Eddie grumbled, but since Wyatt had taken all of the risks, he didn't push the matter.

'Mate,' he said instead, 'what you want to do is hijack a drug deal. That's where the real money is.'

Then he saw the coldness in Wyatt and shut up. Wyatt refused to handle drugs or drug money. In Wyatt's experience, dealers and suppliers took stupid risks because there was so much money at stake, and they could be vicious and unpredictable if they were also users. He was an old-style hold-up man: cash, jewellery, paintings.

Wyatt thought about that as he cleaned his pistol, or stood at a window and watched the twilight leak away. The trouble was, technology had outstripped him. He no longer had the skills to bypass high-tech security systems or intercept electronic transfers and was preternaturally wary of going into partnership with anyone who did. So here he was, obliged to carry out small-scale hold-ups and burglaries.

And it was more than advances in technology. To Wyatt, one of the main qualifying factors in any robbery was the merchandise itself—not only its value, and how that might be realised, but also its size and weight. Cash was bulky, gold and silver jewellery settings were heavy, and you couldn't exactly slip a painting into your pocket. Besides, precious stones didn't always hold their value, most paintings of any worth were listed on national and international registers, and the police knew how to track the serial numbers on stolen currency.

And there were the problems of finding, funding and outfitting a good team, dealing with aggrieved and unpredictable personalities, and offloading the gear without being shortchanged.

Another man might say to himself, 'Time I had some good luck,' but Wyatt didn't believe in luck, only in recognising opportunities.

Like that time in Tasmania.

He'd been casing a rural bank from the front window of a local-history museum on the other side of the street when an old farmer had walked in and plonked a charred, smoke-stained cash box on the curator's desk. 'I was pulling down a stone ruin and found this stuck inside the chimney,' the farmer began. 'Thought you might like to—'

'I'm sorry,' the curator said, 'but we have several similar boxes in fine condition.'

'Not the box, what's *inside* the box.'

Wyatt drifted closer, peering at a glass case of decorated hatpins and thimbles, silver pillboxes, carved emu eggs and Boer War medals. He watched from the corner of his eye as the farmer tipped out the contents of the cash box.

The curator peered. 'Are they certificates of some kind?'

'Bank notes,' the farmer said. 'Fifteen of them.'

The curator lifted one to the light. Even from some distance away, Wyatt could appreciate the unfaded green colour tone and black scrollwork.

'Bank of Van Diemen's Land,' read the curator, 'one pound sterling…'

'Dated 1881,' the farmer said. 'Interested?'

'Well, yes, yes I am,' the curator said, showing some cautious excitement. 'I wouldn't mind putting them on permanent display. We have colonial-era coins, and some pre-decimal currency, but no notes from the period before federation.'

They shook hands on it. Wyatt forgot about the bank. He returned to the museum after dark. There was no security: the curator, a retired primary school teacher, had locked the notes in a drawer. The curator wasn't Wyatt, or he'd have known that the notes were worth up to $25,000 each. Wyatt stole all fifteen of them, together with knick-knacks that he later tossed into a dump bin. As the years went by he sold them off, always in one of the mainland cities, sometimes using the old farmer's story, sometimes posing as a collector. He was never doubted or questioned, so he assumed that any report from the museum break-in was gathering dust in the local police station.

Wyatt still owned a couple of the bank notes. They sat in a safe-deposit box in Darwin. He'd like to 'find' another cache like that. In fact, what'd he'd really like to do was find an 1817 Bank of New South Wales ten shilling note in fine condition. One of those would net him a cool million and not weigh his pockets down as he climbed out of a window.

But that was unlikely. People were cannier now and he couldn't go around looking inside old stone chimneys.

There were few public phones left in the city, but Wyatt knew of one in Elizabeth Street and Eddie Oberin of another in the student union at the university. On Friday afternoon, seven days after escaping the law in Frankston, Wyatt walked back across the river to the central business district. A mild spring day and he was ready to work again.

He found his phone, dialled Eddie Oberin's number, said 'Call me' and hung up. He waited, picturing Eddie leaving his North Melbourne house and walking to the campus. Both men had stolen mobile phones that were good for a few days, but mobiles can be pinpointed and intercepted. Public phones were better suited for the calls they had to make. Next month they'd move on to another pair of phones.

Wyatt's phone rang and Eddie said, 'Heard the harbourmaster went pear-shaped.'

'Yes.'

'Sorry, pal.'

Wyatt said, 'Anything else for me?'

There was a pause. He could hear indistinct background voices on Eddie's end of the line, probably students grabbing coffee before an evening in the library. Now there was a scraping sound as if Eddie had cupped his hand around the mouthpiece. 'There *is* something,' Eddie murmured. 'Jewellery. But not much of a window, only a few days.'

Wyatt thought about it. 'Okay.'

'Free Sunday morning? Someone I want you to meet.'

Wyatt went still. He'd come to value the quality of Eddie's information, but was wary of meeting the people who supplied it. Wyatt preferred to work alone; he trusted only his own plans. But the big scores always involved others: those he could rely on, those he'd never met before, those who could finger him, those who might cross him.

He said, 'Neutral territory, you know the drill. Don't bring him to my place.'

'Botanical Gardens. And it's a she,' Eddie said.

7

At eleven o'clock on Sunday morning Lydia Stark saw the taxi again.

It first showed at 10.45 when Eddie Oberin came for her in his ageing Audi. She paid it no mind, a taxi pulling into the kerb at the end of her street, and climbed in next to Eddie. But later, when she stripped off her cotton jacket and reached around to place it on the back seat, she spotted that same taxi on their tail.

She didn't say anything but found reasons to lean into the gap between the front seats and engage Eddie in animated conversation as he steered out of the back streets and onto Johnston and then Hoddle. The taxi was always there, in the corner of her eye, a couple of car lengths behind.

She lost it on the narrow streets around the Botanical Gardens, where the good people strolled or jogged or crawled by in their cars, looking for somewhere to park. Eddie crawled too, then steered into a side street signposted resident parking only. He switched off and the Audi died with a bark and a shudder and plenty of smoke. Lydia smiled crookedly to herself: nothing had changed. Eddie loved Audis and Mercs but could only afford the ones with too many hard miles on them.

She watched him lock the car. It was odd, visiting the gardens with him again. They'd liked to do it when they were married, but that was almost a decade ago. Four years of marriage, three years too many. But she hadn't hated him then, didn't hate him now. He was generous, often amusing, and sharp when he was putting a score together. At all other times, he wasn't sharp. He liked the horses and the cards too much, and seemed genuinely astonished when she complained about the women. 'But they don't mean anything,' he'd say. 'You're the one I love.'

And so she'd left him. And now she was here because she didn't know anyone else who could help her rob Henri Furneaux. She glanced towards the end of the little street and the gardens beyond, and saw the taxi creep by.

There was a chill in the air so she shrugged into her jacket, then followed Eddie to the corner, where they waited for a gap in the traffic. The taxi was on a yellow line a hundred metres away. Lydia thought of a couple of explanations: Eddie owed money, or he'd pissed off someone's husband. The little disappointments that did their marriage in. It was as if Eddie had the brains and the nerve to pull a tricky heist, but not to manage his life. Which was why, in the end, she'd walked out. She hadn't so much grieved as suffered a wearying sense of miscalculation. But that was a long time ago. She'd scarcely thought of him in the intervening years.

They crossed the road and entered the gardens. Soon they were heading downhill through the lovely old trees and Lydia was letting her gaze sweep ahead of her and left and right, Eddie still unaware, treading lightly beside her, his face crinkled good-humouredly, as though the brisk air was a tonic. She didn't see a man who might be Wyatt. She didn't see the taxi driver.

Eddie clamped his arm around her shoulders, squeezed, let her go again. 'Remember?'

'Yes,' she said, biting the word off.

But he didn't pursue the memories and she was grateful. At the bottom of the slope, where parents and small children surrounded the pond and the angled sun barely penetrated, she shivered inside the thin cotton of her jacket and glanced uneasily back at the tree line. It was a sensation of being watched on all sides, and she said to Eddie, 'By the way, someone followed us here.'

She told him about the taxi, and liked the way he listened and flicked his gaze all around. That was the Eddie she'd loved in the old days, not the Eddie who liked gambling and other women.

'I can't see anything,' he said, his face full of hollows and doubt.

She gestured at the hidden streets above. 'Up there somewhere.'

'We'll have to tell Wyatt,' Eddie muttered, not liking it.

Lydia was taking in the pond, the approach paths and the kinds of people who like to picnic and look at trees. She was looking for the kinds of people who don't, and locked on Wyatt immediately. He'd been standing very still and now he approached from a patch of dappled light.

He was tall and hard inside the Sunday morning shirt, trousers and polished shoes. The hardness was there in his loping stride and self-sufficiency, not his size, for he was wiry, stripped down, bones close to the surface.

Lydia waited with Eddie. The man named Wyatt was unhurried and, like her, he was aware of his surroundings, watching for the things that didn't belong. But that didn't mean she was ready to trust him, or trust Eddie's judgment of him. She'd wait and see. After all, she'd never heard of the man until yesterday, when Eddie said, 'I know a guy.'

Typical Eddie. Almost three months had passed since she'd come to him with her idea, and no mention of who or how or when. But the French courier was back in town. It was time.

'I know a guy,' Eddie had said, and now here he was, with the kind of eyes that take and give nothing.

8

The agreed time was eleven but Wyatt had arrived at ten and waited where he wouldn't be noticed. His gaze was restless, looking for traps, directional microphones, anything or anyone that didn't belong.

He saw Eddie Oberin arrive, wearing black trousers and a charcoal grey jacket over an open-necked black shirt. Neat, elegant, his longish hair lifting in a mild, eddying wind, he might have come from one of the big houses on the hill above the gardens. He was with a slender woman wearing a skirt, sandals and a cotton jacket over a vivid white T-shirt, auburn hair loose on her shoulders. Feeling the wind a little, arms wrapped around herself. The pair stopped at the pond and while Eddie gazed at the water, the woman gestured back at the tree line. Eddie stiffened. Then the woman searched, found Wyatt, and fixed on him.

He walked down from the shelter of the trees and said, 'Let's walk.'

Eddie grinned at the woman. 'What did I tell you? A warm, engaging guy.'

Wyatt waited for the nonsense to end. Oberin was about forty, with a thin-lipped, ascetic kind of arrogance that some women found appealing. Normally he was close-mouthed and wary, so the jokiness made Wyatt suspect a history with the woman. He needed to know if Eddie could separate the job from her in ways that mattered.

Eddie gestured. 'Wyatt, Lydia Stark. Lydia, Wyatt.'

Stark was about thirty-five, with an edgy scowl that said she wasn't ready to trust anytime soon. Wyatt liked that: suspicion was as natural to him as breathing. 'Somewhere quiet,' he murmured.

She surprised him. 'Know anyone who drives a taxi?'

He watched her, his thin face tight. 'Tell me.'

'I live in Abbotsford. Eddie came by to pick me up, the taxi came by. Tailed us all the way here.'

Eddie opened his arms wide. 'If she saw it, she saw it.'

Without seeming to, Wyatt scanned the area. He didn't see anyone who didn't belong but somehow he trusted the woman. 'Let's talk.'

They found a clearing and sat on the grass and no one was around. Eddie said, 'It's Lydia's score.'

'First things first,' Wyatt said. 'How long have you two known each other?'

The woman watched Wyatt with cold interest, legs outstretched, arms propping up her trunk, and said in a soft growl, 'Years. We used to be married.'

Wyatt thought about it: bitterness, jealousy, old scores to be settled. Then he tried to put Lydia Stark together with Eddie, who had the faintly flashy look of a gallery owner who liked nightclubs and gambling. Clearly she hadn't come from that world.

'An earlier me,' Eddie said, reading his mind.

'You stayed in touch?'

'Not exactly.'

'You're in touch now.'

'Look, I can vouch for her, right?'

Stark placed a slender, olive-toned hand on Eddie's forearm. 'It's okay, Eddie.' She looked at Wyatt. The scowl was gone and he guessed it had been an unselfconscious camouflage. Now he could see appealing configurations in her face and manner. He scanned the trees and grassy slopes again, and waited.

She said, 'I contacted Eddie because I need his help. I don't want anything else from him. I don't want to remarry him or get inside his pants or get revenge or anything else.'

She paused. 'He has expertise. He tells me *you* have expertise.'

'She came to me with an idea for a job,' Eddie said. 'I could see it had legs, so we scoped it out for a couple of months. All the groundwork's done.'

Wyatt wondered if this job would prove to be no more than someone with an itch and a way in. The sun was mild on them now and Lydia Stark removed her jacket and propped herself on it by one elbow. Her bare arms were taut, her neck and shoulders shapely. Wyatt turned away and saw movement in the trees.

'Something?' she said.

'Yes.'

'You're not going to do anything about it?'

'It can wait. Tell me about the job.'

She weighed it up and said, 'Until a year ago I worked for a jeweller in—'

Wyatt got to his feet. 'Inside job. No thanks.'

Stark swung gracefully onto her knees and seized his arm. 'Don't get your knickers in a twist.'

She was laughing and Wyatt felt uncomfortable. 'Sit,' she said, tugging him down.

He complied. 'Convince me.'

'When Eddie and I got divorced—ten years ago—I moved to Mildura. Found work with a jeweller, eventually got to be chief buyer and assistant manager.'

Wyatt knew the river town, its extremes of rich and poor. His first thought was market gardens, corruption and the Calabrian Mafia, but he waited, wanting to see where she was taking him.

'It was a good business. The locals bought from us,' Lydia said. 'You've heard the stories: some old Italian gent walks into a car showroom, holes in his pants, shoes held together with fencing wire, and plonks down eighty grand cash to buy a Mercedes? It was like that for us, sometimes.'

Wyatt didn't like the Mafia whiff. And he wasn't impatient, exactly—he knew people liked to spin narratives casting themselves in the central role—but he had no use for suspense right now. 'And?'

'We didn't make or design our jewellery; we bought from a manufacturing jeweller, Furneaux Brothers, here in Melbourne. High end stuff.'

'Were you sacked? If we hit this crowd, they'll come for you.'

Stark flinched at his coldness, the dark, prohibitive cast of his face. 'Not sacked. About fourteen months ago my boss died of a heart attack and his wife closed the business. I came down here to live. I'm not on the Furneauxs' radar.'

'Tell me about them.'

It was Oberin who answered: 'Henri Furneaux's the brains behind the outfit. His brother Joe's the driver, the muscle.' He paused. 'Joe's a beer short of a six-pack.'

Lydia snorted. 'They're both creeps.'

It was probably important to know these things. Wyatt raised an inquiring eyebrow and she said, 'Touchy-feely, the old tit-grab and crotch-rub.'

Wyatt understood that at one level she wanted revenge. He didn't think much of it as a motive for robbery. In his world, you took revenge when you were doublecrossed. You did it coolly, and you always made it final. It was business, that's all. When emotions were involved, things could go wrong. So, had Lydia Stark made a fuss? Enough to make an impression, so that the Furneaux brothers would remember? If so, someone—the cops or Furneaux—would link her back to the robbery eventually.

She read his mind. 'I put up with it. But at the back of my mind I was calculating how to bring the bastards down.'

Wyatt shrugged, accepting what she said. 'You're thinking a hit on their store or warehouse?'

She shook her head. 'We hijack a delivery.'

'Henri likes to deliver the gear himself,' Eddie explained. 'He's notoriously tight-fisted. Won't fork out for a security van or guards or extra insurance cover.'

Lydia leaned forward, placing her thin hand over Wyatt's forearm, a way of saying this was her story. When she removed her hand his skin missed the contact and he was distracted. He heard her say, 'They have clients all over Victoria and southern New South Wales. Every few weeks they make a long round trip of jewellers in Geelong, Ballarat, Bendigo, Hamilton, Mildura, Wagga, Albury-Wodonga, places like that.'

'Armed muscle?'

'Only Joe.'

Wyatt turned to Oberin. 'Why are you interested?'

Eddie shrugged. 'Because it's Lydia, because I need the money. Because her idea chimes in with information I already had.'

Wyatt knew that, as a fixer, an agent, a middle-man, Eddie could sit on a half-formed plan for years until the right circumstances came along. But, as Wyatt said now, 'This time you want an active role?'

'Yeah.'

'Guns, Eddie. Fast cars, sirens...'

Eddie's stone face twitched. 'Hear us out, Wyatt.'

Wyatt turned to Lydia, who said, 'They deliver the shipments in an Audi four-wheel-drive with secret compartments in the back. We hit it before the first drop-off.'

Wyatt twisted his mouth. 'Secret compartments? Drugs.'

'Not drugs. Jewellery.'

Wyatt went on ruthlessly, 'We intercept a delivery, what then? You suggesting we fence it—rings and necklaces that are unique and recognisable? We'd be lucky to get twenty cents in the dollar. Ransom the gear back to this Furneaux character, maybe? Sell it back to him after he's claimed the insurance? We'd get peanuts, and it would take too long. Even if we melted the settings down we'd only end up with a smallish puddle of gold or silver. Too much hassle for too little reward.'

Eddie showed a little heat, nostrils flaring, and Wyatt thought he might get to the heart of the score. 'Fuck off, Wyatt. Don't you think I've thought of that?'

Wyatt watched Lydia's reaction. He liked the way she calmed Eddie with a glance and her cool fingers.

Turning to Wyatt, she said, 'That's where the Frenchman comes in.'

Wyatt was recognising something of himself in Eddie's ex-wife. She was naturally wary and assessing, and silence was probably her natural state. There, under the spreading trees and coins of sunlight, he gave her a faint, assenting nod.

'His name is Alain Le Page,' she continued. 'A legitimate courier of cut and uncut stones, gold chains and small ingots to Australian manufacturing jewellers. Several times a year he flies in, books into the Sofitel, spends a few days doing the rounds, flies out again.'

'You tailed him?' said Wyatt. A good courier would know how to spot a tail.

'He didn't know I was there,' said Eddie defensively.

Lydia touched his forearm to shut him up. 'The Furneaux brothers buy their raw materials from Le Page, make it up into fancy jewellery, and sell it to retailers. The thing is, about eighteen months ago, things changed.'

She paused. 'The brothers arrived at our shop, as expected, but this time Le Page was with them. Until then, I hadn't known he existed. Anyway, he was introduced as their supplier, I said hello and bought some of Henri's designs for the shop, and then

Henri and Le Page took my boss out to their car, all very secretive.'

'Not you, the boss?'

'That's right. Next thing you know, we're displaying some fabulous rings, necklaces, earrings and watches in our estate-jewellery window, some of it antique, all of it pretty scarce and expensive.'

'What did your boss tell you?'

'He was a nod-and-a-wink kind of guy.'

'Mate,' Eddie said, 'it's *stolen* gear.'

Wyatt got it. 'Le Page smuggles it in from Europe, concealed as part of a legitimate shipment.'

Eddie grinned. 'That's the beauty of it—we rob a robber.'

Lydia said, 'We're talking Rolex, Piaget, Patek Philippe, Georg Jensen, Raymond Weil, Breitling, Tiffany, stuff like that.'

'Not stuff you'd melt down,' Eddie said. 'A gold Rolex from the 1950s? Worth up to twenty or thirty grand to a collector.'

'The boss always had a good story to account for the stuff,' Lydia said. 'He'd tell people it came from the estate of a wealthy outback widow who'd liked to travel.'

Wyatt thought ahead. 'You were not their only client.'

'No.'

'Homework,' Eddie said. 'I tailed them a couple of times, window-shopped the estate jewellery before and after delivery. They must have a dozen similar clients around the state.'

'You weren't seen?'

'Count on it.'

Wyatt counted on nothing, but he followed the threads of thought. 'It's all stolen in Europe, so therefore doesn't appear on stolen-property lists here.'

'Exactly,' Lydia said. 'We can pose as the legitimate owners and no one's the wiser.'

'We can't pull this without you, pal,' Oberin said.

Wyatt had heard that before. Other people's endorsements meant nothing to him. He didn't even measure himself by himself. He was a thief and hold-up man, that's all. He was good at it because he thought and planned, and then thought and planned all over again, until he was satisfied. He was honest enough with himself to acknowledge his mistakes, but he rarely had to do that. Other people let him down. Eddie Oberin would let him down eventually.

Still, the well was running dry and the harbourmaster job had failed. 'There's something you're not considering.'

'What?'

'It all hinges on who the Furneaux brothers really are. You know as well as I do, organised outfits from the old Iron Curtain countries are moving in: major heists, human trafficking, drugs. Do we want to antagonise these people? Even if the brothers are working freelance, maybe they've been sanctioned by one of the organised outfits, kicking back a percentage of their proceeds as payment for protection and sponsorship. We don't want to hit an operation like that. Sooner or later they'd find one of you and they'd hurt you and you'd give me up. I don't want to spend my time looking over my shoulder.'

Eddie scowled. 'I did my homework, bud. You know me: I hear things, I learn things. The Furneaux brothers are running their own operation.'

Wyatt would check that independently. 'I take it these guys are about to make another trip?'

'Wednesday next week,' Eddie said, 'returning on the Friday.'

'Gives us ten days,' brooded Wyatt.

'Should be enough,' Eddie said.

Wyatt was thinking about the mystery taxi, about envy and loose lips. 'From now on we use pre-paid mobile phones and payphones, one use only. And I want you both to drop out of sight until it's over. Motel, hotel, guesthouse, something like that.'

'Paranoid, Wyatt,' Eddie said.

But Lydia Stark was also thinking about the taxi, and said, 'No, it makes sense.'

Wyatt flipped open his mobile phone. 'Who are you calling?' said Eddie suspiciously.

'Someone who can hurt or help us,' Wyatt said.

9

After tailing Eddie Oberin and some woman to the Botanical Gardens, Tyler Gadd sat for a while, flipping through a skin magazine and watching the spot where they'd disappeared from view.

The taxi belonged to a guy who owed Ma $2000. When Tyler had come to collect, the guy—thick accent, pouchy face, eyes too far apart, garlic stink—blubbered that he didn't have two grand, didn't have two bucks. Tyler had been smacking him around out of habit when he paused in mid-punch: a taxi is your perfect surveillance vehicle.

That was four days ago. Tyler had got himself a cab, the ethnic guy an extension on his loan.

Stage two was poking around in Ma's laptop files. Normally that would have been impossible: Ma was always close by when Tyler helped at the market, or she was sending him out in the van—Gadfly Flowers—to buy from wholesalers or strongarm the losers who owed her money. But the old girl loved the horses, meaning she was often gone for hours, across town at Caulfield or Flemington in her old white Bentley, betting in the thousands and coming home with tens of thousands. So one day, when she was out at the racetrack, he fired up her Toshiba.

And found a North Melbourne address for Eddie Oberin. Given that tailing Wyatt was too risky, Oberin was the next best thing.

Not that he was able to do it full time. Tyler worked as a bouncer at Chaos Theory, so had no idea what Oberin did at night, but late one afternoon he followed him from his rundown little house to a stretch of High Street, Armadale. Here Oberin had paced up and down and stared both ways along the street and even checked the alleyway behind the shops, dressed in a fashionable lightweight suit and narrow glasses with thick black frames, looking as though he belonged to the area. Tyler couldn't work it out: doors were shut, lights off, blinds drawn. The guy wasn't on a shopping expedition, and there were none of your usual hold-up targets on that stretch of the street, no banks, credit unions, TABs or Medicare offices. Only a wine bar, a bookshop, a joint full of ricepaper screens and other oriental crap, a shoe shop—and Furneaux Brothers Fine Jewellery.

The more Tyler watched, the more he was convinced. Oberin was scoping the jeweller's. Trying for nonchalant, but the way he rubbed his neck, and talked on his phone, he had something on the boil.

And now this, Oberin at the Bot Gardens with a chick he'd collected from a house in Abbotsford. Was this a date, a stroll in the spring sunshine, Eddie and his sweetheart? Tyler believed in body language and he hadn't seen any when the pair entered the park, no hand-in-hand or hand-in-the-crook-of-the-arm or hand-in-the-small-of-the-back.

Tyler was betting on some kind of rendezvous. Curiosity getting the better of common sense, he locked the taxi and crossed the road. A minute later, standing in the speckled shade of a massive tree, the trunk veined and knobbly, roots like anacondas and the air loamy all around it, he spotted Eddie and the woman, and they were with Wyatt.

Tyler swallowed involuntarily and his heart went bang-bang-bang and he retreated from there, quick smart.

He headed back to the house in Abbotsford, where the air is more of your stagnant stink, and learned the woman's name from the address slip on an unopened RACV magazine lying under a lilac bush in her front yard. Lydia Stark. Meant nothing to him.

Tyler spent the rest of Sunday morning collecting loan repayments for Ma: $500 from a nurse who wailed and scratched because she'd intended to score with it, and $275 from a PhD student who failed to show the proper respect until Tyler ripped the gold hoop out of his earlobe.

Then he returned to the market. 'Got some money for ya, Ma.'

She whacked him. She had hands like waffle irons and he fell among her buckets of field carnations, two bunches for $5. 'That's from Wyatt.'

Tyler blinked to clear his ringing head. 'What?'

Ma wheezed, 'He *saw* you, you moron. Stay away, I mean it, Tyler. This time he did me a courtesy. And you. Next time, well, use your imagination.'

Tyler, awash in scummy water, tasted blood on his tongue.

10

As Wyatt heard about the Furneaux Brothers' jewellery operation, Henri Furneaux was in his cousin's suite at the Sofitel on Collins Street in the centre of Melbourne, saying, 'Are you sure?'

Le Page, standing at the window, sighed and repeated, 'No one followed me from the airport yesterday.'

'You're absolutely certain?' said Henri, his pouchy face working, his hands washing. He was fifty, moistly plump, smooth and sleek with his wealthy customers but nervy around his cousin.

Le Page ignored him. He looked down on Collins Street, insulated by thick glass from car horns, tram bells warning the jaywalkers, shoe leather snapping against the pavement. He'd spent the rest of Saturday sleeping off his jetlag and looked and felt relaxed.

Henri felt unrelaxed. 'Alain,' he said, wriggling forward on a club chair, resting his belly on his thighs, 'I went on-line after you e-mailed me last week. A guy was *knifed*. Was that you? Interpol will be all over this.'

'If we act quickly we can move the bonds before they think to look here.'

'But—'

'I am a legitimate courier,' said Le Page over his shoulder, 'in and out of this country all the time.'

'But what if they're already looking for you?'

Le Page pointed down at Collins Street. 'They call this "the Paris end"?' He shook his head in disgust.

'Alain, please.'

Le Page turned from the window and sat on the end of the bed. 'Listen to me. The Russian is dead. If the police knew anything I would have been arrested by now.'

'Russian?' said Henri weakly, glancing at the treasury bonds stacked on the coffee table between them.

He chewed the inside of his mouth. As always, his cousin looked fresh, crisp and scary, his bony head severely groomed, his face tight and fleshless. If Furneaux was any judge, Alain was wearing $1000 shoes. Silk jacket, linen trousers, cotton shirt—all slightly baggy, to conceal the 9mm Glock and holster. Every time Alain flew in from Europe, Henri was obliged to provide him with a pistol. Same pistol every time, from his office safe.

'The Russian is *dead*,' repeated Alain, 'so you must not worry.'

The inside of Henri Furneaux's cheek was raw. 'Interpol...'

His cousin said, 'Listen. I have never been arrested. Never. Anywhere. Never questioned or detained. Never suspected of anything.'

He gestured in emphasis. Le Page looked very French to

Furneaux, who for thirty years had been no closer to France than his morning croissant. He looked contemptuous and arrogant, an impression reinforced when he went on to say, 'I will spot any tail. I will lose any tail. That is what I am good at. One of the many things. In fact, I will be the one who watches.'

It was all elegant European gangster bullshit to Furneaux, the thing he'd always hated most about his cousin. He hauled himself out of the chair, crossed to the window and looked out. The view stretched southeast, way down the coastline. Beneath them were the River Yarra, the rail yards at Jolimont, parks and gardens and endless tiled roofs after that. From up here the city seemed dramatic and full of promise. When you were on the ground you felt duped, life reduced to small disappointments and nasty surprises, with little that pleased the eye. Not like Sydney. Furneaux could imagine moving to Sydney. He was wearing a $3000 suit but beside Alain Le Page he felt provincial, as if the suit had dated and was inappropriate anyway. Alain often did that to him.

Returning to the coffee table, Furneaux found his cousin idly fiddling with one of the tiny tracking transponders they used whenever they moved valuables around the country. 'I get to keep some of the bonds?'

'Naturally,' Le Page said, stowing the transponder with the bonds and taking out his Glock.

Furneaux watched him eject the clip from the butt and ram it home again. He closed his eyes, opened them again and said, 'Look, I honestly think we should wait a few months. Give me time to find more clients.'

In the five days since the e-mail, Henri had made contact with his richest and greediest clients, promising huge potential profits. They were interested, and had funds available, but were suburban and regional jewellers who scarcely knew the difference between a Rolex and a Swatch, and would commit to taking only one or two bonds at a time.

'Some of these expire soon,' Le Page said, casting a slender hand over the bonds. 'Interpol will eventually think to search for them in this country. We must strike while the iron is hot, as they say.'

There was a knock on the door. Room service. Le Page casually scooped the bonds into a couple of document wallets while Furneaux opened the door and watched as a tray was wheeled in. Silver cutlery, a rose stem in a crystal vase, thick starched napkin and tablecloth, an open bagel, salmon and capers, on a broad white plate, and mineral water. Le Page tipped the waiter and tucked into his lunch, Furneaux suddenly ravenous and wishing he'd eaten before coming here.

'Eat,' Le Page said, reading his mind.

Henri tore off a corner of bagel and balanced salmon and capers on it. 'But I've only got confirmed buyers for about sixty per cent of the bonds.'

'Did you play on their greed?'

'Yes.'

'All that's necessary is nerve and an accommodating bank manager,' Le Page said. 'The words "Bank of England" will unlock many doors.'

'Sure, but—'

'A person of confidence should have no trouble exchanging a Bank of England treasury note for clean money,' Le Page continued. 'Or purchasing real estate or valuables. Or paying off debts. Or securing loans.'

'The clients know all that,' Henri said.

'Maybe when I show them the bonds their greed will grow,' Le Page said.

Furneaux doubted that. Le Page unnerved the clients. 'You needn't stick around,' he told his cousin now.

Le Page masticated, swallowed and dabbed at his lips. His voice when it came was a cold rasp. 'Don't be stupid. There is too much at stake. Do you know what to do if a client steals from you or threatens to inform the police? Will you be the one to slice through an ankle tendon, so they do not walk again so well? Then the other ankle, if that should prove to be necessary, followed by one knee, the other knee, one elbow, the other elbow?' He paused. Patted his lips again with the heavy napkin, so stiff it held its shape from lap to mouth, and said, 'Although one ankle is generally sufficient, in my experience.'

Furneaux realised that he loathed Alain: the hold that Alain had over him, and what Alain did to him. Spend time with Alain and you started to think like him. 'Okay.'

At that point the building swayed in the high winds that flowed around it, and that seemed to underscore everything.

11

'Ma promised to put the fear of God into him,' said Wyatt on Monday morning, 'but after a day or two he'll feel hard done by and decide to tail us again.'

'Or he'll ask his mates to do it for him,' Lydia Stark said.

Wyatt nodded. 'So we keep it low key, watch our backs, stay out of sight.'

It was 10 a.m. and they were in a fast food joint on Swanston Street in the heart of the city. Lydia and Wyatt were nursing coffees; Eddie's narrow face was hunched over a hamburger, which he'd been eating with tiny nibbles, as though to spin out the pleasure. Wyatt knew it was a prison mannerism. Eddie looked like Mr Suave but the old habits were still there. Wyatt had eaten muesli and bananas for energy some time earlier, and wouldn't eat again until late afternoon. He knew the gulf between himself and Oberin, but maybe the woman would make a good thief.

They were sitting where Wyatt could see the street. That meant that he couldn't watch his back, but if anyone came it would be through the front door. He'd been watching the cash register idly. Most people were paying by card. Where could a man like Wyatt lift cash these days? Money was moved around electronically. If cash was used, it was stored and protected by the kinds of high-tech security that he couldn't hope to crack or bypass, not without the help of experts and costly equipment. That left paintings and jewellery, which were also highly protected and could only be shifted by a fence who'd give you a few dollars and then sell you out.

But if Eddie and Lydia were correct and the Furneaux brothers were moving valuables stolen in Europe, some of the risk had been removed.

He opened his other senses. All around him was the cacophony of any diner in the world: plates slamming together, orders being shouted, bloated parents striking their bloated toddlers, who bawled about it and got beaten again for bawling. It was a useful screen for the conversation he was having with Eddie and Lydia. He narrowed his senses without closing them entirely and entered the calm place where his mind operated best.

'So what first?' said Lydia.

'Where do they start the delivery run?'

'The shop in Armadale.'

'Have you ever been inside it?'

She shook her head. 'They'd recognise me.'

'Both brothers hang out there?'

She nodded. 'With Le Page, when he's in town.'

'They own other stores?'

'Lygon Street and Chadstone,' Eddie said, finishing the hamburger.

Wyatt thought it through. 'We need some elbow room,' he said, with a smile like a slash in his face.

That evening, at six, they staged a car hijacking. The manager of Henri Furneaux's Lygon Street store had locked the rear door and was heading for her cute little Alfa hatchback when two tall, silent men jumped her from behind, one clamping an arm around her throat, the other snatching the keys from her hand. Collars up, caps low over their brows, sunglasses and whiskers, that's all she was able to tell the cops. One man said, 'All we want is the car.' She thought to say, 'In that case, let me go,' but didn't say it. Maybe she was their insurance. For a while after that nothing else was said by either man.

They were desperate, possibly on drugs, because the one driving made a mess of it. Too fast, too erratic. She was in the back seat with the other one and screamed at the driver to slow down. The other one jabbed her hard with his elbow, but then he started screaming at the driver, too. In the end they crashed her car and ran away, leaving her badly shaken.

After arranging a tow and going to the hospital for a check-up and giving a statement to the police, she was a mess. 'I won't be coming in tomorrow,' she told her boss tearfully. 'I ache all over and my nerves are shot.'

'Take a couple of days,' Henri Furneaux said. 'Me and Joe will look after the shop.'

Tuesday morning, Wyatt sent Lydia in to the Armadale store. 'Browse for a while, maybe buy something cheap. I need to know where the obvious cameras are, the layout of the showroom, anything else you can gather. Maybe fake stomach cramps, your period: ask to use the bathroom. We need to know how many rooms are behind the showroom, doors in and out, security on the back door and windows.'

They met again that evening. Lydia was wearing a new gold chain that looked garish under the McDonald's fluorescents. She hooked it with a finger. 'Can I claim expenses?'

Wyatt gave her a sharkish smile. 'Maybe.'

'The only person I saw was the manager, young, blonde, not a twit, name of Danielle.'

'Security?'

'Plenty of it, all high-end. Motion detectors, bars and alarms at the rear, newish safe.'

Wyatt shook his head. 'Not looking good.'

Eddie Oberin rubbed dry palms together. 'So we don't break in. We steal the Audi when it's got the gear on board, either from under their noses or hijack it once they're on the road.'

Wyatt nodded but didn't want to be drawn or rushed. To a man like Oberin, Wyatt was patient and plodding beyond all reason. This was a broad-strokes conversation: the detail would come later and not in a diner.

On Wednesday afternoon Wyatt and Lydia wore shorts, hat, bum bag and hiking shoes to High Street. She carried a Lonely Planet guide, he a digital camera. They looked American or possibly German, and sauntered in the street for a while, licking ice-creams. Once or twice, when Lydia hooked her hand in the crook of his elbow, Wyatt tensed, thinking that he liked the sensation, thinking that he was unused to it, thinking that it was part of their cover, and wondering if that's why she did it.

She did it again as they window-shopped outside Furneaux Brothers. Dim inside. Then she gave Wyatt a little push, and he entered, began to browse. 'Just looking, ma'am,' he drawled. The woman named Danielle smiled, busied herself. He peered at the estate jewellery. 'People buy this old stuff?'

She smiled again, a little tighter, and turned away.

At once he took several photographs of a man's watch, Jaeger-Le Coultre, and left the shop.

That night he found the watch on the Internet. Pink gold, dating from 1996, one of a limited edition of 500. It had been stolen from a Lyon banker.

On Thursday Wyatt told Oberin, 'I want to check out the rear of the building and the layout of the nearby streets.'

'Mate, what do you think I've been doing over the past few weeks?'

Wyatt stared at Eddie. 'New road works,' he said repressively, 'one-way systems further out, speed bumps...'

Eddie shrugged. 'Suit yourself.'

They started in a coffee shop diagonally across from the store. Wyatt had green tea, Eddie a long black and a muffin. To avoid being spotted and perhaps remembered by the men they intended to rob, they were not seated by the window, but had an unobstructed view of the jewellery store nevertheless. Eddie talked, Wyatt watched. The eastern half of the greater sprawl of Melbourne was crosshatched with long roads that chopped the suburbs into postcodes. This part of High Street was situated in one of the better postcodes and the shops were full of antiques, dresses, homewares and jewellery. Every third or fourth building was a bistro or a coffee shop and the cars were perky imports: Audis, Minis, Peugeots.

'The main thing I'm noticing is the traffic,' Wyatt said.

Eddie nodded. 'No high-speed getaway.'

'A getaway needn't be speedy if it's accurate and efficient,' Wyatt said. 'Vanishing, that's the thing, and that means anticipation.'

Eddie looked bored.

Wyatt said, 'Let's take a walk.'

'I haven't finished my muffin,' Eddie complained.

He was wearing a leather jacket over a cotton shirt buttoned at the throat. As Wyatt stood then, looking down, he saw, in the narrow gap between Eddie's neck and shirt collar, a hint of discolouration. The guy had a love bite. *No contact*, Wyatt had said. 'You and Lydia are in separate motels, right?'

Eddie looked confused. 'Yep, just like you said.'

Wyatt didn't pursue it. He stalked out and headed along the street away from the vicinity of the store.

Eddie caught up. 'Where are we going?'

'I want to see what's parallel to High Street, I want to check the laneways.'

He walked on, Oberin struggling to keep pace. Eddie was lean and elegant but unfit. He was also the kind of man who needs to add to the general racket of horns, muzak, mobile conversations and engines surging uselessly: he talked. And sneezed from time to time, checking the evidence in his handkerchief. 'You may not know this,' he told Wyatt, 'but Melbourne's one of the worst cities in the world for air quality.'

They were parallel to High Street and doubling back. The laneways, Wyatt realised, were narrow, narrower still where dump bins and cars waited.

'You've got pollens from all the surrounding grasslands, and no prevailing winds to blow the factory shit away.'

Wyatt ignored him. 'Let's take a drive.'

'Where?'

'Everywhere.'

Wyatt caught his first glimpse of the main players on Friday morning, watching with Lydia Stark as two men emerged from Furneaux Brothers, one plump and soft-looking, the other tall and circumspect. 'The fat man's Henri Furneaux, the other is Le Page,' Lydia said.

Wyatt discounted Furneaux and measured Le Page, noting the European cut of the suit and shoes, the bony insolence of the face, the unmistakable language of the human form concealing a handgun. But, more than anything, it was the walk Wyatt noticed. All of his senses came on hard and he watched Le Page nod goodbye to the jeweller and stride towards a waiting taxi, unhurried, as though everything in life was settled and nothing would ever stop him. He noted other characteristics, too, probably because he shared them with the man: nerve, economy, containment. The taxi pulled out and crawled away in the direction of the city. Furneaux re-entered the shop.

'Le Page stays at the Sofitel?'

'Yes.'

Wyatt grunted. He said, 'I want to show you something.'

'What?'

'A park.'

'You've been looking at parks?'

It didn't require an answer. In the car, Wyatt asked in a neutral voice what she did in the evenings.

She was puzzled. 'Nothing. Why? Low profile, right?'

'That's right.'

The weekend passed. They amassed more information and didn't spot Tyler Gadd anywhere.

On Monday morning Wyatt took another pass along the alley behind the store, then spent the last of his money on bullet-proof vests, latex gloves, balaclavas, pre-paid mobile phones and a pistol for Eddie. He'd been away for many years, but some of his old suppliers were still in business.

Late that afternoon he met the others in Lydia's motel. It was a struggling, sun-blasted structure on a flat, windy street near Sydney Road, a street of extremes, pretty evident at that time of the day: young Muslim women carrying lecture notes, Turkish widows in black, Goths, business types in suits, labourers returning home from building sites, a handful of junkies. The other buildings ranged from small factories and rundown terraces of the 1880s through to expensively restored 1920s bungalows, 1970s tan-brick apartment blocks and a handful of immigrant-made-good monstrosities with pointless white columns, backyard pools and plenty of wrought iron around the perimeter. There was nothing remarkable about the motel, therefore. In that neighbourhood, there was nothing remarkable about Wyatt, Eddie or Lydia, either.

He told them what happened in the alley behind the jewellery store.

Lydia snorted. 'Joe saw you?'

She lay sprawled on the bed, chin propped on the palms of her hands. A framed poster advertising a Matisse exhibition hung from the wall above her bed. It was a good reproduction, adding colour to the dingy room, but Wyatt couldn't see the point of buying, framing and hanging a reproduction, let alone a poster with names and dates on it. He smiled at her, his habitual twitch. 'I pretended to be drunk.'

When he'd wandered down the Furneauxs' alley that morning, there was Joseph Furneaux in the little yard, waxing the Audi four-wheel-drive, an ugly vehicle, high and bloated, with a low window line and a lift-up rear door.

'The gate was open,' Wyatt continued, 'so I staggered in and asked for a smoke. He told me to fuck off.'

Lydia laughed, a friendly, uncomplicated laugh, acknowledging ironies. But her air of completion and contentedness bothered Wyatt. He swung his gaze upon Eddie Oberin for a long moment. He failed to pick up anything. Eddie was Eddie, twitchy and impatient in one of the room's chairs.

Maybe Lydia felt content because the job was coming together. Wyatt saw her sharp mind working. 'That back yard is where the Furneauxs feel safest,' she said, 'yet it's where they're most vulnerable.'

Wyatt agreed. 'They expect to be hit on the open road, not at home.'

'Did you get a good look inside the yard?'

'The gate shouldn't pose a problem. The rear of the shop

itself is well secured: bars on the windows, a camera, a steel door with a good lock.'

'So on Wednesday morning we hijack the Audi,' Lydia said. She turned to Oberin. 'Eddie?'

He'd been fiddling with a small, black electronic device. 'This will override the locks, alarm and ignition.'

They continued to talk through the plan, their voices backgrounded by traffic noises and the permanent music of water tinkling through a faulty valve in the bathroom. This wasn't the kind of place where the management would wonder why the water bill was so high.

Lydia rolled off the bed and pulled on one of the bullet-proof vests. 'Let's hope we don't need these.'

Wyatt nodded. He passed Eddie the pistol.

Eddie grimaced. 'I never used a gun in the old days.'

Wyatt didn't bother with a reply. A job was a job and required tools. He distributed the disposable phones, gloves and balaclavas.

'I don't get a gun?' Lydia said.

'You're the driver.'

Wyatt watched her shrug off the vest and swing neatly to a sitting position on the bed. He'd brought maps to the meeting. She gathered them into her lap. 'You want me here?'

Wyatt stood beside the bed. The street he'd taken her to on Friday curved around a patch of green parkland five kilometres from Furneaux Brothers, and she was indicating, with a shapely forefinger, a guardrail above a steep slope that bottomed out in a clearing concealed by trees.

'And you dump and torch the Audi *here*.' She tapped the clearing.

'Yes.'

'Let me see,' said Eddie.

They examined the map, the two men and the woman, knowing the job was moving beyond idle speculation.

'I won't be able to see you until I see you,' warned Lydia. She'd said it on Friday, too.

'Keep the motor running,' Wyatt said.

12

Ma Gadd was watching Tyler like a hawk these days.

'Where do you think you're going?' she'd say, whenever he set out in the delivery van. It was clear she didn't trust him to leave Wyatt alone.

So he'd tell her the truth, he was delivering flowers, buying plastic buckets from K-Mart, doing the rounds of the sad wankers who owed her money, collecting tulips from the airport, KLM, direct from Amsterdam. Ma would cast him a doubtful look from her pudding face and say, 'I want you to come straight back, okay?'

'Yeah, yeah.'

Every day for a week.

Tyler got his chance in the second week, Tuesday morning, a delivery of funeral wreaths to the Monash University chapel, all over and done with in record time. He stopped in Armadale on the way back and, seeing no sign of Wyatt, Oberin or the woman, peered through the unsmeared display window of

Furneaux Brothers Fine Jewellery. Plenty of glass-topped counters, revolving display cases, velvet drapes and shadows. He went in.

The chick behind the main counter looked him up and down as if first gauging his dollar value, then sizing up his cock. Nice tits.

She blinked, stepped behind one of the glass counters. 'May I help you?'

Tyler smiled, deciphering the body language. She was using the counter as a barrier. But—big but—*it was see-through*, meaning she wasn't blocking him off completely. He ran his tongue around his lips and said, with heat and a hint of a growl, 'Just looking.'

Hands behind his back, he idled along the display cabinets, paying attention to the diamonds. Maybe arouse a little stab of jealousy, here's this cool guy buying not for me. At the same time, he was scoping the place for cameras, alarms, doors, windows.

'See anything you like?'

He straightened and stared at her name tag and cleavage. 'Danielle. Cool name.'

'Thank you.'

'Could I see that tray of rings, what are they, engagement rings?'

'Certainly, sir.'

She bent gracefully, more tit, reached in and placed the tray on the glass top. 'Sir has a good eye.'

Plastic smile, plastic voice. Tyler felt rage bubbling and leaned forward, pointing past her hip to the floor behind her. 'What's that? You drop something?'

With no change of expression or manner she snarled, 'What, a snatch and grab? Get lost, loser.'

And a voice in Tyler's ear. 'You heard the young lady.'

Tyler jumped and spun around. The guy sounded foreign, and that bony European look, a hawkish nose carved from granite, you could feel the menace coiled in him. Must have been in the showroom all along, lurking in the shadows. Tyler swallowed. 'Just going.'

He turned for the door and long, dry fingers clamped his neck and the hinge of his jaw and then he simply blacked out, waking on the floor in terrible pain and numbness. Bony had found some kind of pressure point. How long was I out? wondered Tyler.

The chick smiled.

13

Furneaux Brothers Fine Jewellery, Wednesday morning, 8.30. The young store manager contemplated her boss.

Sly and sleazy were the words that usually came to Danielle's mind. Henri Furneaux's face was saturnine, his fleshy jowls dark and closely shaven. Dark eyes and eyebrows, down-turned mouth. Dark forearm and knuckle hairs. Always a black suit and a sombre tie. Manner gravely courteous to the rich, pointless women who bought their jewellery from him. He'd be a convincing undertaker, she often thought.

But this morning he was fired up. She guessed it was agitation and anticipation, in equal doses. He got that way every time he and Joe made the rounds of the regional buyers. The imagined problems stirred him up, the knowledge that he was going to get richer put a spring in his step, and all that emotion always got him aroused. He'd stand close and she'd feel his shoulder press against her if she were standing too, his meaty thigh if she were sitting. Right now, as she took rings and necklaces from the safe and arranged them in the display cabinets, his groin brushed her hips and behind as he manoeuvred around her in the narrow spaces of the shop. He murmured, 'Excuse me.'

As Danielle bent to slide a $4000 diamond ring in under the glass counter top, Furneaux's partial erection pressed against her hip. Otherwise the day was beautiful, sunny, a lovely spring morning. Sure, there was plenty of bumper-to-bumper traffic, as always at this hour of the day, plus kids in their school uniforms overrunning the footpath and bus stops, but they'd be gone soon. She avoided Henri's cock adroitly and stepped through an inner door to the tearoom. The guys would want coffee before they left.

That creepy French guy was there, draped elegantly in a plastic chair, sitting in utter stillness. Danielle avoided meeting his gaze but could feel it licking at her. Normally he flew in, flew out again. Never stuck around. She finished making the coffee and returned to the showroom, doing her job. The French guy followed her and took up position in a dim corner.

Then Joe appeared from the yard, saying, 'All done.' He had dry, whistling lips and bloodshot eyes and wore jeans, a T-shirt that read 'What Did Your Last Slave Die Of?' and gaudy purple, white and yellow running shoes. And sunglasses, resting on top of his shaved head. He looked nothing like a man who dealt in fine jewellery.

But he did look like a van driver. Henri glanced at his watch, then at Joe. 'Will we need fuel?'

'Filled up yesterday,' Joe said.

Danielle continued to arrange the display cabinets. She was enveloped on both sides by powerful odours: Henri's expressive body lotions, and Joe's perspiration, the latter leaching various toxins into the air—alcohol and amphetamines, at a guess.

'Got your mobile?'

'Yep,' said Joe.

'Fully charged?'

'Yep.'

'Clothes, toothbrush…'

'I'm not a kid, Henri,' said Joe Furneaux.

Danielle kept a straight face and loaded the till with coins and banknotes as Henri said, 'That's all, then.'

He was stepping from one foot to the other.

Joe was supremely relaxed, maybe chemically so. 'No worries, bro.'

Henri snapped his fingers. 'Snack bars? Bottled water? I don't want you falling asleep at the wheel.'

Joe shrugged.

'You need sustenance, Joe,' Henri said. 'Danielle?'

She straightened and looked at her boss. 'Yes, Mr Furneaux?'

'Staffroom fridge. Grab a few protein bars and bottles of mineral water, take them out to the Audi.'

What am I? thought Danielle. Clearly not the manager of an exclusive shop on High Street. She knew that in a certain light she looked her age—twenty-five—and wasn't the brightest jewel in the store, but she had the legs and breasts of an eighteen-year-old, and that had been enough for Henri Furneaux to hire her and teach her the job. Which included being treated like shit.

'Come on, gorgeous, get a move on.'

'Yes, Mr Furneaux.'

When she got to the yard she saw Henri's soft-top Mercedes

and the open gate but not the four-wheel-drive. Then she heard hissing, and a soft, metallic complaint, and realised the Mercedes was sinking gently on its suspension. There was a faint hint of diesel hanging in the air. Maybe the Audi was in the alley? No, empty in both directions. She dragged her heels for a while, wondering if she'd misheard Henri, before wandering back inside with a worried look and an armful of snack bars and bottled water. 'Excuse me, Mr Furneaux.'

He gave her his empty smile, then spotted the snacks and drinks and his true nature showed itself: irritation and a hint of the bully. 'Out to the Audi, I said.'

'Not there.'

It took him a few seconds to register this. He went white. 'What do you mean, it's not there?'

Joe put in, 'It was there five minutes ago.'

'It's not there now,' Danielle said. 'The gate's open and the Audi's not there.'

The French guy gave her a long, flat look, then strode past her with a kind of creepy grace, the Furneaux brothers pushing after him. Joe's boot clipped her ankle. She spun and teetered from the force of it and her ankle began to drip blood. The three men disappeared through the door leading to the rear of the building and the alleyway.

A moment later Henri and Joe came barging back, Joe insisting, 'But the gate *was* locked, Henri. I swear it was locked.'

Danielle gazed at the brothers—Joe perplexed and sulky, Henri transformed by anger and panic—and ventured a question. 'Would you like me to call the police?'

Furneaux snarled. 'Sure, I can just see them dropping everything to tend to a stolen four-wheel-drive.'

'Maybe it was kids,' Danielle said. 'You know, opportunistic. Maybe the gate was open and they thought, "Hey, cool."'

'Then wouldn't they be more likely to steal my car?' screamed Furneaux, while Joe looked aggrieved and said, 'The gate was fucking locked, I tell ya.'

Henri ducked behind the cash register and came out with an automatic pistol. 'Mr Furneaux!' said Danielle, her hand to her mouth, although she thought that everything was suddenly way cool.

He ignored her, patting his suit for his car keys, pulling them from a pocket and saying, 'Let's go.'

'Are you going after them?' Danielle said.

'Too right we are,' Joe said.

Henri nodded, telling Danielle, 'Sit tight here until we get back. Don't call the police yet. In fact, shut up shop and wait in the staffroom.'

But Henri, they let down your tyres. 'How will you know which direction they took?' said Danielle, enjoying herself.

Joe touched his nose, trying for clever but looking comical. 'Global positioning.'

'Shut the fuck up, Joe,' Furneaux said, shoving his brother towards the back door.

But Le Page materialised there, holding the tracking monitor from Henri's Mercedes and looking so hard at Danielle that she buried her emotions. He turned to Henri. 'They have slashed your tyres.'

Danielle, far removed from it all, watched Joe gape and heard Henri snarl, 'Fuck.' Meanwhile Le Page continued to stare, and to deflect it she said, 'Shall I ring the police?'

Le Page shook his head. 'No. Stay here.'

Henri and Joe followed him out onto High Street, where they climbed into Le Page's car, a black BMW from Prestige Rental. Danielle watched them tear away. Switching the front door sign from 'open' to 'closed', she figured they'd lost about ten minutes. A big part of her wanted that to be enough.

14

'Anything?' said Eddie in the passenger seat of the Audi.

Wyatt glanced at the rear view mirror again. 'No.'

It was 8.50 and they were clear of Armadale now, heading east through Malvern along the side streets. Here and there they encountered glossy Volvo and BMW wagons, but it was local traffic, mothers on the school run. Everyone else was in a train, bus, tram or car, choking the main routes into the centre of the city, another day at the treadmill. No one was heading east.

'Anything?' said Eddie again.

The guy was too antsy. Wyatt didn't like it. 'When there is something,' he said, 'I'll tell you.'

He said it in a way that would shut Eddie up. He never talked for the sake of talking. People like Eddie talked to fill some gulf, he supposed. He checked the mirror, feeling very alive. He never ate or drank before a job and so the blood was flowing smoothly within him and all of his synapses were firing.

Eddie pitched about in his seat, tugging at his upper clothing. 'Hate these bloody vests.'

Wyatt ignored him. If Eddie didn't know to expect this level of outfitting, he'd been out of the game for too long.

'Fucking uncomfortable,' Eddie said.

Wyatt drove along Wattletree Road, but got caught behind a tram. The tram made every stop, and there were plenty of those, and it seemed to wallow at every stop for extended periods, so Wyatt turned right into a region of leafy streets, box hedges and red tiles, then headed east again. They passed Central Park. He'd examined it as a place to torch the Audi, just as he had many other parks in a five-kilometre radius of Furneaux Brothers, but Central Park was too small and public. Only one park had what he needed. He got onto Malvern Road for a short while, then crossed the freeway and Gardiner's Creek. He was heading in stages for Buckingham Park, on Glen Iris Road. Lydia was already there, monitoring the police band.

'Check your phone,' he said.

Lydia would send a text message if she had to abort her part of the operation or heard anything that would endanger them. Eddie fished out the mobile and pressed buttons and said, 'Nothing.'

Wyatt thought about the location. The well-heeled people who lived out here had the wallet power to demand stretches of public grassland yet you'd not see many of them out walking or running at this hour on a weekday morning. The other benefit of Buckingham Park, confirmed yesterday, was that it offered plenty of cover from the nearby streets.

He slowed the Audi, ready to turn off, and said, 'We've got company.'

Eddie contorted in his seat, trying to find the tail in his side mirror. 'The black Mercedes? But you let the fucker's tyres down.'

Wyatt concentrated. 'Get your gun out.'

Eddie patted himself. 'Shit, left it behind.'

It was an icy silence Wyatt gave him, and he babbled, 'Must have been subconscious. You know I hate guns.'

'Watch the Merc.'

'Okay, all right,' Eddie said. Then relief shuddered in his voice. 'False alarm, it turned onto a side road.'

Wyatt drove on. 'I bet we have a GPS transmitter somewhere on board, if not with the jewellery then on the vehicle.'

'Meaning?'

'We hurry.'

Reaching the park, Wyatt jerked the wheel to take the Audi bumping over gutter and footpath and down across a grassy slope to wind among trees. As he understood it, navigation, tracking and global positioning systems are mostly logical and unimaginative, seeing a city as a series of grid patterns. Supposing Henri Furneaux or the police got their act together quickly, and started tracking the Audi, there was no way a monitor screen could pick a route off the bitumen and down through trees and rocks.

He bumped across the grass, over walking tracks and around park benches, and came to a little grove enclosed by vast, leafy trees. He braked hard. 'Lydia's up there somewhere,' he said, indicating a grassy bank leading up to guardrails and a street.

They got out and hurried to the rear door of the bulbous Audi. Wyatt swung it open and stood back for Eddie, who ducked in, fiddled with clips and lifted the false floor to reveal the concealed compartments. Inside them were a pair of titanium cases. He shoved these into a gym bag, and stepped away to let Wyatt toss petrol around the interior and throw in a match.

Wyatt retreated, turned, saw that Eddie wasn't alone. Then he saw the gun. Then a bullet smashed into his chest and he went down and out.

15

'*Head* shot, remember?' shouted Eddie. 'Not body.'

Khandi Cane shrugged, animating her unholstered breasts. 'This time I tried to anticipate the kick, but it threw my aim off.'

'What do you mean, *this* time?'

But she was straddling Wyatt's prone body, her long legs in a micro skirt and slinky boots. Her smile was glassy. 'Taking a bead on his head, Khandi squeezes the trigger.'

Voices beyond the trees, somewhere up on the road above the hollow, and Khandi was just standing there. '*Shoot,*' urged Eddie.

'I did.' She looked at the end of the barrel. 'This gun is shit. It just jammed on me.'

Wyatt groaned on the ground. 'We haven't got time for this,' screamed Eddie, close to hyperventilating. He grabbed Khandi's arm. 'Where's the fucking car?'

She pointed. 'Up there, where you told me.'

Parked where Lydia wouldn't spot it. 'We need to move.'

Leaving Eddie to carry the titanium cases, Khandi strode up a parkland slope to a faded white Commodore and got behind the wheel. Eddie, gasping after her, stowed the cases in the boot and climbed into the passenger seat. 'Go!'

But Khandi merely grinned at him, the white streak in her hair more demonic than ever.

'Will you fucking go?' shouted Eddie, peering down into the park, certain Wyatt was after them, the unstoppable cunt.

'Don't be such a wuss,' said Khandi, pulling away from the kerb, leaving rubber on the road. 'Everything's cool.' She placed her hand and her gaze on his cock.

Eddie grabbed the dash. 'Watch where you're going.'

He'd been wheelman on a couple of hold-ups a long time ago and one day it had all gone wrong: he'd clipped a bus, flipped the getaway car, and had never quite got his nerve back. Now here was his sweetheart driving like a maniac.

He shrugged off his bullet-proof vest and tried for calmness. 'We don't want to get noticed by the cops. We don't want Wyatt after us.'

Khandi smirked but removed her hand. 'Can't help it, I'm all wet,' she said, glancing at him, making a feint at his groin, shooting them off course.

'Time and place, babe.'

'You're no fun,' Khandi said.

She corrected the car with a flick of her wrist and told him how she'd swiped the Commodore from the all-day zone of an outer suburban railway station and fitted it with plates swiped from another Commodore parked in the next station along, to fool the cops. A Commodore because you saw them everywhere.

'Good one,' nodded Eddie.

Suddenly she braked, swung to the kerb. He couldn't believe she was doing that. 'Fuck's sake, Khandi, get us out of here.'

Instead, Khandi swung the car around in a squealing U-turn that took them back to a point in the road above the scene of the shooting. Not only that, she braked again. Eddie could see the screen of trees, evil black smoke roiling out of the little glade, a couple of curious onlookers.

Sirens in the distance.

And there was the getaway Camry, Lydia still waiting.

'What the fuck are you doing?'

'You'll see,' Khandi said, pulling up next to the Camry.

He saw, all right: Lydia slumped over the wheel, blood splashed on the glass, the shattered driver's window. 'You shot her?'

Khandi smiled one of her smiles and floored the accelerator.

He shook his head. 'You shot her.'

Her crazy jealousy, that's what it was. Not part of the plan.

The plan was, he and Khandi would kill Wyatt, grab the gear, hop into the Commodore and speed off.

All over in less than two minutes.

Meanwhile he'd call Lydia by mobile phone, tell her it had all gone pear-shaped. He'd say Wyatt had tried to doublecross them and he'd been forced to shoot the guy. He'd say they struggled and the vehicle caught fire before he could grab the gear. He was on foot, couldn't risk joining her. 'Get out now,' he'd tell her. 'I'll contact you in a few days.'

Instead, he'd be with Khandi somewhere tropical, long beaches, palm trees and piña coladas. Lydia would start to wonder after a while, discover that he'd sold his house, feel betrayed, but she'd get over it. He was nothing to her any more. No real pain for anyone—except Wyatt, and he didn't count.

Simple.

Except for the Khandi factor.

Eddie chewed on his bottom lip. Lydia hadn't deserved to die. She'd been a good sort, game for anything, and she'd dropped the Furneaux job in his lap. He'd loved her once, and yeah, thought for about five minutes they could get back together, but that was a non-starter. She'd changed anyway, and then Khandi came along.

'You didn't have to kill her.'

Whack. Khandi backhanded him.

Eddie rubbed his cheek. Big mistake, telling her about Lydia. Jealousy at the insane end of the spectrum.

He glanced back over his shoulder, expecting to see Wyatt on their tail. 'Quit twitching,' Khandi said.

'Quit hitting me in the face.'

'I haven't seen you for *days* and—'

'I told you, we had to keep our heads down.'

'Haven't seen you for days,' growled Khandi, 'and all you can talk about is your fucking ex-wife.'

Eddie swallowed. He'd met Khandi at Blue Poles, a club in the city. She'd begun paying him special attention one night, writhing around her pole before crossing to the edge of the little stage, which was slightly above his ringside table, and squatting, legs wide apart, to present her gorgeous, shaven slit.

He fell for her, fell hard. He liked women, liked sex, and even Lydia had been hot in her way, but no one was ever hot like Khandi. He'd tried explaining this to Khandi and she'd got it into her head that he still loved Lydia. '*You're* the one I love,' he insisted.

'So how come you're seeing so much of the bitch?' she screamed.

Doing homework, Khandi. Preparation for the job.

Twisting again in the passenger seat, squinting through the rear window, Eddie said, 'You don't know Wyatt. He'll come after us.'

'He's just a guy,' Khandi said.

'Just a guy? He's like a shark, he doesn't stop.'

Eddie faced forward again, laying it out for her. 'Never been arrested. Good at planning, good with a gun, a fucking incredible heist man. You can trust him, even if he never trusts you. Despises drugs and junkies. A guy who'll kill you if you cross or attack him.' He glanced at her sideways. 'But not a thrill killer.'

'What, he's got rules?' sneered Khandi. 'Rules get you nowhere.'

'Maybe. But everything just got a lot more complicated.'

Khandi gestured with her left hand, slim, brown and loaded with gold. Little tiger-stripe transfers on her fingernails, which were nicely hooked and perfect for scooping cocaine. 'Didn't know I'd taken up with a wuss,' she said.

About the worst thing she could have said to Eddie. He glanced out at the blur of fences, houses and cars. Being Khandi's lover was precarious. She'd entered his life on long legs sheathed in leather boots, fascinating, scary, alive. Beautiful, violent, unpredictable. He wanted it to last but doubted it would, and that frightened him. He didn't know what she saw in him. It was a miracle.

Meanwhile she'd landed them right in the shit. 'You need to know who we're dealing with,' he said.

'Look,' said Khandi, 'your little cutie pie's out of the way and we're heading for Queensland, okay? The guy's not going to look for us there.'

'I wouldn't bet on it.'

Khandi jammed on the brakes, leaving more rubber on the road and terrorising pedestrians and other drivers. She leaned across, opened Eddie's door. 'Get out.'

'Khandi, for fuck's sake, all I'm saying is we need to watch our backs.'

She pursed her wide red mouth and pretended to weigh a few facts. 'I hear you,' she said, and sped off again. Presently she laughed. 'The look in Goldilocks' eyes.'

Eddie was stony-faced.

Khandi sensed it, shrieking, 'Did you tell her about me?'

'Do we have to do this now?'

Big mistake: her slim, bejewelled hand lashed out again, reddening his cheek. 'I'm sensing some reserve, lover boy. Were you and that skinny cunt going to pull a fast one on me?'

'Christ, no, nothing like that,' Eddie said. He paused, trying to find the right words. 'But me and Lydia shared a history, you know?'

Another big mistake. Without changing expression, Khandi whacked him once more. 'I thought you were finished with that dried-up twat, that fucking white-bread virgin, thought her shit didn't stink.'

'Long ago.'

'Well, you are now,' snarled Khandi. 'What I meant was, finished *emotionally*.'

'We've had this discussion.'

'Do you love me?'

'You know I do.'

'Say it.'

'I adore you.'

Khandi whacked him across the kisser again. 'To adore is not to love. I'm talking about love.'

'I love you,' said Eddie, gulping.

Khandi's face was always mobile. Huge smiles wreathed it and she reached out her lovely striking hand and rested it on his crotch. He was instantly excited, so she removed her hand. In that, and many other ways, she continued to wield her power over him.

She checked his expression, checking for backsliding. Irritated, he twisted to glance through the rear window again. 'The cops will be all over this.'

'We knew that. We factored that.'

'We didn't factor Wyatt getting arrested and spilling his guts. We didn't factor the cops tying Lydia to me. Why the fuck did you shoot her? A straight hijack and we'd have been home free.'

He braced himself for another belting, but Khandi was fishing around to adjust the lie of her considerable breasts. 'Quit snivelling.'

Khandi and her fucking jealousy. The cops would tie him to Lydia, come knocking and find his place empty, publish his photo and watch for him at airports, train stations, bus depots, seaports. Then someone at Blue Poles, seeking a bit of ready cash, would tell the cops he'd been seen with Khandi Cane, who incidentally hadn't shown up for work recently.

His mind churned. 'We can't head for Queensland just yet. We need to lie low for a while.'

Suddenly Khandi was crying, wet and gusty. 'You love Lydia,' she gasped. 'Not me. Not truly.'

'Christ, Khandi, don't do that.'

'Then don't be so negative,' she said, recovering instantly. 'Support me. We're in this together.'

'Together,' Eddie said, squeezing her knee, removing his hand when the Commodore veered out of control.

Khandi recovered and kept to the speed limit. Then she yanked on the wheel and cut into a side street, stopping at a small rise half-way along. Eddie, wondering what fresh misery she had in mind for him, reached for the door handle, but Khandi surprised him. 'Tracking device,' she said.

'Good one,' said Eddie, remembering Wyatt's warning, back at the park.

He joined Khandi at the rear of the car, where she was keying open the boot. The titanium cases nestled there but Khandi leaned in and removed the spare tyre. 'A prop to explain what we're doing here.'

'You're not just a pretty face,' Eddie said.

The tyre against the side of the car, they turned their attention to the cases. Khandi popped open the nearest lid. She went still.

'What the fuck?'

A bulky document wallet. Reaching past her, Eddie opened the second case. Another wallet.

'We've been had.'

But Khandi was shaking the contents into the boot cavity, sheets of heavy-grain paper. 'Don't speak too soon.'

Bewildered, Eddie tried to read the Gothic script. 'Certificates of some kind.'

'Bearer bonds,' breathed Khandi. 'Treasury notes. Worth *millions*.'

A small metal object tumbled out. 'Tracking device,' she said, dropping it onto the asphalt, smashing it with the heel of her fine boot.

'Now what?'

'First things first,' said Khandi, 'we need to get out of here.'

Eddie directed her along side streets until they reached the Maroondah Highway, which would take them further east, away from the stink and the tension. Out there somewhere was the Yarra Valley, a region of art-and-craft towns, wineries, farmlets, hills and his aunt's cabin. The plan had been to stay the night, start heading north tomorrow. He knew people in Sydney and Brisbane who'd give him a good return on watches and jewellery, but bank paper?

It was scary, the way Khandi picked up on his thoughts. 'This is a bit out of our league, Eddie.'

'We'll think of something.'

'What, walk into a bank and exchange the stuff for cash? They'd take one look at us and—'

'Exactly. So we should stay here for a few days and work something out.'

'You sure this aunt of yours isn't going to turn up?'

'She's in an old folks' home.'

Khandi shrugged as if she'd never had an aged relative or indeed any family at all. 'Cousins?'

'No. We'll have the place to ourselves. We hide out until

the heat dies down, monitor the news. Make, umm, wild and passionate love.'

The last phrase came out hoarsely. 'Love' was a word that tangled Eddie's tongue, but Khandi, in her present mood, needed to know that sex with him was more than mere lust.

It seemed to work. She squeezed his thigh—and turned volcanic again. 'Did you ever take wifey-poo there?'

'Of course not,' lied Eddie.

Khandi changed in a flash, saying softly, 'Our own cabin in the woods.'

'Yep.'

Eddie didn't tell her that it was a gloomy, fibro-cement structure that sweltered in summer and froze in winter. It sat on a dirt road halfway up a hidden gully. No electricity, no running water. 'First we stop in Yarra Junction and stock up on supplies.'

'Okay,' said Khandi.

They drove. Khandi kept the pistol within reach and used it to scratch her calf from time to time, and once she tapped the barrel against her teeth. She was fearless and very fine. Time passed, and they left the city behind them, passing through farmland and in and out of shallow valleys before reaching the little town of Yarra Junction. 'You stay here,' said Eddie, pretty sure the likes of Khandi had not been seen in the Yarra Valley lately. He went from shop to shop buying eggs, bacon, milk, bread, beer, tequila for Khandi, cornflakes, and a $12 radio to keep up with the news. Back at the Commodore, he was relieved to see that Khandi hadn't driven off without him.

She snarled, 'What's that look for?'

'What look?'

'You thought I might run out on you.'

'No I didn't!'

'Don't lie to me, never lie to me,' Khandi said, yanking the car into drive and planting her foot.

Eddie directed her along barely remembered back roads into the hills surrounding the town. The landscape was tilled and green, but here and there were hovels with abandoned cars bedded in thick spring grass, pale nude dead trees and signs advertising New Age crackpots. Eddie didn't dare comment: he had no idea if Khandi was into all that shit. He'd only known her for six weeks. How did she get that name? Eddie felt nervous out here. It was a world apart from the inner city and his local pub.

They arrived and Khandi said, 'You've got to be joking.'

The cabin was as depressing as Eddie remembered it. 'I guess Auntie Elsie didn't get out here much.'

'Fuck your Auntie Elsie,' said Khandi, stamping around in the flowering weeds and throwing furious looks at Eddie and the grime, cobwebs, rot and mould.

But the cabin was intact. The key was up on a veranda rafter and, although the air inside was stale, there were no signs of vermin or recent visitors. Still, Eddie knew that he had to forestall further explosions so he wrapped his arms around his lover, full of tenderness and heat.

Khandi shrugged him away, heaving the titanium cases onto a wooden table coated in dust and grease. 'Later. Right now we need to think of a way to turn these into cash.'

Eddie deflated. 'Maybe if I put out some feelers...'

'The less people who know about this, the better,' said Khandi, 'otherwise your pal Wyatt will find us.'

'True.'

Khandi knuckled him on the chest to protect her nails. 'No banks, Eddie, no words dropped in certain ears.'

She had an idea, and Eddie waited for it.

'We ransom the bonds back to the man they belong to.'

16

Wyatt stirred. The vest had saved him, but the slug had delivered a cruel punch, knocking him flat, leaving him stunned. And he'd lost time. Seconds? Minutes? Awareness of his surroundings and his capabilities returned. Hearing sirens, he pushed into a crouch and to his feet. Beyond the screen of trees were houses, people walking their dogs, joggers. They would have heard the crackling of the flames, seen the black smoke corkscrewing into the sky. Soon the fuel would ignite. He couldn't afford to stick around.

Wyatt checked: he still had the pistol. Tucking it into his waistband he clambered up the slope, emerging from the roadside trees to find a handful of people standing around, hesitation painting their faces. There were no steps or path down into the park from this point, but a young woman in jogging shorts had stepped over the guardrail as if to slither down and investigate. She stopped when she saw Wyatt. She stared and the others stared—two middle-aged women, an old man with a dog, and a young man pushing a child in a stroller. The sirens were deceptive—close and loud, as if the police or the medics were lost or trapped on the network of side streets and bike lanes.

'I'm a police officer,' Wyatt called.

That would hold them for a while. He scanned the street: driveways sloping up to brick houses set in terraced gardens. There were a couple of cars visible in these driveways, but he was more interested in the pale blue Camry straddling the footpath, warning lights flashing. He strode towards it.

Lydia's head lay propped on the steering wheel and the side window was shattered. A lot of blood. He felt the beginnings of distress, didn't like it and tamped it down. Speculating about who and why would come later. Wyatt acted on reason and instinct: he had to know if she was dead or alive, and then he had to run.

He leaned in, the tensing of his spine and torso aggravating the bruising in his chest. A head wound: that explained the blood. A nasty crease above her right ear. She was lucky, Wyatt thought. She must have sensed the presence of the shooter at the side window and turned her head. And maybe the glass slowed and deflected the bullet. The noise, glass chips and flowing blood told the shooter the job was done. He felt for a pulse: it was strong and steady.

But she was unconscious, she was bleeding, and he figured that if he left her here the police would arrive and call an ambulance and she'd be patched up and then the questions would start. Who shot you? What were you doing near a burnt-out four-wheel-drive delivery vehicle belonging to Henri Furneaux? Sooner or later she would talk. Pain, painkillers and heavy questioning would break down her resolve and she'd offer up names.

He glanced back at the onlookers. They hadn't yet noticed the bloody mess in the Camry so he went around to the other side of the car, opened the door and dragged Lydia into the passenger seat. Then he returned to the driver's door, opened it and called out, 'When my colleagues get here, tell them a four-wheel-drive has plunged off the road and down among the trees. It's burning too fiercely to rescue anyone.'

They gaped at him. He got behind the wheel and drove away.

Wyatt parked the Camry in the slot reserved for his first-floor apartment, grabbed Lydia's shoulder bag and walked around to the passenger door. Perching her on the edge of the seat, he hoisted her over a shoulder in one motion and carried her to the service elevator. The underground car park was dim and toxic. Late morning; there was no one about. When the doors opened he swivelled in and pushed the button for the eighth floor, where he kept his second apartment. He was careful not to smear blood anywhere. It was all over his upper body, but he didn't want it on the doors or wall panels of the elevator.

On eight the door pinged and he shot his head out for a quick, scouting glance both ways along the corridor. Empty. He carried Lydia to his door and took her through to the bedroom. He realised that he still wore the Kevlar vest. He shrugged it off. The relief was palpable, even if his chest still ached. Then he fetched a damp cloth, bandages and a tube of antiseptic cream and cleaned Lydia's wound. It was a furrow as deep as the surface of her skull and the blood ran. He taped a thick compress to it, the fabric reddening before he'd finished removing her vest, jeans and shoes. She lay slackly in knickers and a bloodied T-shirt, unconscious but breathing evenly. He pulled the bed covers to her chin.

Now he had time to speculate.

One: until it was safe to do so, he shouldn't go back to the apartment he'd been living in. Eddie knew about it and might send the shooter there—exactly the kind of scenario that had prompted Wyatt to buy a second apartment in the same building. If he was ever traced to the first-floor apartment, and no one had seen him come and go from the *eighth* floor, he had the perfect bolthole. Anyone watching for him to return to the first floor would eventually assume that he wasn't coming back. It was like hiding in plain sight.

Two: what to do about Lydia? She wouldn't die but she needed attention. He couldn't take her to a hospital.

Three: he'd have to get rid of the car.

Four: who was the shooter? Eddie had intended to rip him off from the start, that much was evident. Eddie, wanting him dead, had stashed a shooter in ambush. Wyatt didn't spend much time exploring this line of thought. All he knew was that Eddie and the shooter had to die. They'd wanted *him* dead, so that was the right payback. It was business. He didn't feel hurt, shocked or dismayed at being cheated and left for dead. Those were the kinds of useless emotions that led a man to lash out and make an error of judgment. He would kill Eddie and the shooter and get on with his life.

Five: how involved had Lydia been? She was in pain and he could probably make use of that when she regained consciousness, but he didn't think it would be necessary. She'd been crossed, too. Besides, she was unconscious and couldn't talk yet.

Wyatt made a phone call, then left the apartment and took the stairs to the first floor, where he paused to listen. Satisfied that the corridor was empty, he walked to the shadowy end and his apartment door, listened again, let himself in. No one had been there yet. He turned on a couple of lights, figuring that an apartment that is dark for a long period is going to attract more attention than one with a few lights burning inside.

He let himself out and took the stairs to the basement. He drove the Camry to a quiet back street near the river in Abbotsford and set fire to it. He took a taxi back to Flinders Street station and walked across the river to his apartment building. Almost two hours had passed since the robbery.

Lydia was still unconscious. He sat and watched.

Thirty minutes later, the downstairs buzzer sounded.

17

Le Page and his cousins lost the GPS signal at 8.55 a.m. They spent an hour prowling around the park, attracted by the smoke and sirens, before joining the onlookers and asking what had happened. An accident, someone said. Involving a stolen vehicle, said another. A third had heard a whisper: a hijack, professional job.

Just as the three men climbed back into the BMW, Henri groaned. 'Oh, Christ.'

'What?' said Joe.

'Look who's come to the party.'

'Bloody Rigby,' said Joe.

Le Page's cousins were staring at a plain-looking woman, mousy hair, cheap, ill-fitting pants and jacket. She was a hundred metres away, getting out of an unmarked Falcon and teetering down the embankment.

'Who is she?'

'Local CIU detective, the bane of my existence,' said Henri.

Le Page leaned over from the driver's seat and grabbed his shirt front. 'You are under suspicion? The police are watching you? Tapping your phone?'

'I have the line checked every week.'

'You have not answered the question.'

'I had a bit of trouble a couple of years ago, okay?'

'What kind of trouble?'

'I was accused of handling stolen goods. The charges were dropped.'

Le Page released him, stared at him. 'But this woman watches you?'

'No. She comes into the shop sometimes. Makes a few snide remarks to piss me off, then leaves. Doesn't question me, doesn't turn the place over, just wants to remind me I'm on her radar. Happens to everyone. Bet it happens to you.'

'No,' Le Page said. He paused. 'So she will come knocking on your door now, this woman.'

'So what?' Joe said. 'We were robbed, the real thing.'

Le Page shook his head. It was now after 10 a.m. He started the BMW and they drove back to High Street, Le Page slotting the car next to the Mercedes in the yard behind the store. They got out, Henri and Joe subdued, Le Page fuming. Were Henri and Joe ripping him off? Did the detective, Rigby, know about his business here? He began to search the yard.

Henri put his hands on his hips. 'What are you doing?'

'What do you *think* I'm doing?'

Joe was affronted. 'Jesus, Alain.'

Finding nothing in the yard, Le Page moved on to the tearoom, the poky bathroom, the ceiling manholes and Henri's office, his cousins trailing him morosely. The bonds were gone. They'd been in the Audi.

'See?' said Joe, returning to the yard to smoke a cigarette.

Le Page wasn't finished. 'Come with me,' he told Henri, heading into the showroom.

Danielle watched them enter. She'd been waiting for this. The front door was locked, the 'closed' sign displayed. She knew the police would be along soon, and they'd have questions for her, but right now she could see that the French guy had questions, too. She slid a tray of engagement rings into a display cabinet and eyed him warily. She didn't know his exact connection to Mr Furneaux except they did business together. Slight accent. Old, yeah, but not as old as her boss. Maybe thirty or forty. Mr Furneaux was, like, fifty or more, and he was kind of sweaty and nervous. Danielle guessed the robbery had done that to him, but there was something else too, and then she got it: her boss was scared of the Frenchman. It was like Mr Le Page was the boss, and all this time she'd thought he was just some guy that Mr Furneaux bought stuff from.

She swallowed. Frenchie was fixing her with a look so steady and cold that it made her cringe. Her hand flew up to the commas of hair on her cheeks and she chewed the ends and turned her mini-skirted groin away from that cruel scrutiny, before straightening her back and deciding to brave it out. She'd been looked at before. Guys were scared of her, not the other way around. 'You got a problem?'

'Danielle, please,' said her boss, who was hovering behind Le Page.

'Did I do something wrong?'

'You're not in any trouble, Danielle,' her boss said.

Le Page said, in a low, burning way, 'We cannot be sure of that, Henri.'

He advanced on Danielle, stopping just a metre away from her. She stepped back. He ran his gaze up and down her body with glittering intensity. She swallowed and said, 'I don't work for you, so piss off.'

He laughed. Mr Furneaux uttered a kind of laugh. She hated them both. Then Le Page's hand shot out, found her nipple and gave it a squeeze and twist. The pain crippled her. She hunched, jerked and began to cry.

'Jesus, Alain,' her boss said.

'Shut up,' Le Page said.

With one hand over each breast, Danielle began to kick Le Page. He slapped her. She slapped at him. 'Enough,' he said.

'I'm gonna tell the cops on you,' she said.

'I do not think so,' he said.

'Mr Furneaux, make him leave me alone. It's not fair. What have I done to him?'

Furneaux, standing to one side and behind Le Page, shrugged as if to say it was out of his hands.

'I hate you both,' she said. 'I quit, and I'm telling my dad and my brothers and the police.'

Le Page fished around in the pocket of his jacket and held out five $100 notes. 'Do I have your attention?'

Danielle sniffed. She took the money after the merest hesitation. There might be more if she played her cards right. 'I didn't do anything,' she said.

'Let us suppose that I believe you.'

'It's *true*.'

'You are aware that Henri and Joseph sell their jewellery to other jewellers, are you not?'

'Yes.'

'You knew that another delivery was planned for this week, leaving today and returning on Friday?'

'Yes.'

Le Page said flatly, 'Did you tell anyone about this? A friend, lover, brother, cousin?'

The cold manner intimidated Danielle. Her only defence was to screw up her face and say, 'No way. Who do you take me for?'

'Perhaps you mentioned it in passing to someone. Perhaps you are not actively involved after all.'

Danielle shrugged, but fabric slid over her ravaged nipple and reminded her of where she was and who she was with. 'Told no one,' she muttered. 'Leave me alone.'

'You were the first person to arrive this morning, no?'

'So what? That's my job, unlocking the shop, putting stuff on display.'

'You opened the alleyway gate for your friends.'

Danielle frowned, looked at Mr Furneaux, then past him at the front window, seeing one of their regulars, an expensive idle women like many of the others, frown at the closed sign and get back into a sports car. Danielle couldn't see any comfort anywhere. 'No! Anyway, Joe was out there, getting the Audi ready.'

She waited for Le Page's response. There was a shift in the clouds above Melbourne and the mid-morning sunlight was quenched for a few seconds. The light dimmed and the lovely stones in the display window lost their lustre. Then the sun returned and Le Page said, 'Are you a stupid girl, Danielle, or is it, how do you say, all a pretence?'

She'd been asked that plenty of times by schoolteachers. She flushed and snarled, 'I'm dead honest. Ask anyone.'

'Dead honest or dead,' said Le Page. 'One or the other.'

'You're scaring me.'

Mr Furneaux said, 'You're not in any trouble, Danielle.'

'Shut up,' Le Page said. He turned to Danielle again. 'Do you ever discuss your employer's business with your friends?'

'No.'

'Perhaps you are angry with Henri. He doesn't pay you what you are worth.'

Danielle shrugged. 'It's okay.'

'Okay?' echoed Henri. 'I pay you more than enough.'

'Shut up,' Le Page said.

'Well, I do.'

Le Page said, 'Perhaps you are angry with Henri because he cannot control his urges and this offends you.'

Danielle blinked. 'Pardon?'

'He touches your titties and pussy and you wished to have revenge, no?'

Danielle wanted to please the guy and get another wad of cash off him, but she knew almost nothing about the robbery. Her world was small, and she rarely noticed anything that did not impinge on it. She knew a bit about blokes. She knew she wouldn't quit this job or report Le Page for hurting her. She'd been hurt before, hit by more than one boyfriend. Guys did that to get their own way or when they were frustrated. Knowing that about them gave her a hold over them, a sense of satisfaction.

That's when Eddie Oberin popped into her mind.

She said, marking time, 'Look, Henri and Joe deal with heaps of other businesses. You telling me they're all straight? I don't think so. Pick on someone else.'

Le Page turned to Furneaux, still standing behind him, and said, 'I am beginning to understand the limited workings of her mind, to understand her limited grasp of the English language. She is incapable of giving "yes" or "no" answers, or saying "I don't know". Am I correct?' he demanded, whirling around on Danielle again.

'Fuck off.'

His hand shot out and she cringed and wailed, 'No, don't. I don't know anything. It's not fair.'

Le Page gestured in irritation. He was finished with Danielle. He said to Furneaux, 'A waste of time.'

Danielle swallowed, wondering what would happen to her now. More pain, more cash, or nothing at all? One thing for sure, she shouldn't mention Eddie Oberin.

As if in answer, Le Page turned to her and said, 'You will say nothing of this to anyone. You will not talk to your family. You will tell the police that you know nothing, am I clear?'

'What did I ever do to you?' said Danielle sulkily.

But she was watching Le Page's hands. Sure enough, they reached into his pocket again and a moment later she'd added a further $250 to the morning's takings.

'I have to tell the police something,' she said.

Le Page thought. 'Joseph went into the yard to, to—'

'Henri asked him to wash the Mercedes.'

'Yes. He discovered the gate open and the other car missing.' A pause. 'This is very important: a delivery had not been planned. The stolen vehicle was empty.'

'Joyriding teenage boys,' Danielle said, alert for more cash.

'Very good.'

'How come?' said Henri.

'The police, they will look too closely if they suspect a jewellery robbery.'

'Got you,' Henri said.

Le Page dragged him to the back yard, where Joe was leaning against the Mercedes, surrounded by cigarette butts. He gave Joe the story—wash the car, gate open, kids, nothing valuable aboard—and had him repeat it.

'But there was something valuable aboard.'

Le Page ignored him, glowered at the brick wall. After a while, he said, 'They will not so easily move the bonds, these people.'

'They probably expected to find watches and rings,' Henri said.

'So we wait,' Le Page said. 'You have contacts, yes? Ask them to listen, as you say, on the street.'

'Offer a reward?'

'Are you mad?'

Danielle appeared. 'The police are out the front.'

Henri groaned. 'Rigby?'

She shook her head. 'Uniforms.'

'They need not know about me, Danielle,' said Le Page, starting his car.

Danielle shrugged as if it might earn her another couple of hundred dollars.

18

Wyatt's wall-mounted security unit showed the grainy face of a man with a bag outside the building, staring up at the camera above the main door.

Recognising Dr Lowe, Wyatt said 'Eight-oh-five' into the grille and pressed a button to deactivate the lock. Rather than wait behind a peephole he stepped into the corridor and stood where he could watch the lift doors and the staircase entrance. The lift peeled open, and the man who emerged saw the pistol and froze.

'You won't need that,' he said to Wyatt.

Wyatt nodded, pocketed the gun. 'Doc.'

'Good to see you again, Mr Wyatt.'

Wyatt nodded, gestured Lowe inside and shut the door behind them. The doctor was about sixty, short and slight with a potbelly the size of a basketball. He wasn't the kind of doctor who treats criminals under the radar—he wasn't an addict, didn't have a gambling habit and hadn't been struck off the register—but he was in Wyatt's debt. When Lowe's wife subjected him to a restraining order and a punitive divorce settlement, the doctor hired Wyatt to steal back three paintings he'd paid a lot of money for: a Sidney Nolan, a David Hockney and a Francis Bacon, worth a total of five million dollars. 'That's just the start,' he'd said at the time.

'Through here,' Wyatt said now.

'So much for the small talk.'

Wyatt gestured, almost in irritation, and the look that passed across his face seemed to sober the doctor. 'Gunshot, you said?'

'Creased the side of her head.'

The bedroom was peaceful, sunlight showing in gauzy bands on the carpet and bedspread. Lydia had tossed a little in unconsciousness. The pillow was smeared with blood.

Lowe examined her. 'She should really be in a hospital.'

'Not going to happen,' Wyatt said. 'Not yet.'

'I can stop the bleeding but she needs monitoring.' Lowe peeled back her eyelids. 'I don't think she's concussed,' he murmured, 'but—'

'Can you patch her up? I need a few days. If she enters hospital like this the police will come sniffing around.'

'I'll see what I can do,' Lowe said. He brooded on it. 'When we get her admitted we can say she fell off a motorbike, hit her head on an iron spike of some kind.'

'Thanks, doc.'

'The wife's also got a Bill Henson I wouldn't mind getting my hands on.'

'Don't push your luck,' Wyatt said.

Lowe dressed the wound and handed Wyatt some pills.

'Sedatives, painkillers. She'll be out for a few hours. Let me know if there's any change.'

Then he was gone.

A few kilometres east of Wyatt's apartment building, Alain Le Page had swapped the rented BMW for a pale blue Ford from the nearest Hertz agency and was seated behind the wheel, nursing the portable GPS monitor and watching the activity at Furneaux Brothers. The rest of the morning passed, the police dawdled, and still no GPS signal. He'd banked on the thieves finding the main transponder, but not those he'd concealed inside the thick carry handles of the document wallets, so something else must have gone wrong. Some kind of signal black-spot, environmental interference, problems with the satellite?

Danielle emerged from Furneaux Brothers at twelve-thirty, carrying a bag and a light-weight jacket. Le Page saw her stand there and chew on her lower lip, and when she moved he tailed her to a little red Mazda parked in a narrow lot behind a supermarket.

This could go any way. It went the way Le Page expected. He knew Danielle lived in Highett, but instead of heading home, like anyone who's suffered a distressing couple of hours, or to a café for lunch, she drove across town to North Melbourne and a hangdog little house on a narrow sloping street. Angling his rental car behind a dump bin, bumping the front tyres over the kerb, Le Page switched off and powered down his window. He propped a Nikon fitted with a telephoto lens on the sill, and snapped Danielle opening a gate and knocking on a white door.

*

There was no answer, and the house felt empty. Danielle hovered, wondering what to do. Go home? But she needed to know if Eddie Oberin was behind the robbery, needed to know if her big mouth was to blame for it. Eddie had sweet-talked her into confiding about work and the creepy brothers who employed her. Pillow talk. Now she felt stupid and scared, stupid for getting fooled, scared of Le Page's creepy fingers, the way they had hurt her, then paid her in hundred-dollar bills.

She tried telling herself she hadn't really done anything wrong, or not deliberately. Also, it was ages ago, two, three months at least. She'd moved on, other guys, other experiences. When Eddie stopped returning her calls, she shrugged, no big deal. If you don't invest much, you don't lose much.

She recalled the way he just appeared at the gym one day, a good-looking older guy with a twinkle in his eye. Calm, collected, well-dressed, not some try-hard twenty-something loser. She let him chat her up, spend some money on her. The sex was good without being spectacular; an older guy, he knew how to take his time and pay attention to a woman's needs. Gave her a little coke, some speed from time to time.

He liked to lie with her afterwards, with her head on his chest or in the crook of his arm, and they'd talk about everything under the sun. She told him about the hidden compartments in the big Audi. She told him about Le Page's visits, how they coincided with the Furneaux brothers' sales run and the new stock in their estate-jewellery display.

Sneakily done, she thought now, the bastard. Eddie had told her some stories about bosses *he'd* endured over the years, scams he'd twigged to or been part of. He drew her in, flattering, patient, and she fell for it. Then he stopped calling and she supposed there was another woman but she wasn't going to humiliate herself over it.

Eddie didn't like to use his place. 'Bachelor pad,' he said, 'a side of me you don't want to see.' Ambiguous, yeah? Like maybe he'd welcome a change in status sometime? So they fucked at her place.

But she knew where he lived. So as soon as the cops finished questioning her, and Henri said she could take the rest of the day off, she'd headed straight here to Eddie's.

And the bastard wasn't home.

Le Page photographed the girl several times in the act of knocking, and again when she returned to her car and drove away.

He elected to stay. Danielle was the known quantity. The unknown was the person who lived behind the white door. 'I need to talk to Danielle again,' he said, into his mobile phone. 'You will detain her for me.'

'She's not here,' Henri said.

Le Page closed and opened his eyes. 'I realise that. I want you to seize her at her house.'

'I'll send Joseph,' Henri said.

Le Page settled in to wait.

Wyatt was edgy after the doctor's visit. He could be patient for long hours if there was a score at the end of it, but nursing an invalid brought him nothing. He needed to move.

Maybe Eddie Oberin was hiding in plain sight. Pocketing Lydia's house keys, Wyatt darted through a brief sun shower to the underground car park of an adjacent apartment complex, where he kept an old Falcon. It meant a handy $100 a month to the Malaysian accountancy student who rented the slot to him.

The building was on a corner, meaning two exits, one onto the street that passed Wyatt's apartment building, the other onto the street at right angles to it. Wyatt drove out of the second one, wearing a baseball cap and dark glasses. Then he steered into his street and prowled along it, blessing the speed bumps, which obliged him to drive slowly and gave him time to eyeball the parked cars. They were all empty and at that moment the footpaths were clear of pedestrians. There was only a woman in uniform delivering the mail, and she'd been working in this part of Southbank ever since Wyatt had moved into the area.

Satisfied, he drove to Abbotsford. The little river suburb was mostly prettified cottages now, but brewery and river odours still lingered at the back of a man's throat, dingy factories and weatherboards still crouched in the side streets. Here and there the sun penetrated, coaxing dirty rainbows out of greasy potholes. Dirty old town, Wyatt thought.

Lydia's house was a semi-detached cottage dating from the 1890s, heritage stripes on the little veranda roof but otherwise in need of upkeep. He watched from the car for thirty minutes, then let himself in. After making a rapid sweep of the interior, he took a closer look at her letters, calendars, computer files, wardrobes, drawers and bathroom cabinets for signs of a hidden life or partner. Finding nothing that didn't belong, he began to select changes of clothes for her, cramming a garbage bag with underwear, T-shirts, jeans, tops and shoes. The fabric moved softly in his grasp, leaving him faintly unmoored.

*

While Wyatt searched and packed, Le Page waited. His rental car ticked as it cooled. Still no GPS signal from the transponders he'd stowed with the bonds, no sign of life at the house with the white door. Meanwhile pedestrians wandered by, and they all glanced in at Le Page sitting there. He knew that some of them would wonder, it would grow and niggle at them. With a curse, he left the car, taking the camera with him.

Opposite the house with the white door was a small, two-storey structure, vaguely Mediterranean villa in style, with creamy rendered walls and fat columns. A woman dressed in black was watering the concrete in front. Le Page advanced on her in his stylish clothes, his fleshless face severe, and flipped open his wallet. 'Police. I need your upstairs front room for a couple of hours.'

He'd made a snap judgment, seeing a widowed Turkish or Lebanese woman who would naturally fear all kinds of authority. She wouldn't interfere.

'You live alone?'

She shrank away and stared at the garden path, so he let himself in and made a rapid search of the house, finding only unoccupied rooms outfitted by the kinds of furniture barns that advertise on late-night TV. Plenty of chunky dark wood, gold plaster and velvet. It must be universal, Le Page thought, recalling the homes of the Algerians he'd known in Marseilles. He stationed himself at the window above the street and stared out with all the patience in the world. The time was 1 p.m.

Wyatt parked in the customer-parking zone of a Subway store two blocks from Eddie Oberin's house, rear bumper toward the wall so that he could get away quickly. He kept a gym bag of props in the boot of the car: tools, some generic items of workmen's apparel, official-looking forms and a hand-held gauge. Shrugging into a yellow safety jacket, he pocketed a glasscutter and set off on foot, carrying a clipboard. A clipboard is one of the oldest props and the most effective. It made Wyatt invisible. He was a meter reader, maybe, or a guy checking for potholes.

He made one rapid pass of Eddie's street, striding along as though bound for a particular house at the far end. Then he came back slowly, looking at numbers and making nonsense notations on his clipboard with a ballpoint pen, trying to imagine Eddie living here. Not all of the houses up and down the gentle slopes and tightly packed streets had been gentrified. Mean little brick and weatherboard cottages crouched here and there, unaltered in a hundred and forty years, behind verandas and light-choking hedges. Old battler couples lived in them, too poor and hidebound to renovate or move out. Where would they go, anyway? Far away to the edges of the city, to some new estate where there was no love, pride or public transport? And so they stayed until they died. Eddie's parents had died fifteen years ago and Eddie had moved back into the tiny weatherboard where he'd been raised.

The place was a ruin but this was North Melbourne and the location was worth a fortune. Even so, Eddie had told Wyatt he had no intention of selling. 'I'd only gamble or piss it away,' he said. 'Besides, I love the joint.'

Love it enough to return to it after this morning's debacle? Wyatt walked to the other end of the street, the early afternoon sun around him lying bright on asphalt, parked cars and dispirited front gardens. The owners of those gardens were at work, young professionals mostly, with large salaries and larger mortgages, in love with the idea of life in the inner suburbs, close to the university which had insulated them when they studied there, and engendered in them a fearful narrowness of range. If lured to powerful jobs elsewhere, they would always come back, to architect-designed boxes alongside the student houses in which they'd first smoked dope and lost their virginity. That made them like everyone else, in Wyatt's view. Afraid to roam, an instinct for the herd.

He walked to the other end and back again, checking every car, a mix of student wrecks, old codger Holden sedans from the 1980s, Saabs, Golfs and Subarus, and a Hertz Falcon. No engine heat rising from any of them. No one sitting behind the wheel, pretending to read a newspaper or make a phone call. Two young women entered the street, wheeling prams, one with a toddler clinging to her jeans. They entered a house midway along. Two guys were hammering a new roof onto a house half a block from the main road, but they'd clearly been there for days. An old couple sat behind a screen of vines and creepers on a nearby veranda. That was all.

Le Page saw the man stroll with an easy lope up and down the street. The clipboard was reassuring, but the covert examination of every car wasn't, and no man with a clipboard was this dark and sinuous. Le Page went on full alert and snapped off a few photographs.

The woman came in behind Le Page and said, 'Coffee or tea, sir? You are hungry?'

He ignored her. The stranger was making another pass of the little street.

'Sir?'

'Get out.'

Wyatt turned his head to the side, catching a brief glimpse of the right flank of Eddie's cottage; then he was passing along the front; and now he caught a glimpse down the left flank. The place looked shut up and empty. A hedge on either side divided it from the neighbours, one a 1970s house of pale yellow brick and the other a new, pastel-grey structure that looked like a stack of corrugated iron cubes, the kind to have his'n'hers Peugeots in the driveway. Wyatt walked to the end of the street and came back again.

Shortly after that, the old couple went indoors. Wyatt opened Eddie's gate, closed it behind him and mounted the front steps.

Le Page saw the man knock on the white door, just as Danielle had. He tried to imagine their motives. They have come to divide the spoils but their partners have doublecrossed them. They have come to ambush the thieves. They were betrayed and seek revenge.

Now the stranger was hunting for something.

19

First Wyatt searched for a spare key, turning over Oberin's garden rocks and pot plants, running his hand along the top of door and window frames, fishing around inside the fuse box.

It was an old-style fuse box, with gauges, metres and needles. Just a trickle of power showing—probably the refrigerator. He turned off the main switch and darted into the shelter of bushes at the side of the house to see if the alarm would sound and Eddie Oberin come charging out with a gun.

Nothing happened. Wyatt edged around to the rear of the house. The back yard was a tangle of weeds. The sunlight revealed a garden shed in bright aluminium, a clothesline and a wheelbarrow loaded with grassy old bricks.

It was a nasty place to get trapped in, so he checked the back fence, which overlooked a narrow lane of bluestone cobbles, jasmine-draped fences, cat piss and sodden drifts of cardboard. The gate was unlocked, but the bottom edge struck a cobblestone and wouldn't budge. He tested the fence: the rotting boards left a scum of green-black mould on his hands. He wrenched a couple of boards away, making a hole he could slip through into the lane.

Wyatt returned to the yard and settled to watch the house from the shelter of the little shed. He scarcely moved. Most people are poor sentinels, but Wyatt's life was built on stillness, watching and thinking. The waiting and thinking were steady and natural, like breathing. He was comfortable inside his skin. The wind moaned, and the city charged on around him, and he tried to visualise Eddie Oberin in the aftershock of what had happened that morning. He asked himself what Eddie knew or guessed, and what, consequently, he would do. No doubt he'd monitor the radio and TV news. He'd wonder why there was no mention of bodies being found at the scene of the burning Audi. That would throw him off balance. If he thinks I'm alive, Wyatt thought, he'll be scared. If he thinks I'm dead, he'll wonder why the cops aren't saying anything.

There was also Eddie's relationship with Lydia. Was shooting her always part of the plan? Had the mystery woman been brought in later, or was she in it from the beginning? Perhaps Eddie hadn't known that his partner would start shooting and bring the whole thing undone.

So, would Eddie risk coming back to this house? It seemed to Wyatt that Eddie's thinking would hinge on Lydia. By now he's assuming the police have identified her, he thought. He'll know the police can link her to him, and he'll know not to come back—especially if he thinks there's any chance I'm still alive.

Satisfied that he'd be able to pick over Eddie Oberin's life without interruption, Wyatt looked for a way into the house. He started with the back door, which was heavy, behind an iron and wire mesh outer door. Both doors had been fitted with top-class locks. He checked the windows. They were all locked and alarmed—a thin, unbroken metal strip ran around the perimeter of every glass panel. If he broke the glass and severed the metal strip, an alarm would sound. It hadn't sounded when he turned the power off because it had its own power supply.

The solution was simple. Using the glasscutter on a window at the side of the house, Wyatt cut out the entire panel without damaging the security strip and propped it on the sill. He saw a narrow room, grimy carpet, nothing else. He climbed through and dropped to the floor.

Wyatt waited again. It was a house of shifting joists and rafters, but none betrayed the presence of Oberin or his friends or pursuers. And the air was stale. Admittedly the guy had spent the past week in a motel, but the house felt abandoned. Wyatt stepped into the corridor and then from room to room. The sensation intensified.

There were some scraps of furniture, but nothing of any worth, such as TV set, sound system, refrigerator, computer. The remainder pointed to a life of unrealistic and disappointed aims. Wyatt found lottery and raffle tickets, betting slips, some weary porn, a crusted sock in a dusty corner, a rickety wardrobe with a busted door. Nicotine painted the walls and ceilings of the main rooms and furniture shapes shadowed the carpet. Over the kitchen sink was a cobwebby electric clock, evidently worth nothing to a second-hand dealer and the reason why the meter box had shown a slow seep of current. The time was 1.20.

A couple of business letters and flyers lay inside the front door. A letter from Optus confirmed that the phone had been cancelled and the account closed with a nil balance. A bank had written: for the foreclosure to be official and final, Mr Oberin's presence and signature were required, at his earliest convenience.

Wyatt went through the place again and found a strip of matches, the flap vivid navy with a writhing black silhouette, the words 'Blue Poles' in gold and an address in Flinders Lane.

There was a knock on the door.

20

Then another knock, and a voice calling, 'Eddie? You there? It's Danielle.'

Wyatt nodded to himself, putting it all together. He yanked open the door, clamped his fingers around the woman's forearm and pulled. When she was over the threshold he slammed the door. Now his fingers were around her windpipe and she was backing up the wall, climbing onto her toes. The odours of scorched meat and spicy sauce were caught in her hair, on her clothes and hands.

He released the pressure. 'Did you come straight here from work?'

'What? Who are you? Where's Eddie?'

But it was feigned. Her eyes were hooded; she was looking for angles to play. Wyatt didn't have time for it and choked her again. 'Did you come straight here?'

He saw her switch gears. He stood back and watched her swallow and stroke her throat and finally shake her head.

'Not exactly. I was here earlier.'

'And?'

She shrugged. 'No one home, so I went to get some lunch and saw you.'

Wyatt thought. 'The Subway parking lot? You recognised me?'

'Yes.' She was half-proud, half-scared to admit it.

Wyatt dragged her away from the door. 'We have to leave. Right now. Out the back.'

She struggled against the steel of his fingers. 'Ow. Why?'

'You were probably followed.'

'Followed?'

Wyatt ignored her and took her at a stumbling run through to the rear of the house. 'You're hurting me,' she said.

He opened the back door, glanced into the miserable yard and used her as a shield down the steps to the flourishing weeds. Men were shouting somewhere on the street in front of the house. He hauled Danielle through the grass to the rotted planks of the alleyway fence.

'This jacket's ruined,' she said on the other side, holding the torn, moss-stained fabric away from her hip.

'Shut up.'

'*You* shut up.'

He slapped her hard. 'You were feeding Eddie information.'

'Ow.'

'Come on.' He wanted her moving.

'I didn't mean to. It was over ages ago.'

Wyatt hustled her over the slick cobbles to the alley mouth but kept her close to the backyard fences and tendrils of jasmine.

'Whether or not you actively helped Eddie, you're a suspect.'

'I didn't *do* anything.'

Wyatt felt close to the edge on this. He said savagely, 'Someone will have followed you, the police or Le Page. Surprise, surprise, you don't go home but straight here, to the house of a man with a criminal record.'

She was silent. Wyatt flattened against the end wall with her while he stuck his head out. Then he glanced back along the alley, which remained clear. He didn't understand the shouting in the street or the silence that had followed it. When a taxi drew into the kerb on the cross street, he ran to it in a crouch, Danielle's slender wrist still in the steel clamp of his fingers.

'Ow.'

'Shut up.'

They piled into the back seat and Wyatt said, 'Southern Cross.'

The central railway station. From there he could choose a train in any direction. The taxi merged with the flow of afternoon traffic and passed the entrance to Eddie Oberin's street. Three young men were chest-shoving Le Page and that was all Wyatt saw. He settled back in his seat and, almost like a lover, pulled Danielle against his upper body and murmured in her ear, 'Le Page. I saw him back there.'

She went rigid. Still like a lover he said, 'It's dangerous for you now. He'll hurt you. Don't go home.'

She nodded and tears splashed onto her shirt front.

Wyatt went on pitilessly, 'Eddie appeared one day, friendly, charming, you started going out.'

'I swear I didn't know he was pumping me for information.'

'Did you give the police his name? Le Page?'

'No! I swear, I didn't twig till later, and...'

Wyatt let her talk. It probably did her good. When she asked him how he was connected to Eddie or the robbery, he said nothing but crammed a few dollars into her hand and got out at the next set of lights.

21

Leaving Khandi to sleep after her hectic morning, Eddie headed back down to Yarra Junction and asked around for the library. Eddie hadn't knowingly been near a library since he'd left school, and just stepping inside this one, a small branch library behind the village shops, brought back memories of dreariness. He averted his eyes from the stacks of scuffed hardcovers and went straight to the main desk.

'I'd like to use the Internet.'

He glanced across at the small cluster of computers. Every unit was taken—retirees, by the look of the grey heads. Old geezers and chooks tapping away with one finger, searching the net to see if they had convicts in the family tree.

The librarian ran her finger down a booking sheet. 'I'm afraid we won't have a computer ready until two o'clock.'

Giving him an hour for lunch. 'That's fine,' Eddie said.

He walked to the pub, where he ate a mixed grill and nursed a beer. He wanted a clear head when he returned to the library. There was a TV set bolted to the wall above the bar, tuned to a talk show. When a news update came on, Eddie strained to listen. He'd heard the midday news back at the cabin, but details of the robbery and the Audi fire were sketchy. Eddie wanted visuals. He peered at the screen.

Good: film of the park and the Audi's blackened shell, cops, bystanders milling around, fire engine some distance away— but no body bags, no ambulances, no mention of a man and a woman with gunshot wounds.

He couldn't let himself think that Lydia was alive, that she'd talk to the cops. Or Wyatt. Would she remember the cabin after all this time? He struggled to finish his beer. All flavour had disappeared from it and his tastebuds, mouth and throat wouldn't work. He ordered a scotch.

At 2 p.m. he was seated between an old guy looking at images of World War II battleships and a girl of fifteen Googling song lyrics. She had rolls of visible midriff, electric blue hair, rings in the cartilage of both ears. Edging his chair away from her, Eddie clicked on Internet Explorer.

For the next hour, he searched permutations of 'bearer bonds', 'treasury bonds', 'Bank of England' and 'theft'. Pretty soon he was reading about a recent snatch, big-time, a courier knifed on a London street in broad daylight. He tingled inside, admiring the nerve. *£260 million* worth. Who had the rest? He read on and learned that Interpol, acting on a tip-off, had arrested four couriers and recovered bonds worth £60 million in the suitcase of an Irish woman travelling from Toronto to Rio, £40 million in a New Delhi locker, £55 million during a routine search of baggage aboard a Los Angeles flight bound for Peru, £13 million in a Cape Town hotel room. But that left bonds worth £92 million unaccounted for. Given that the couriers had travelled to multiple locations before being arrested, it was the opinion of Scotland Yard and Interpol that the missing bonds had been distributed widely. Some would expire soon, but not before unscrupulous people exchanged them for loans, cash, real estate, paintings...

Eddie made a note to himself: check expiry dates.

He read on. A couple of mysterious deaths.

Sitting back, staring at the ceiling battens of the library, Eddie wondered what he and Khandi had let themselves in for. Maybe the Furneaux brothers were big-time after all. If so, they wouldn't respond well to a ransom demand. On the other hand, there was no one he knew or trusted to buy the bonds or broker a deal for him; definitely no way he or Khandi could hope to fool a bank manager. So her plan was probably best: ransom the bonds back to the Furneaux brothers.

Before he left the library, Eddie checked the websites of the ABC, Channel 9 and the *Herald Sun*. Scarcely anything on the torched four-wheel-drive, still nothing about gunshot victims. Either the cops hadn't found any bodies, or they had and were keeping it quiet.

He wiped his palms on his jeans, found the number for Furneaux Brothers on line, quit and headed for the post office, where he bought a pre-paid mobile phone. He dumped the phone Wyatt had supplied into a bin.

Back at the cabin, Khandi was climbing the walls, an amphetamine buzz on, the streak in her hair looking more disordered than dangerous.

'Where the fuck have you been?'

'I'm here now,' Eddie said.

She flung herself against him, hot, squirming and desperate. 'I thought you'd left me. I thought you didn't love me any more.'

'Baby,' said Eddie, inadequate to the task of returning so much passion, hoping it didn't show, 'I wouldn't run off—*you* had the bonds.'

Whack. He staggered and the world yawed a little. 'The money means more to you than I do?' shrieked Khandi.

'Of course not,' he said, blinking to clear the numerous Khandis floating before his eyes. She was mad, lethal, focused when she needed to be and unpredictable, but two things were constant: she loved him and she always turned paranoid when she was on the gear. Eddie put his loving arms around her and took her to the sofa. Dust rose as he held her and nuzzled her neck for a while.

She shoved him away. 'What did you find out? Were you looking at porn?'

Eddie went on high alert. The slightest thing could make her wildly jealous. He couldn't even let his eyes pass a billboard of a chick in her knickers—and how do you avoid that these days? 'I don't think you can look up porn in a library—not that I'd want to,' he said hastily. He told her about the London robbery.

'Two hundred and sixty *million*? Where's the rest of it?'

'Cape Town, Peru…you name it. Some of it came to Henri Furneaux, and he was going to off-load his allocation here,' guessed Eddie.

Khandi fetched him a can of beer and the tequila for herself and they sat outside in the sun for a while. Eddie fiddled with the pistol, surprised himself by clearing the jam. Then Khandi placed a lissom foot in his lap and he had trouble concentrating.

He took a swig of beer. 'There was nothing on the news about Lydia or Wyatt.'

'That bitch,' hissed Khandi.

'Sweetness, it means trouble for us.'

'Like how? I offed wifey, and Wyatt can't find us.'

Eddie crushed his empty can and hurled it at a blue wren. 'You'd think there'd be something in the news.'

'It's some cop thing,' Khandi said. 'They're keeping it quiet.'

Eddie brooded. 'What I think happened is, the vest saved Wyatt and he made his way back to the car. Found Lydia, shoved her into the passenger seat and took off before the cops arrived.'

'Will you just quit it?'

'You're not listening to me. If Wyatt finds us, we're history.'

Khandi cuddled him violently. 'I've got a bullet for the prick and I know where he lives, so chill out, okay?'

He'd shown her the Southbank apartment one day when Wyatt was scouting around looking at parks. But would the guy be stupid enough to go back there?

They drank some more and watched cloud shadows pass across the valley folds. Mellowing as the day dwindled, Eddie said, 'I think we should contact Furneaux right now and get our money before Wyatt finds us.'

'Wyatt, always Wyatt,' Khandi screamed in her fine, insane way, then calmed abruptly. 'Good thinking, I guess.' He showed her the pre-paid mobile, and she dialled the jeweller's number with her dexterous, tiger-striped thumbs.

22

Picking up his office phone to hear a woman announce she was calling about his bearer bonds, Furneaux nearly lost it. 'You've got a fucking nerve,' he snarled.

The voice screeched in his ear. 'Whoa, whoa, Henri, let's establish who has the upper hand here.'

Furneaux checked the display. An unfamiliar mobile phone number. 'Danielle?'

'Who the fuck's Danielle?'

Furneaux shook his head. 'Who is this?'

'I'm your guardian angel. I've got your stuff, it's safe and sound, and you can have it back for a million bucks.'

'You must be joking.'

'Call you back in an hour.'

The phone went dead. He checked his watch: 3.45. A moment later, more shit piled on his head. His mobile rang and Joe said, 'Can't find her anywhere.'

'Who?' said Henri, rattled.

There was the kind of silence that said Joe was sifting through the recent past to find where he'd got Henri's orders wrong. He said, in a low voice, 'Danielle?'

'Forget it. Come on back.'

Then a fist pounded on the front door. Lynette Rigby, the detective sergeant flashing her badge at him through the glass. He unlocked the door. 'I might have known you'd show up eventually.'

'Nice to be wanted, Henri. A few minutes of your time?'

'It's not really convenient right now.'

Rigby laughed, ducked past him and strode through the showroom to his office. Settled into the chair that faced his desk, waited for him to sit across from her. 'We've already given statements to the uniform boys,' he said, glancing at his watch.

'Are you expected somewhere, Henri? Late for an appointment? Waiting on a phone call?'

Furneaux shot his cuffs, folded his arms and stared at her. 'I'm not getting any younger.'

'Or any richer, apparently.'

Was she talking about the bonds or the Audi? 'Quit hassling me. Month after month.'

She opened her arms in astonishment. 'But Henri, I'm investigating a crime. You were robbed this morning, remember?'

'Look, there's no need for CIU to get involved. Joe left the bloody gate open and some joyriding kids stole the Audi and torched it, that's all.'

She gave him one of those big empty smiles the police are so good at. 'Really? Stole that ugly great four-wheel-drive instead of your cute sports car?'

He shrugged. 'Maybe it was easier to break into.'

'And they cut your car tyres so you wouldn't follow? Kids? I don't think so. Made some enemies, Henri? Up to your old tricks?'

'I'm straight,' Furneaux muttered. 'Have been for years.'

'Just let me check our records,' Rigby said, flipping through some pages in a folder. 'Oh yes, here we are…receiving stolen goods.'

'That was years ago.'

'Oh, and you have a brother who's done time for burglary and assault. Leopards never change their spots, Henri.'

'Don't call me Henri, Lyn.'

'*Mr* Furneaux.'

He couldn't get a clear fix on her shape under the pants and jacket. Dryish shoulder-length hair, short, bitten fingernails, no wedding or engagement rings, murky, shallow eyes. But he knew she was ambitious, unimpressed and, in her way, tough. And a distraction right now. Furneaux wanted her out of his office so he could let Alain know about the ransom demand.

He glanced at his watch again. Almost four. 'How much longer?'

He pictured the hard, bony stillness of his cousin. Alain would know what to do. If only Rigby would get a move on, finish her questions and piss off back to the cop shop.

'A lot of things don't add up,' Rigby said. 'You glimpsed the thieves driving away?'

'Enough to see it was a pair of kids.'

'Like I said, kids clever and ballsy enough to steal your flash four-wheel-drive and let down your tyres so you couldn't follow.'

It was a statement, not a question. Furneaux shrugged. 'Kids these days.'

'Oh, you're a wise old man now, Henri?'

'Fuck off.'

'How do you know they were kids if you didn't get a close look at them?'

'Their clothing, size, stuff like that, okay?'

His mouth felt dry. He could see the bearer bonds and treasury notes disappearing forever. It would have been so easy to wash them into legitimate cash and secure bank loans, but now some mad woman had them. Wanted a million dollars for them. Where the hell was he going to get that kind of money? And who the fuck *was* she? She'd sounded off her head.

'I guess it's reasonable to suppose that it *was* kids,' Rigby was saying, musing.

'I've told you all I know.'

'Oh, I don't think so, Henri.'

Furneaux gazed at her.

'There's the matter of your missing jewellery.'

'What jewellery?' said Henri, guessing their forensic people had been poking around in the ashes and hadn't found any molten gold or silver, any stones, and were thinking *jewel robbery*.

'Does this sound like an inside job to you, Henri? Someone who knows you deliver your goodies around the state in a luxury four-wheel-drive?'

What did she know about his delivery runs? 'Couldn't say.'

'Try.'

Furneaux shrugged again. But his mind was racing. The thieves had expected a jewellery shipment, found themselves with paper instead, didn't know how to offload it, and were ransoming it back to him.

They're desperate, he thought, feeling calmer now. Desperate people make mistakes. Their big mistake was going to be Alain.

'Look, the Audi was empty. Not making a delivery till next week. It was kids, I'm telling ya.'

'Fair enough. Leaving aside the question of the *source* of the goods you transport, is it possible one of your clients decided to hit you before you left the city?'

That's what Furneaux wanted to know. He said nothing but stared past Lynette Rigby's shoulder at his bookshelf, books about art and design, jewellery making, histories of famous manufacturers and designers. 'Like I said, no delivery planned, joyriding kids.'

'Someone heard shots,' said Rigby.

Well, that creeped him out. 'Not here. We didn't shoot anyone, or anything.'

'Do you own a gun, Henri? Did you in fact tail the thieves to the park and shoot it out with them?'

Furneaux didn't want her asking him about guns. 'Fuck it, *no*. Probably glass cracking, the fuel tank exploding, that kind of thing.'

Another of those empty smiles. 'A man was seen leaving the park and getting into a blue Camry. One witness mentioned seeing blood and broken glass. The man said he was a policeman. We've checked: no suspicious shooting, burns or accident victims have been admitted to hospital anywhere today. No cops unaccounted for, either.' She paused. 'Do you or Joe own a blue Camry, Henri?'

He smirked. 'You are joking.'

'Isn't it in your best interests to help me? We're on the same side, aren't we?'

'You're the detective. Go and detect. I merely make and sell jewellery.'

'What can you tell me about Danielle?'

Furneaux tried to meet Rigby's gaze. 'She's honest.'

'A man in your profession would want to do a background check on potential employees, wouldn't he?'

'She checked out okay.'

'She was interviewed by a uniformed officer this morning. Now she's uncontactable.'

'I sent her home. She was upset.'

'How did you follow the Audi, Henri? How did you know which way it went?'

'We didn't follow it.'

'A man like you, prosperous jeweller, you'd want to keep track of your vehicles, wouldn't you? GPS and so on. Maybe you tailed the thieves, shot it out with them, hurried back here and slashed your own tyres to cover it up?'

'Don't be ridiculous.'

Furneaux was getting pissed off with her. Like a lot of cops, Rigby was driven by self-love; you could see it in her smartarse expressions. Meanwhile the woman who had his bonds was about to call back and he still hadn't told Alain and he didn't have a million bucks. 'Like I told you, it was a couple of thieving little bastards who let my tyres down.'

'Kids.'

'Yeah.'

'Where's your brother, Henri? I thought he'd be here with you.'

'Had a delivery.'

'He told the uniformed officers that the back gate was locked.'

'He's just trying to protect me. It's instinctive.'

'Protect you from what?'

'Insurance hassles.'

'Yeah?'

'It's true,' Furneaux insisted. 'He's not the sharpest knife in the drawer, but he's solid.'

'He likes to beat people up, Henri. Put them in hospital with brain damage.'

Furneaux flushed.

Rigby leaned across the desk and patted his wrist. He'd been leaning his forearms on the pristine blotter there, fiddling with a paperclip. Her fingers were cool and dry but they felt like burning brands and he jerked back from her touch.

'No reason for CIU to be involved.'

'Then I'll find a reason,' Rigby said.

'What, you're going to fit me up?'

It came out heated and cranky. It was getting late and he needed a scotch. Plus, he'd missed lunch. His shirt was sticking to him. Please god Joe wouldn't decide to wander in before Rigby left. The only good thing was, she didn't seem to know about Alain.

'Fit you up, Henri? You've already done a pretty good job of fitting yourself up.'

23

After ditching Danielle, Wyatt went shopping and returned to his apartment in the role of jogger: running shorts, singlet, Nike trainers. He didn't think he'd been tailed, but the defensive measures were instinctive. Lydia was still unconscious.

Late afternoon, she stirred. Her eyes fluttered, opened, and registered pain, bewilderment and grogginess. Her hand went to her ear. Wyatt said, 'You were shot.'

He saw her struggle to remember. He saw the knowledge dawn in her. She shut her eyes for some time.

When she opened them again, Wyatt said, 'Who was the woman?'

The tiny responses of Lydia's face and body said that she didn't have a clue.

'Did Eddie have a secret girlfriend?'

Lydia shrugged minutely.

'Did you ever go to a place called Blue Poles with him?'

She was baffled. 'What?'

Wyatt piled on the questions. 'Did you know that he intended to rip me off? Were you part of it?'

There was a whispered no.

He watched her neutrally. 'I was also shot.'

Her gaze flickered across his face and body.

'The vest.'

He continued to watch her, his eyes bright, alert and empty. 'Tell me about the woman.'

'I swear I—'

'Is she Eddie's sister? Cousin? *Your* sister or cousin or friend? The three of you intended to rip me off, except you didn't know you'd be ripped off, too?'

'No.'

'Convince me.'

Tears were leaking from her eyes. He was watching for the lies and evasions. Struggling against the pain, she said, with minimal movements of her mouth, 'Someone shot me. That's all I know.'

She blinked and tried to sit up. Wyatt propped a pillow beneath her shoulders, another behind her head, but the effort was too much for her. 'My head's killing me,' she said, and slid into unconsciousness again. Wyatt waited. When she stirred he gave her a painkiller and a glass of water. She gulped the water, screwed up her eyes and flopped back on the pillow. 'Such a headache, you wouldn't believe.'

Wyatt was unimpressed. 'Do you know who Eddie's friends are?'

'Clearly not all of them,' she murmured, a knot of bitterness in her voice.

'I went to your house, thinking he might be there.'

Lydia was baffled. 'Why would he be?'

'The question I had to ask myself,' said Wyatt, 'was why *wouldn't* he be.'

'Eddie...' She was distressed. 'Look, the bastard sold me out.'

'Then I went to *his* house. It's empty, been sold.'

She frowned. 'What?'

'You didn't know?'

She shook her head.

'You know what Henri Furneaux's store manager looks like?'

'Yes.'

'Was she the woman who shot you?'

'No. Why?'

'She showed up at Eddie's.'

Wyatt watched Lydia's face. She closed her eyes. 'I don't understand.'

Wyatt pressed on. 'And the Frenchman, Le Page, was there outside Eddie's house. Know anything about that?'

Lydia groaned. 'Why would I?'

'I think he followed the store manager, but encountered some locals before he could kill us.'

His voice offered no comfort, so she said, desolately, 'Is that what you're going to do, kill me?'

Wyatt allowed himself a trace of irritation. If it was necessary to kill her, he would. But it wasn't. Only fools let it be the solution to everything. Right now, killing Lydia would compound his problems. 'What aren't you telling me?'

'*Nothing*,' she said hoarsely, straining again to lift from the pillow.

The motion, minute and exhausting, finished her. She fell asleep. Wyatt let her sleep. He walked to his window high above the streets and watched the lengthening shadows. Realising that he was hungry, he zapped a microwave dinner and ate it at the bare table, closed off from the world by walls and heavy glass. Lydia would have to stay here until he'd taken care of Eddie Oberin and the female shooter. Then it would be safe for her to be admitted to a discreet private hospital or nursed at home. She'd mend. Apart from a scar she could hide under her hair, she'd be herself again.

He listened to the news-radio station and to the chatter on his police scanner. Only a little about the torched Audi and none of it new. When Lydia surfaced again he helped her to sip water, even some soup. The spills he mopped from her breasts with a soft towel. She watched him helplessly as he dabbed. It was almost a lover's touch. Lydia was dismayed to feel her body responding, even as she sensed his distance, distance of the worst kind, not respect for her condition but coming from a far place where he felt nothing at all.

24

Khandi was ticking over nicely. Pumped since the call to the jeweller, she couldn't wait for the call-back. The only downer was Eddie. Khandi guessed he was thinking about his skinny fucking bony fucking slag of an ex-wife. She felt the need to point out some home truths and so, in the dim main room of the shack, amid the dust, cobwebs and old frying-pan grease, she gave Eddie a few slaps and kicks. 'You think bitchface was just going to let you disappear? Doesn't work like that.'

She rolled a joint, took a hit off it, passed it to Eddie. 'Go on.'

Eddie took the joint from her fingers and stared at it absently. 'It's just, I thought we agreed...'

There was only so much treachery of the heart that Khandi could take. She said savagely, 'The skinny cunt would of found out about you and me and gone to the cops, Eddie, jealous cow. She'd of given you up.'

'I told you, there was nothing between us.'

Khandi took a ferocious hit off the joint. She didn't know why, but she actually loved Eddie. But that could change, mate, she thought, factoring in the money. She glared at him. He still looked gloomy. Counting the good times? Guilt, regret, now that it was too fucking late?

Another thought popped into her head: maybe Eddie and bitchface had plans of their own. Khandi stewed on that for a while. What's done is done, she thought, staring at Eddie. It was time the weak prick focused on her, not that scrawny, dried up, frigid, cuntfaced, pissflapping bitch of a professional virgin. Khandi, doing what she did best, reached over and fished around inside Eddie's pants.

Afterwards, chasing the scum with a slug of tequila and another joint, she said, 'Besides, you heard the news. Nothing. No dead bodies, no one knows where to find us and we have the gear. So chill out Eddie, okay?'

'Okay.'

'I mean it.'

'I'm fine.'

'I want you focused: me, and the job at hand.'

'For fuck's sake,' said Eddie, grabbing the joint and focusing on that.

'Time to see what Henri Furneaux has to say,' Khandi said.

Wednesday afternoon, 4.45.

Khandi destroyed the mobile phone. Her initial call to Furneaux had been too brief to monitor or triangulate, but the jeweller might have alerted the police or hired a security company in the meantime, so she and Eddie went looking for a public phone. Driving out of the hills, they headed west to

Ringwood and its endless used-car yards. Inside the vast expanse of Car City was a public phone where she'd not be noticed or remembered, and where Eddie could keep watch in case the cops descended. If that happened, they'd fade into the crowd like some young couple down on their luck and looking to buy a cheap rustbucket.

The phone was bolted to the outside of a café, alongside a cluttered wall map of the complex. Furneaux answered and Khandi said, 'Got our money ready?'

'It's not your money, it's my money.'

'Oh, hello, Mr Defiance. Well, have I got news for you,' Khandi said, meanwhile wondering where the guy's resistance had come from. 'I just now posted you an envelope.'

'What envelope?'

'An envelope containing ashes, if you know what I mean.'

She hadn't. It had only just occurred to her. Good idea, though. Burn one of the bonds—better still, scorch it. He wouldn't be able to cash it and he'd know she meant business and wasn't just sending him the ashes of that morning's *Herald Sun.*

He was silent. 'I haven't got a million,' he said. 'I can't *get* a million.'

'I'm very sorry to hear that,' Khandi said.

'Where are you calling from? A public phone? I thought I heard a PA announcement just then.'

'Stop stalling.'

'Look, I can rustle up ten grand,' Furneaux said.

'You must be joking.'

'Fifteen.'

'It's going to be cold tonight,' Khandi said. She was in lycra tights, heels and a pink waisted jacket, genuine vinyl, over a singlet top. She looked good to the late afternoon tyre kickers wandering around Car City, being glared at by Eddie Oberin. She was a magnet. The gawkers kept doubling back, finding excuses to buy takeout coffee or read the wall map beside the public phone on which she was trying to get a lot of cash out of a crook.

'Cold?'

'Might have to light a fire to get warm,' Khandi said. 'You know, kindling, *paper…*'

'Who the fuck are you anyway?' demanded Furneaux.

Why wasn't the guy grovelling? One of Khandi's tsunamic rages swamped her. Her fingers tightened around the phone and with her other hand she traced the outline of her .32 Beretta through the leather of her shoulder bag. The only thing that saved her was the look on Eddie's face: her sweet man—insanely jealous of the guys who were eye-fucking her—was making throat-cutting gestures with the flat of his hand, telling her to get off the phone. Khandi turned all of her rage and grief into a sweetly chilling voice. 'I'd better go, Henri. Keep an eye on the mail.'

'Wait.'

Khandi turned her perfect behind to the world and chirruped, 'Bye now.'

'Fifty,' said Furneaux.

'Pal, I can add. Bonds and treasury notes worth millions, and you're offering me fifty grand?'

'Sixty.'

'Sounds like desperation to me,' Khandi said. She glanced around uneasily. This was taking too long. Were they tracing the call?

'I know where the stuff comes from,' she went on. 'A street robbery in London, correct?'

Furneaux was silent and that answered her question. Behind her Eddie was saying to some guy, 'Eyes off, pal,' and that was a balm to Khandi just then, after his doubts and sulks earlier. Being in love and staying in love were hard work. Meanwhile she still had a job to do. 'But what I *don't* know,' she told Furneaux, 'is how come *you* got your hands on some of the stolen paper.'

Silence.

'You must be working for, or with, some pretty powerful people. International people.'

Silence.

'I bet they don't like stuffups, do they? And, boy, have you stuffed up, Henri.'

There was some conviction, not a lot, in Furneaux's response. 'The stuffup's yours, not mine.'

'What will these shadowy people say or do when they learn you let yourself get robbed?'

'Hundred grand. That's my final offer. That's all I can raise.'

Khandi put her palm over the mouthpiece and turned to Eddie, who was standing close against her now, while the clouds slipped across the sinking sun and the plastic pennants snapped in the wind. 'Hundred grand,' she murmured.

'Get one more raise,' he said promptly, 'then agree.'

Khandi returned sweetly to the phone and said, 'Maybe instead of burning the bonds I could send them to the cops. You would of handled them, right, Henri? Your prints would be all over them? Are your prints on file, Henri?'

'Hundred and twenty,' said Furneaux with a little yelp of strangled emotions. 'But I need time.'

'You have all day tomorrow to raise the cash,' Khandi said. 'I'll call you late morning with the details. Oh, and be a good boy—no cops or we destroy the gear.'

That's when she saw a cop car come creeping in from Whitehorse Road and lift its snout as it prowled over the speed bumps. Khandi kissed Eddie, snuggled her waist against his thigh, hooked her hand into his back pocket, and walked him into the café, which was all glass. She watched the patrol car cruise once through the cramped grounds of Car City and out again and she relaxed and grabbed Eddie's cock under the table.

Le Page was loading the images from his digital camera onto Henri's office computer. 'It was the woman?'

'Yes.'

'Now that you have heard her a second time, did you recognise her voice?'

'No.'

'You're certain it was not Danielle.'

'Positive,' Furneaux said.

His control brittle after the day's debacles, Le Page tried some slow breathing, tried telling himself things weren't all bad. They'd lost the bonds, but now looked like getting them back. The Turkish widow had called his bluff—phoned her sons to come and turf him out—but he'd had the sense not to pull his gun or his knife. He'd lost the man with the clipboard, but had his photograph. And he'd learned who owned the house with the white door.

He leaned over the desk and reached past Henri to scroll through the images. 'This is the house. According to a neighbour, it belongs to a man named Edward Oberin.'

'Oberin, Oberin. I've heard of him,' Henri said, 'but I'd always thought he was a fence, a back room kind of guy.'

'Here we have Danielle knocking on his door. Some time later, this man appeared.'

Le Page operated the zoom function until the face filled the screen, a dark force in the room. 'I have no idea who that is,' Henri said, flinching a little.

Le Page grunted. 'You can put together one hundred and twenty thousand dollars?'

'Yes, but—'

'Tomorrow morning you will gather this amount and wait for instructions.'

'Christ, we're not paying, are we?'

'We need to get close,' snarled Le Page, 'if we want the bonds and the money.'

Henri Furneaux's courage had been ebbing all day. Now it came creeping back. 'Okay.'

'Sorry, sorry,' Joe said, barging in and looking hot and bothered. Seeing Le Page there he blanched and retreated. 'Sorry. I'll come back.'

Le Page grabbed his wrist and yanked on it. 'Sorry for what?'

Joe swallowed. 'I think Danielle's done a runner.'

Le Page didn't care about that. He pointed at the monitor screen. 'Do you know this man?'

Joe peered, recoiled. 'Jesus, that's Wyatt.'

'Who is Wyatt?'

Joseph launched into a nervy explanation but, at the end of it, all Le Page had was a name and the configurations of a myth.

25

Lydia was feverish overnight, tossing in pain, sometimes calling out. Wyatt went to her each time, stood watching. He didn't want a dead body on his hands. He was also not sure that he trusted her. He was curious to find himself capable of a range of fugitive emotions, old, lost and new. Desire was one of them. She was hardly beautiful—in distress, her head lolling—but he was intensely aware of her.

Thursday morning saw him ragged with sleep loss. When she awoke he was observing her from a chair in a corner of the room. Her fever had passed, her colour was better. She croaked 'Hello' but then he saw her eyes close, her fingers clench, as the pain hit.

He stood over her and said nothing. She opened her eyes again. 'What day is it?'

'Thursday.'

She said, 'My head still aches. Like it's in the bone.'

'The doctor will call again later today.'

Lydia patted the wound dressing with the slim fingers of her right hand. 'Tell me again what happened.'

'I think you turned your head to face the window just as Eddie's girlfriend pulled the trigger, so the bullet creased you. If you hadn't, you'd be dead.'

Her gaze flickered past his face, taking in the room. She said, barely moving her lower jaw, 'I need to eat and drink, but I feel if I move anything it's going to hurt.'

'Yes.'

Tears came into her eyes. 'I need a bath. I stink.'

'Eat and drink first.'

He fed her soup and sugary tea. Some of the fluids ran from the sides of her mouth and gathered in the hollow of her throat, to escape beneath her shirtfront, which rose and fell as she breathed. He mopped her dry unselfconsciously and all was silent bar the sounds of her throat and the spoon tapping her teeth.

He took the dishes to the kitchen and then he ran water into the bath. He returned to the bedroom in time to see her sit up, swing her legs out until her feet touched the floor, and reel, both hands going to her temples. He went to her and helped her to stand.

'How are we going to do this?'

'You'll get undressed and into the bath and I'll wait out here. Leave the door open. I need to see that you don't faint.'

She looked at him and decided that she trusted him. 'I need fresh clothes.'

'I collected some from your house yesterday.'

She didn't know what to say. It sounded like a kindness but she didn't suppose it was. Like her, he was tall and thin; she could have borrowed his tracksuit pants and a T-shirt, even if she swam in them a little. She said, 'Thank you.'

He walked her to the bath. He tested the water and turned off the tap. Her back to him, Lydia stepped out of her knickers. She grabbed the hem of the T-shirt and pulled it gingerly up over her face, her voice muffled as she said, 'Ouch.'

Her trunk was slim and pale, the hair damp and limp on her neck, her spine knobbly. The skin on her back was creased here and there from tossing in bed all night. Buttocks and thighs, too. As a courtesy Wyatt stepped away from her and began to turn, so that when Lydia swayed and stumbled he was late getting to her. He caught and steadied her, helped her to step over the side of the bath, then settle into the water. Her skin was warm but the bath warmer, and he saw the fine hairs stand up from the temperature difference. She bent her knees to conceal herself and he turned to leave the room.

She stayed in the bath for thirty minutes. Now and then she ran the hot water and he could hear soapy splashes and long silences. During the silences she would sometimes call out, 'Still alive.'

As he waited for her to finish, Wyatt brewed coffee and tried to place himself in Eddie Oberin's shoes. Thinking that women were a constant in Eddie's life, he went to the crack in the bathroom door and said, 'Does Eddie have a sister?'

'In Perth. They don't speak.'

'Female cousins?'

'I have no idea.'

'Old girlfriends?'

'Only about five hundred of them. You know what he's like.'

Wyatt did. He also knew that Eddie Oberin was a creature

of many habits, and exercising them probably accounted for how and where he'd met the shooter. 'You didn't know about the store manager?'

'No, I swear.'

'Anyway, she's in the wind now,' said Wyatt.

Lydia said nothing.

'And Eddie never mentioned a club named Blue Poles?'

'No.'

Splashing sounds, Lydia saying, after a pause, 'Yesterday you said you saw Le Page at Eddie's house.'

Wondering if she'd only just remembered it, or had some stake in the matter and needed to know what he knew, Wyatt said, 'Yes.'

Silence.

'If he followed the girl, they must suspect an inside job.'

'Yes.'

Another pause. 'It won't be hard for them to learn Eddie's name.'

'No.'

'And eventually mine.'

It was all true, so Wyatt didn't say anything. He was about to move from the door when he thought of another question. 'Did you and Eddie have a favourite holiday place?'

'Wyatt, that was ten years ago.'

'Where?'

'He liked the Gold Coast, I liked the Sunshine Coast.'

Her voice saying so was a little lost and desolate, but Wyatt wasn't ready to feel or express sympathy. She hadn't known she would be left for dead by her ex-husband, but she might well

have thought Wyatt would be. As he turned to go he heard
angry splashing. He stood at the door. 'Do you need help?'

Her voice was teary. 'My hair.'

He understood. Her head wore a bandage, but she wanted
to wash her hair. She needed his help and that was a final stroke
of humiliation and vulnerability. She hated to be like that and
just then she hated him. 'Get dressed,' he said, 'and let me wash
your hair over the basin.'

He waited and she relented. 'You sure?'

'Yes. Do you need help getting out?'

There was silence again. 'Yes.'

He found her on her knees in the water, spine bowed and
glistening, shoulder blades poking back as she braced her arms
on each edge of the bath. He crouched and lifted her out in
stages, first to a standing position and then, before she could
recover and stiffen against him, out onto the bathmat, where
he mopped her with a towel.

He waited a moment while she rocked on her feet. Presently
she recovered and began the gentle motions of drying her back.
The bath sheet concealed all but her head and her slender calves.

'Your clothes,' he said, pointing to a pile on the white cane
basket beside the basin.

'Thanks,' she muttered.

The room was scented and steamy. He supposed the scent
was from his soap. He'd barely noticed it before.

He returned to his note pad and empty cup. Before he could
brew fresh coffee, she called, 'Ready.'

Sensations came to him as he washed her hair, sounds,
images and textures. Perhaps he'd seen other women bent like

this over a basin, although he was certain he'd never assisted them. Or perhaps his mother had done this when he was a child. To him? His sister? That was a long time ago and he didn't know them any more, or even if they were alive or dead. He didn't trust his memories. He had no use for memories like these. He made himself concentrate on what he was doing with Lydia's hair, the water and the shampoo and the rinsing off. But if this ever became a memory, he wouldn't push it away.

'Coffee?' he said when he was finished.

She was patting her face with the towel, patting dry the damp bandage tinged now with blood. She was pale and in pain and he said, 'I'll call the doctor.'

'Yes,' she said, and fainted.

And so the long morning passed. This time he didn't watch over her but fell into a deep sleep.

26

In the CIU office, Lynette Rigby's inspector was saying, 'I want you to drop it.'

Rigby kept a damper on her feelings, which were anger, disappointment and sulkiness. 'But boss—'

'No wire taps,' he said, 'we don't have the money for it. No search warrants, we don't have the evidence. And no, you can't have a couple of uniforms.'

'These guys are up to something,' Rigby muttered, shifting in the chair opposite his desk. Her bra didn't fit; coffee burned like acid in her stomach. She loathed the guy's family, their sunny smiles and well-adjusted personalities looking out at her from the picture frames on his desk.

'I don't doubt it,' he said. 'Plenty are. But their lawyer's going to argue they were simply the victim of vehicle theft yesterday morning. There's no evidence that a shipment of any kind was in the vehicle or that it was hijacked by professionals.'

'They're bent.'

'I know they're bent,' the inspector said, 'but we need evidence.'

'How can I get evidence if you won't authorise a wire tap or a search?'

'Sergeant,' the inspector said.

'Sorry, sir.'

A glass-ceiling thing, Rigby thought. Bright women make their male colleagues nervous and envious.

'I said no to everything yesterday,' the inspector said, 'and I'm giving you the same answer today. Blame your lefty pals in government. We're short of money, time, equipment and manpower. And you want me to mount a full-scale search and surveillance on a couple of crooked jewellers? Get on with something that will bring results.'

'Yes, sir.'

Rigby went to the ladies' toilet, slipped her bra off through her sleeve and splashed water on her face. She returned to her office and put in a request to Interpol, anything they had on the French courier. Then she signed out an unmarked white Falcon and drove to High Street. Before long she picked up Henri Furneaux making the rounds of three banks, one on High Street, the others in Malvern and Toorak. The time was 10 a.m.

After tailing Furneaux back to his shop, she returned to the banks and flashed her ID and bluffed about warrants. The jeweller had made largish withdrawals from two banks, and asked to use his safe-deposit box at the third. She wondered how—or if—it related to the torching of his four-wheel-drive. Had he lost a shipment yesterday? Drugs? Guns? Jewellery? Maybe he needed to buy new stock? Or was he working with hard people who wanted their money back?

To hell with her boss. Watch and learn.

Meanwhile Khandi had torn through the glove box, rear seats, floor and boot of the Commodore. Slamming back into the kitchen, she said, 'No fucking street directory.'

Eddie crinkled his eyes at her through the smoke drifting from his cigarette. 'So we steal one.'

But the Yarra Junction newsagent went on full alert when they walked into her shop, hovered over them, her hands on her hips. 'Bitch,' said Khandi, out on the footpath. 'What now?'

'Check on-line,' Eddie said.

But all of the library's computers were taken. 'That's just great,' Khandi said.

Eddie hated it when she was like this. He fronted up to the main desk. 'Got a Melways, by any chance?'

'It can't leave the building,' the librarian said, reaching around to a shelf of telephone books and street directories.

'No worries.'

With all of the main tables taken by the geriatric genealogists, they were forced to sit at a knee-high table in the kids' section.

'We need an open space,' Khandi said, 'with plenty of escape routes, near roads that will get us back here quickly.'

She flipped through the Melways in a kind of fury. She hated the library, the street directory and the general imposition of restrictions, and was generally pissed off at the effort everything was costing her. Finally she finger-stabbed the maps on a two-page spread. 'Ringwood,' she said. 'Jacaranda Park. There's a lake, footbridge, walking tracks, and it's right on Whitehorse Road.'

Whitehorse Road became the Maroondah Highway and was one of the main routes through the eastern sprawl of Melbourne, eventually running out through farmland to the Yarra Valley. Khandi traced it with a hooked talon. 'We can be back at the cabin in no time,' she told Eddie. 'Meanwhile, look at all the intersecting routes near the park: Warrandyte Road, Wantirna Road, Mount Dandenong Road, Whitehorse Road itself. They won't know where the hell we've gone.'

Photocopying was twenty cents per page, A3 thirty cents. Fuck that: Khandi ripped out both maps, shoved them into her knickers and said, 'Let's go.'

They returned to the cabin for further planning, but first she wanted sex to release built-up tension. Then, moist and still amorous, she placed the creased pages on the greasy table and bumped hips with Eddie. 'How do you see it, big boy?'

Eddie was staring at the maps. She watched him, appreciating his unshaven Hollywood look, and rubbed her tingling groin against him. His slender forefinger traced the paths, lake, barbecues, scout hall and parking areas. She waited. She'd already seen the answer.

'We use motorbikes,' Eddie said.

Khandi drew his face to her breasts, which were fifty per cent real. 'Good thinking, Batman.'

Late morning they contacted Furneaux from a public phone outside the post office in the next town and gave him the instructions. 'Ringwood? That's way out in the boondocks.'

'Seven this evening,' Khandi said. 'Come alone.'

'You're not getting the money until I see the bonds.'

'You're not seeing the bonds until I see the money,' Khandi said.

'Where in the park?'

'The footbridge over the lake.'

After that it was about waiting. Khandi hated to wait.

'Ringwood,' said Henri Furneaux, replacing the handset.

On the other side of his desk, Le Page was dead-eyed. 'So?'

Henri shook his head. His world was old-money suburbs near the river. Ringwood to him was like a hellish foreign country, an endless tract of uninspired family homes, highways and used-car yards.

'Where in Ringwood?' said Joe.

Joseph Furneaux was a mess, his buck teeth prominent, his lips dry and his breath whistling, his eyes streaked red, his hair arranged in tufts and knots, all marks of guilt for leaving the back gate unlocked, not finding Danielle and being a general fuck-up. He needed to make amends. 'I know Ringwood pretty well,' he said. 'Buy all my cars out that way.'

Henri grunted. Joe's last car was a heap of shit. He dug a street directory out from the bottom drawer of his desk, snatched it back when Joe tried to take it from him. 'I can do it.'

'Only trying to help,' Joe said.

'Well don't.'

Henri scanned the index, opened the pages to Jacaranda Park. 'Here.' He shook his head. 'Seven o'clock: the traffic will still be heavy.'

Le Page's expressionless gaze swung from the map to Henri. 'Heavy for the thieves also.'

Furneaux glanced involuntarily at his office safe. He kept thirty grand there on a daily basis, but this morning he'd added another ninety grand, all in hundreds, scrounged from various accounts as soon as the banks opened. He still couldn't see the reason for putting the ransom together. 'I don't understand why we have to pay these people. Can't we just ambush them?'

'Yeah,' Joe said.

Le Page gave them his pitiless look. 'And if they do not have the bonds with them? Or only some—as proof? Or photocopies? And if they do not appear but send an agent in their place? And if there are many of them, all armed? We first wait and listen.'

'We risk losing the bonds *and* my cash,' Henri said.

Pouring coffee only for himself, Le Page said, 'Forget about the cash. If necessary, I will cover you—but it will not come to that.'

Joe had been scratching his head, raining dandruff. 'How about me and Henri put a GPS thingy with the money? Different frequency, so it won't stuff up your signal?'

That made sense to Le Page. He would monitor the bonds, the brothers their precious cash. 'As you wish.'

'That way,' said Joe, warming to his plan, 'we can coordinate with each other if they try to rip us off.'

'Either way,' Le Page said, 'I will follow and eliminate.'

A short while later, he headed downtown and used fake ID to rent a Subaru Impreza from an agency that specialised in sports and high-performance cars. Mounting the GPS tracker, he returned to his hotel and paid a valet $50 to keep the car close by. Back in his room he examined the Subaru's street directory until he knew the main and minor streets adjacent to Jacaranda Park. His head ached. He stood, stretched and walked to the window. Everything about the country affronted him. The Australian suburbanite had no aesthetic sense; the middle class was aspirant, vulgar and ignorant. No wonder the cities were bland. He vowed never to visit the place again; there would be no need to once he'd retrieved the bonds.

Le Page returned to the hire car, started the engine, and decided to delay his examination of Jacaranda Park. Instead, he drove to Danielle's poky flat in Highett, then to the house with the white door. He didn't expect to find Danielle, or the men named Oberin and Wyatt, but knew that neglecting to look would eat at him all day. Danielle was gone but maybe the others would return when they received the cash this evening.

Finally Le Page drove to Jacaranda Park. He spent an hour walking and driving around the area. The layout—narrow paths, narrow footbridge—would oblige both parties to approach the exchange point on foot. The nearest car parking was fifty metres away from the bridge, which was open to view from all sides. It was that fifty metres that bothered Le Page. Henri would be vulnerable as he walked across to the bridge. On the other hand, so would the thieves—that's if Le Page were to hit them at the time of the exchange instead of following them to whatever burrow they had been hiding in. He was pleased to have the Subaru. Speed and manoeuvrability would be the deciding factors this evening. He finished scouting around. He would return to the park at 5 p.m. and claim a secluded area behind a hedge on the other side of the road. When the light faded from the sky and the shadows blurred, he would use night-vision binoculars.

27

Wyatt spent the rest of Thursday in fruitless pursuit of Eddie Oberin. He could be frightening and persuasive, but mostly relied on reading faces and body tics for evasions and lies, and realised that no one was protecting Eddie, no one knew where he'd go to ground. The guy's parents were dead. He tracked down the Perth sister, but she cut him off in mid call, saying she no longer had anything to do with her brother, and wanted nothing to do with Wyatt. Also, many of Wyatt's old contacts had died or moved or regretted ever knowing Eddie Oberin.

But he did arrive at a short list of names, single names: Sherry, Blinda, Lexus, Chelsee, Aymee, Mindi and Khandi. Made-up names and spellings of the kind that hookers and strippers had always used but now also given to little girls destined to become respectable wives and mothers. Wyatt began to hit the lunch-hour strip clubs and lap-dancing joints, armed with Eddie's photograph and the last of his cash.

As the long day progressed he learned that Chelsee was in jail, attempted armed robbery. Aymee and Blinda were tagging along behind workers building a natural-gas pipeline in central Australia. Lexus had died of an overdose six months earlier.

The matchbook connection was Mindi, a dancer at Blue Poles, in Flinders Lane. 'That bastard,' she told Wyatt, giving Eddie's photo back to him.

She'd taken a five-minute break to wander among the punters. They were mostly $5 and $10 punters, so Wyatt's $50 encouraged her to linger a while at his table. The club was dimly lit, the air hazy as if everything had vaporised: the promise of sex, the different hungers, the disappointments. Mindi's G-string, makeup and plastic breasts meant nothing to Wyatt, and after a while she stopped twitching them at him. 'A real prick,' she said. 'You going to drink that?'

He'd been obliged to buy drinks. 'It's mostly water,' he said.

'What did you expect?' said Mindi, draining her own glass and then his, and chewing the oily ice cube. 'You get dehydrated in this job,' she explained.

'My fifty bucks hasn't got me very far,' Wyatt said. His voice was low and dangerous. It wasn't an act. Wyatt could watch a bank for several days without complaint, but there were other kinds of waiting for which he had no patience.

'Don't get your undies in a twist.'

'How well did you know Eddie?'

'Well enough.'

'Meaning?'

'I lived with him for a few weeks at the beginning of the year, then he went off me and someone said he'd hooked up with his ex-wife. Then a couple of months ago he starts hanging out here again. I tried to rekindle things but he was all over one of the other girls, suggesting threesomes. Prick.'

Wyatt glanced around, staring through the tired lights, fighting the haze to locate the tables distributed close to the stage and in the dark corners, where single men and raucous tables of men and women were entertaining the dancers. 'Which girl?'

'Khandi.'

'She here?'

'Hasn't shown up this evening.'

Wyatt gave his brief nod; it was scarcely there.

'Come to think of it,' added Mindi, 'I haven't seen her for a few days.'

'Know where she lives?'

Mindi examined her nails. Wyatt peeled off another $50.

'Upstairs.'

He glanced at the ceiling involuntarily. 'What's up there?'

'Offices. Storeroom. One apartment.'

'Khandi's?'

'That's what I said, isn't it?'

'Does she live there with anyone?'

Mindi shook her head, jetting a stream of cigarette smoke towards the stage, where a Thai woman was gyrating to an old Stones song. 'Nobody in their right mind would live with that bitch.'

'Why?'

Mindi shrugged and her breasts lifted. 'Unpredictable. Filthy temper. She took a knife to me when I complained about Eddie getting off with her.'

She flipped a wing of hair away from her neck. The scar was small but purplish and cruelly stitched together.

'Nasty,' he said.

'You can say that again,' said Mindi, stabbing out her cigarette. 'Listen, I have to get back to work.'

Wyatt said, 'I need you to be quiet about this conversation.' She shrugged.

Wyatt gave her another $50. 'How do I get upstairs?'

Mindi said nothing but cast her gaze briefly toward a far corner, which was like a black hole, sucking in all light and anything that moved.

'Thanks,' Wyatt said.

'If you're not doing anything later…' Mindi said, and, for just a moment, her life story showed through, the need for some ordinary affection.

Wyatt gave her a nod and a kind smile but no hope at all.

Slipping around a dusty velvet curtain beside a stifling men's room, Wyatt found a set of concrete steps. These led up to a corridor lit by flyspecked bulbs, and a door with a peephole and a plain white business card taped beneath it. He'd found the residence of Khandi Cane. The door was dead bolted, and Wyatt did what he always did, and searched for the key before trying anything else. He found it behind an adjacent door, which housed a hot water service, inside a magnetised box stuck behind a tangle of pipes.

He didn't know what to expect. Sex-shop underwear, candles, New Age crystals, pink stationery and a favourite overcoat? In fact, he did find those things, but he also found a collection of knives, a packet of 9mm cartridges, and a laptop. In the shower cubicle he found Chanel No. 5. Her tiny bar fridge was stocked with French champagne and smoked salmon. Three wigs: red, blonde, brunette. A dozen pairs of shoes. Many magazines and two books: *Own Your Life and Own the World* and *God Loves a Winner*. Some CDs: waterfall music and Emmylou Harris. Two DVDs: *2007 AFL Grand Final* and *Pirates of the Caribbean*. Wyatt couldn't quite work her out. Khandi had hopes and dreams, apparently, but none that would soften a heart.

He fired up her laptop and discovered that she'd been searching the Internet for anything she could find on Henri Furneaux, the jewellery trade and the resale value of antique watches, rings, brooches and necklaces.

Nothing on where she was hiding, however. He tried her answering machine. One message, from someone called Stefan: 'Get your arse down here now or you're fired.'

Wyatt spent another five minutes in the miserable room and had barely stepped out when he sensed a shift in the quality of the air. His nerve endings tingled as he registered the presence of a bulky shape in the shadowed reaches of the grimy corridor, the dully hostile workings of a man's chest and lungs, and the layered odours of hired muscle: sweat, cheap alcohol, cigarettes and methamphetamine. Next he noticed the stance: the guy had been a boxer and he favoured his right arm.

The first rule is to get close. Wyatt surprised the Blue Poles bouncer by not hesitating.

'The fuck you doing up here?'

Wyatt said nothing. The bouncer had spoken because he thought the circumstances demanded it, even though his intention was to beat Wyatt into unconsciousness and toss him into the alley behind the club. Suddenly Wyatt was in his face, so he swung his right arm, his face lit with pleasure now, his bald head gleaming in the weak light, his shirt and trousers straining as his huge limbs and torso began to move.

Wyatt acted in that millisecond before the punch connected, slapping both hands around the bouncer's wrist, turning clockwise and yanking downwards, spinning the man around and driving him nose first into the wall.

He let go, stepped back, but stayed close. He was almost face to face when the bouncer turned to him again. Wyatt could have gone for the man's broken nose, but chose to punish the right arm again, chopping at the clavicle area, where the nerves are close to the bone. He knew how crippling the pain could be. That arm would be numb and useless for several days.

Now he stepped clear of the bouncer. He saw the guy weighing it up, eyebrows knotted with pain but far from finished, and beginning to advance edgeways, clenching his left fist.

Wyatt feinted. He dropped his right shoulder as if readying himself to swing a haymaker, and when the bouncer shifted in anticipation, shielding his upper body, Wyatt pivoted and kicked the man's unguarded lower body, catching him at the side of the knee.

The bouncer hobbled in retreat, almost falling to the floor. By now he was drooling, wheezing, soaked with sweat and shaking his head in bafflement. Wyatt also felt early signs of exertion but knew how to control them. He took shallow, even breaths through his nose. The bouncer was gulping air, taking in too much of it, hyperventilation turning to panic. Wyatt saw it and moved in. He kicked again, the other knee this time. Now the bouncer couldn't run, only hobble. Then, feet spread apart, Wyatt began to punch the man. Using his whole body, visualising a target on the other side of the man's body, he punched through the bouncer, the power coming from his hips and thighs, landing hard. In that way a slight man can defeat a heavy one. The bouncer hit back but didn't know how to move, his trunk static, his right arm useless, his left lacking force and accuracy.

Wyatt wasn't interested in punishment. He was dealing with an obstacle. When the moment presented itself he punched the occipital bulge at the back of the man's head and walked off down the stairs, hearing behind him the smack of heavy limbs on linoleum.

Wyatt didn't acknowledge Mindi as he walked out through the front door of Blue Poles. He returned to his apartment in Southbank and found Lydia asleep in front of the TV. The air was stale and so he opened a window and watched the ribbons of light along the river, the bridges and the streets. The city projected an immense glow onto the clouds. There was no real blackness out there, even though night had fallen.

28

Henri and Joseph were in position by 6.30. Leaving Henri's Mercedes in the public car park, they made a swift reconnaissance of the exchange location on foot, careful not to linger on the footbridge. The sun had recently settled but there was plenty of artificial light in the park. Plenty of people, too: kids mucking around on bikes and skateboards before going home for dinner, joggers, couples, some activity at the scout hall on the far side of the railway tracks. Even a few young families frying sausages on a coin-operated barbecue, clinking plastic cups of champagne, celebrating something.

'I don't like it,' said Joe as they passed a set of playground swings. 'Too open. Too many ways out. Too many people around.'

Henri shook his head. 'It's a good place, from their point of view and ours. We can't afford to try anything and nor can they.'

'Where's Alain?'

'He's here somewhere, don't worry.'

Joe shook his head. 'What's he got us into, bro?'

'Don't call me bro.'

'What do we know about treasury bonds and shit?'

Henri didn't say. They returned to the car, where Joe fiddled with the CD player and Henri sat with the money in a briefcase on his lap. Then it was five minutes to seven and Henri said, 'It's time.'

Joe made to get out. Henri said, 'You stay here.'

'Why?'

'If it goes wrong I need you in the car, ready to roll.'

Joe didn't like it. 'Don't challenge them Henri, okay? Don't piss them off. Don't let on we know their names.'

'What do you take me for?'

Joe ground his teeth. Henri crossed in the dim light to the little bridge and stood in the middle of it, trying to keep from looking around for Le Page. A young woman ran past him, ponytail bouncing, trailed by a dog. Then nothing, then a middle-aged man crossed briskly, not meeting his gaze. The traffic was a constant muted roar on Whitehorse Road. A breeze picked up and swayed the trees all around and Henri felt a little exposed.

He heard it before he saw it, a powerful bike. He glanced around wildly. The bike was on the western approach path to the footbridge, implacably black, rider and helmet. Henri swallowed and wondered if everything had gone to shit. A bike? No way had Le Page anticipated this.

With a little exhaust snarl, the bike rolled onto the bridge. Nothing was said. The rider stopped a metre from Henri, who opened the briefcase, revealing the money. The rider handed over a gym bag and waited, gun in hand, while Henri opened the document wallets and confirmed that the bonds were genuine. There was the suggestion of breasts under the leather jacket; shapely thighs. So this was the woman. Where was her partner?

Henri nodded, then handed over the briefcase. 'It's all there.'

The woman laughed. She rippled each of the bundles with her thumb, as if checking for dummy notes, found the transponder, and crushed it under her boot. Then, instead of taking the briefcase, she removed the cash bundles, crammed them into the pannier and shot past him off the bridge, a sexy black shape on her howling machine. A flare of brake lights at the highway, then she accelerated east, away from the city. Furneaux shook the empty briefcase absently.

Joe Furneaux, window down and bopping to the Red Hot Chilli Peppers, saw the bike howl past. A Ducati, nice set of wheels, he thought. He swung his head back to watch the GPS monitor. Blank.

He looked across at Henri. Another bike had materialised on the bridge, bike and rider all in black.

Eddie Oberin shoved his pistol into the jeweller's soft stomach and said, 'Give us the bag.'

The guy actually resisted, holding the gym bag tight against his chest and twisting away. 'We had a deal.'

'Yeah, well, things change.'

'You bozos can't possibly know how to move these bonds.'

Eddie couldn't believe it. Who did the guy think he was?

There in the crisp air and the tricky shadows, feeling unassailable with a gun in his hand, feeling that he was on the cusp of some kind of indefinable but palpable greatness, Eddie Oberin recalled that Khandi had—more than once—called him a wimp. His orders were clear: grab the bonds and piss off out of there, but he so badly wanted to put a bullet in the guy.

He got a grip on himself. Lowered the pistol. 'Just give me the bag.'

Furneaux said, 'Which one are you? Wyatt? Oberin? We know—'

Jesus Christ. Eddie raised the pistol and shot Henri Furneaux in the throat. He had to wrestle for the bag as Furneaux's fingers clenched. The jeweller slid to the boards. Eddie fired again, forehead this time.

Then, in a fine elation and rage, he accelerated off the bridge and braked at the open window of the Mercedes.

'No,' Joe said.

'Yes,' said Eddie.

One shot to the temple. It felt great.

29

Lynette Rigby tailed Henri Furneaux from his home in South Yarra to Joe Furneaux's poky house in Richmond, and then all the way out here, to this godforsaken little park in Ringwood. The CIU night-shift guys wanted to know when she was bringing the car back. Since she outranked them, she said, 'When I'm good and ready.'

No overtime, this was her dollar. But she didn't have anywhere to be—why not put in the time? She might get some glory at the end of it all.

Rigby parked on a slip road beside the park, settled back to wait. She saw Henri and Joseph wander across a clearing, over a footbridge and past a playground before returning to their car. Thirty minutes passed. The world ticked over. Then, a few minutes before seven o'clock, Henri got out again. If this was a handover, the logical spot was a park bench away from the swings and the barbecues, but Henri strolled onto the little footbridge, carrying a briefcase. Rigby cursed. Her view was obscured by a toilet block.

She reached for the ignition, changing her mind when juddery lights appeared, two motorbikes entering from the far side of the park. Bikes and riders were identical, but heading towards her. No chance of getting the plate numbers. If she started the car, she'd risk spooking everyone. Maybe if she got out and strolled across the park? But Furneaux would recognise her and she needed to know what, exactly, was going down.

Rigby climbed into the back seat for a better view. Not perfect. Then, as she watched, one bike headed at low speed across the park. The other made a wide loop around the perimeter and returned to its original position. She crouched on the floor as it passed her, throttling back. Nothing happened for a while after that. The players were in position but not moving. Rigby waited. She thought about calling for backup but didn't know how she'd explain it if nothing happened.

Moments later, the first rider squirted onto the bridge. Rigby cursed. She disabled the car's interior light so it wouldn't show when she opened the door, got out, turned her back to the footbridge and pressed the door closed with a soft click.

By the time she'd run at a crouch to the toilet block, the bike had fired up again and sped to the other side of the bridge, shooting out of the park and howling east along the highway. She ran back towards the car, thinking she should follow the bike. She'd establish where it was headed, call Traffic to make a stop and arrest, use the rider to get at the Furneaux brothers.

She skidded to a stop halfway to the car. Follow the bike? Call for backup? Detain, search and question Henri Furneaux? She could not decide and felt, suddenly, alone. She retraced her steps to the toilet block. It loomed in the darkness beyond trees and their twisty shadows. She tripped on the humped spine of a root in the dirt, recovered, and heard muffled reports on the other side of the toilet block. The hint of muzzle flashes.

She ran, flattened herself against a wall and peered around the corner. The second rider was speeding across the grass that fringed the little lake. He paused at the Mercedes. This time there was no mistaking the gunshot or the flash in the waning light.

The witnesses Rigby questioned always said, 'It all happened so quickly.' They were right. Her jaw dropped open, a habit of hers, 'catching flies' her colleagues called it. The families around the barbecues were gaping too, one man shouting into a mobile phone.

Rigby shut her mouth and ran back to her unmarked Falcon. She yanked it into gear and headed after the shooter, cursing the tangle of roadways around the park. Scrambling to unhook the radio handset, she called it in, shots fired, officer in pursuit, and named the highway and nearest cross streets.

The bike hadn't escaped the park yet. Rigby saw brake lights flare on the walking path adjacent to the highway, a pair of joggers jumping away in fright and gesturing. Then the gunman righted his bike and gave it full throttle. He shot across to the outbound lanes of Whitehorse Road and streaked away, about one minute behind the first rider.

Rigby followed. It took precious time for her to reach the outbound lanes of Whitehorse Road. The radio traffic was urgent, patrol cars ordered to the park, the duty sergeant wanting her to report in. She left the handset on the passenger seat and planted her foot. The kilometres unwound beneath her. She was far behind the riders and she knew it.

But then she got lucky. She was coming over a rise, way out in Lilydale, when she saw an intersection in the distance, the lights red, and there was one of the bikes. She accelerated. The light turned green. She accelerated some more, just as the bike began to streak away. The guy gave it a standing start, full throttle, the front wheel lifting off the ground. Moron.

Everything seemed to stop. Even from some distance away, Rigby heard an almighty howl and saw bike and rider stall.

The drive-chain had broken.

The rider dismounted, grabbed a gym bag from the pannier and ran, dodging cars as he headed for the neon wash of a Hungry Jack's. Then he was behind the building and Rigby shot across the intersection and bounced over the kerb and into the car park at the rear. She shouted into the radio—location, suspect on foot, armed and dangerous—and ran into a mess of shadows.

She found him seconds later, crouched in the stench of nearby dump bins. 'Stand,' she shouted, grinding her service .38 into his ear. 'Hands on your head and facing away from me.'

He was a tall, morose-looking guy, shocked at the speed of his downfall. She ordered him to put his arms behind his back, and ratcheted the handcuffs onto his wrists as she recited the familiar arrest announcement.

'Suspicion of murder?' he said. 'No way.'

'Shut up,' Rigby said, patting him down. No pistol. No cash or drugs or jewellery, either.

'What did you do with the gun?'

'What gun?'

'Don't give me that. I saw you. It's on the radio, two gunshot victims in Jacaranda Park.'

'Wasn't me.'

'Okay, genius, I'll just have to order a GSR test of your sleeves and hands.'

He struggled and she smacked her palm against his ear. 'Settle down.'

Rigby prodded him into the spill of lights at the front of the burger joint. She was tense. The second rider was unaccounted for, and still no sign of backup. 'What's your name?'

'No comment.'

She cursed him and kept alert for the accomplice as a handful of teenagers emerged from Hungry Jack's and gathered in a half circle. They wanted a show. 'Shoot him,' one of them urged.

'Go and do your homework,' Rigby snarled.

They laughed and wandered away. She turned to the shooter. 'Where's your mate? Done a runner? Left you to face the music?'

'No comment.'

Rigby heard sirens in the distance. The traffic slowed, parted, and blue and red lights were weaving through to save her. Her heart ceased hammering: two patrol cars from Outer Eastern.

Then the handover and the explanations before one car took the gunman away and the other returned to duties. Rigby stayed. She returned to the foetid bins behind the Hungry Jack's, determined to find the gun.

What she found was the gym bag. Her mouth went dry, her heart stopped, to see treasury bonds inside it, the heavy paper embossed and engraved, lots of zeros after the pound sterling symbols.

GARRY DISHER ◆ 192

Rigby felt very alive then. She thought about her credit card debt, mortgage and missed opportunities, the male culture of her workplace, her crap car. She needed a root canal, too. She stowed the gym bag under her seat and stared down the road for a moment, but there was no sign of the first bike, it wasn't coming back, so she made a squealing U-turn and headed in.

30

When Khandi shot out of the park, her Ducati churning up the grass, she was well ahead of Eddie, but as soon as she was on the highway she slowed until he appeared in her rear view mirror. As agreed, they maintained a two-hundred-metre gap as they streaked east along Whitehorse, Khandi leading, her headlight lighting the darkness ahead.

But Eddie was such a fucking show-off. She saw the way he opened out the throttle each time he left a set of lights, rearing up on the back wheel then snapping down again and rocketing away. She began to feel pissed off. She guessed he was getting some kind of sexual glow from snatching back the bonds, the dickhead, but it would get him noticed by the cops.

Then, in Lilydale, it all came unstuck. Her mirrors showed him pull his little stunt, then unaccountably lose speed and wobble towards the kerb. She braked, still watching, and saw him prop the bike on its stand and dart through traffic to a fast food barn.

Cursing him for a fuckwit, Khandi wheeled the Ducati around to go back. And stopped. A white Falcon had appeared out of nowhere, your typical unmarked cop car. It cut across the intersection and a woman got out, running after Eddie and waving a handgun.

They were watching us the whole time, Khandi thought. She glanced around for police backup. The Furneaux brothers told the cops. There was no point in trying to rescue her idiot lover, so she turned again and raced eastwards, headlight punching through the night, feeling shaken by grief, receding adrenaline and the succession of forearm shocks from the road surface. At least she had the money.

The first thing she did when she reached the cabin was light a couple of candles, and the second was light a joint and down a slug of tequila as she paced the main room, pausing only to check the money. More money than she'd ever had. But she didn't have Eddie. That was starting to matter.

At 9 p.m. her mobile rang. She peered at the screen: the caller was using a landline. Only Eddie knew her number, so her heart leapt. 'Hello?'

A voice she didn't know said, 'Susan Roberts?'

That was her real name, but who else except Eddie and the tax office knew it? 'Yes.'

'The lawyer?'

Khandi went to the window and looked out at darkness broken only by a slice of the moon and a solitary light down in the valley. She didn't know how much time she had. 'That's right.'

'My name is Whelan, I'm a detective senior sergeant with CIU at the Outer Eastern police station. We have one of your clients here, refusing to answer questions until he has his lawyer present.'

Khandi's voice had more control than she felt. 'Name?'

'You tell me. We're running his prints.'

'Charges?' said Khandi in the clipped way of lawyers.

'Armed robbery and two counts of murder. He wants to speak to you, and that is his right.'

'I'll be there before ten o'clock,' said Khandi, cutting the connection. She switched off the phone and removed and smashed the SIM card.

She was wired—boy was she wired. Everything she'd done and said with Eddie spoke of their love burning across the sky and into the history books, and he pulls a stupid stunt like this. He must have shot the Furneaux brothers—unless he got into it with the cops. She turned on the radio, but the time was 9.07; no news until ten.

And all the time she was thinking: When he realises I'm not coming for him, he'll talk. She would, in his shoes.

The moon slipped in and out of clouds. Khandi leaned over and vomited, a thin, bitter gruel. Maddened, she hurled a chair at the heavy iron stove and saw it splinter. She was exalted in her fury. She wanted to punch, kick and scratch someone.

But Eddie was locked up and all she had was the mildewed air of his aunt's cabin. Restored a little, she examined her feelings. Reflection was new to her. Usually when thoughts and feelings arose, she acted on them. This time she took note of where her rage was coming from, and where it would lead her.

She saw that she had a right to be mad. For a start, she'd had big plans for those bonds, intending to ransom them to Furneaux a second time and then find a buyer. Maybe she should have discussed this with Eddie, but, by the same token, Eddie should have been more tuned in to her intentions. He'd fucked up what would have been a licence to print money, the dear, sweet, cunt-struck idiot.

And what was that about, two counts of murder? Macho bullshit, probably. To prove he was a stone killer, a hard man. What crap: Khandi could have showed him hard. Incensed to think of what she'd lost, she let out a shriek and threw a frying pan, which stuck handle-first into the plaster wall. Mentally replaying Eddie grandstanding on his bike, like some fifteen-year-old kid, Khandi pulled out the frying pan and demolished another chair.

A voice inside her said, very clearly, 'Eddie's going to spill his guts, save his own skin, because he's weak and he doesn't love you.'

Whirling into motion again, Khandi made a stab at wiping the cabin clean of prints, stowed the money into a backpack and headed down the dirt road to Yarra Junction. She'd drive straight through the night, get as far away as possible, make her way up the eastern seaboard to the beaches north of Cairns and lose herself among the beach bums.

At the main crossroads in town, she stopped on the throbbing bike, her boots planted on either side of the frame. Khandi a beach bum? Sandals, sarong, beads and a tan? I don't think so. She belonged to the night hours, to neon-washed pavements and corner tables.

She accelerated a short distance, stopped again. She should lie low for a couple of days. Sort her options.

Catching sight of a corner pub, a chalkboard sign saying 'Counter Meals', she realised, Jesus, I'm starving. She swerved into the yard behind the Junction Arms, dismounted and clomped into the lounge.

Stowing her helmet on a little table in the corner, hoisting the backpack over one shoulder, she crossed the room, reading the chalked menu.

'When's the kitchen close?'

'Five minutes,' said the young woman behind the servery counter, absently counting till receipts.

'Whiting and chips,' growled Khandi, to make her pay attention.

She paid attention, blinked once, her gaze eating Khandi up.

'Tina', according to her nametag. She was Khandi's height and general shape, but there the resemblance ended. She was so straight-looking, God, rayon slacks and a white short-sleeved shirt with 'Junction Arms' scrolled across the pocket. Short, neat hair. A plain ring and a plain necklace and tiny studs in her earlobes. Looking her full in the face, Khandi said 'Hi Tina,' then let her gaze play across Tina's breasts and groin. 'Come here often?'

Tina looked right back. 'Not often enough.'

Khandi gave her a nod, a smile through parted lips. She sauntered back to her table, selecting a chair that gave her a clear view of the lounge. Tina moved like a woman who knew she was being watched. She took another last-minute order, cleared tables and racked trays. Finally she delivered Khandi's food and purred, 'Enjoy.'

'I intend to,' Khandi purred back. She was exhausted now that she was safe.

After a while the beer, cold and gassy, cut through her torpor as the calories kicked in. She polished off the meal, stretched out her leather-clad legs and absently picked her teeth with a split match. Then she worked a smoulder into her eyes and sauntered across to the servery. 'So, Tina.' Pause, 'What time d'you get off?'

Tina swallowed and her body thrummed. 'Soon.' She looked around quickly. 'I live in a little apartment out the back of the pub,' she whispered, passing a key across the bar.

31

'You'd have to say she was very lucky,' Lowe said, looking indulgently at his patient, who was asleep.

He also meant that he admired his own work. Wyatt said nothing. He didn't see life in terms of luck. There were circumstances, that's all. If you were good at your work, you didn't need to draw attention to how well you did it.

'She'll need a little cosmetic surgery,' Lowe went on, 'but there's no infection. And she was strong and healthy to begin with.'

Wyatt let the man talk. He knew that talking was a comfort to people. It filled the silences in their lives, helped them make sense of the world, assured them they were alive.

Late evening and the doctor was ostensibly on his way home. He'd spent a full day in surgery and then made his hospital rounds, but still looked neat and buttoned down. He seemed inclined to linger. Wyatt didn't know why.

He moved to leave the bedroom. After a moment, the doctor followed. They gravitated to the bank of windows and looked out at the city. The glass distorted everything. The colours swam in the darkness. Lowe said, 'You have anything to do with those dead jewellers?'

Wyatt didn't flinch. 'What dead jewellers?'

'I heard it on the news just now. Two brothers. They were robbed yesterday, and this evening they were shot dead.'

Wyatt processed the information. He didn't know what it meant.

'I wondered if that was you,' the doctor said.

Wyatt said, 'Don't wonder.'

The doctor swallowed. 'Fair enough.'

When the man was gone, Wyatt checked radio and TV broadcasts, monitored the police band and made a couple of terse, cryptic phone calls from one of his unused mobile phones.

Then he poked his head around the bedroom door. 'Khandi Cane: mean anything to you?'

Lydia blinked. 'I prefer the other guy's bedside manner.'

Wyatt didn't have time for this. 'Do you know the name?'

Lydia pulled at her clothes and propped a pillow between her spine and the wall. 'Never heard of her.'

'Eddie's girlfriend. A stripper.'

'Figures.'

Wyatt came closer, perched on the side of the bed, and told her about the shootings in Jacaranda Park.

She was bewildered. 'What's it mean?'

'I don't know.'

'Eddie and his woman?'

'Could be.'

'But why?'

'I intend to find out.'

She looked at him. 'Do you still doubt me?'

'Not really.'

She touched her head as if to ease a pain spasm. 'A ringing endorsement. What if you and I are next on Eddie's list?'

'Lowe and I intend to move you soon. Meanwhile, never answer the landline phone or the door.'

'You're creeping me out.'

Wyatt didn't have time for explanations or reassurances. Handing her an unused prepaid phone, he said, 'This is how we stay in touch. Lowe and I will call you whenever we enter the building. If we call the landline number, you'll know something's wrong. Don't answer, just run.'

She stared at the phone. 'Run where?'

'Somewhere safe,' Wyatt said, returning to the sitting room.

He surfed the TV channels again, alighting on *The Footy Show*, which was celebrating the induction of another cokehead and woman basher into the Football Hall of Fame. 'We break for this news update,' the anchor said, and the screen dissolved to the site of the shooting in Jacaranda Park, and then to an old arrest photo of Eddie Oberin, the reporter saying: 'Outer Eastern Magistrates' Court tomorrow morning.'

Wyatt powered off the TV set and tried to put it together. Had the Furneaux brothers tracked Eddie down? What were they all doing in the park? Had Eddie and the woman fallen out?

And Wyatt thought: Eddie will finger me.

It was like getting his sight back after a period of blindness. He felt light, potent and elastic, and knew at once that he had to clean out his first-floor apartment and destroy everything that pointed to his identity and presence, including his prints.

There was always a chance that Eddie would keep his trap shut, but that wasn't a chance Wyatt could take. And someday the doctor might talk. The police wouldn't get much further than an unoccupied apartment and an untraceable owner, but eventually they'd think to cast an eye over the building's other residents, if only to seek information. In the meantime, the apartment on the eighth floor was safe for a couple more days. There was nothing tying it to the first-floor apartment: they'd been purchased separately, at different times and using different accounts and names. Even so, Wyatt knew the time had come to sell. Together, the apartments were worth close to a million dollars. He'd use two different agencies, and have the proceeds paid into two different account names. Contact strictly by telephone and e-mail. That's how he'd bought each place and that's how he'd sell them.

Wyatt took the stairs. The lift was available, but lifts were a trap. He went straight to the first-floor apartment's concealed safe and removed the contents: spare cash, two sets of false ID and the deeds to both properties. Finally he grabbed the dark suit hanging in his wardrobe. There was nothing else that he wanted to take with him when he left the place forever, no photos, diaries, letters or other keepsakes, for the simple reason that he had no past that he wanted to think about.

32

The shootings hadn't occurred on her patch, but Rigby assured Outer Eastern's CIU head that they related to a case she was working.

'Is that a fact?' he said, unimpressed.

His name was Whelan, a senior sergeant with tar-stained fingers, a restless cough and features cobwebbed from screwing up his face.

'So I wouldn't mind sitting in,' she said.

They were in his office. She'd been in many such offices over the years and there was nothing about this one to mark it out. Citations and certificates on the walls, police regulations spine-out on cheap wooden shelves. She was more interested in Whelan. Was he a rules-and-regulations kind of guy?

'Give me the short version.'

Rigby told him about the torched four-wheel-drive and the Furneaux brothers' form. 'I know what questions to ask,' she continued. 'It'll save time.'

'Well, you did arrest the prick,' Whelan conceded.

Rigby tried and failed to give him a winning smile. 'Thanks. Any forensics in yet?'

'Gunshot residue on his right hand and one sleeve.'

'I knew it. I looked for his weapon, but it was too dark.'

Whelan tilted his head to one side. 'But you found a gym bag.'

'Yep.'

'Containing a couple of Bank of England bearer bonds.'

'That's right,' said Rigby tightly.

'And you don't know his name.'

'Correct.'

Another long stare. Then Whelan unfolded from his chair. 'Let's hope his lawyer can tell us.'

'Lawyer.'

Whelan gave her the smile of a policeman who's encountered too many lawyers. 'Said she'd be here by ten o'clock.'

Rigby followed him along a corridor, glancing at her watch. Almost ten. It had taken time to transport and book the prisoner. Then he'd been printed, swabbed for DNA, stripped of his clothes, tested for gunshot residue. If he wasn't charged or bailed in the next twelve hours, they'd have to let him go.

'Here we are,' Whelan said.

An interrogation room, the blue shape of a uniformed constable showing through on the other side of the frosted glass, guarding the man Rigby had arrested. This was her last chance. 'Do you think we could start before the lawyer gets here? For all we know, his mate is out there, waving a gun around.'

Whelan didn't scotch the idea. 'He won't go for it.'

'Can't hurt to try,' Rigby said, reaching for the door, then remembering her place. 'It can be informal.'

Whelan shook his head. 'We tape it,' he said, and opened the door to the interrogation room.

They went in. Whelan jerked his head at the uniformed constable, who left, closing the door behind him. Rigby and Whelan introduced themselves, sat in plastic chairs at a plastic table across from the prisoner, and Whelan started the tapes rolling. The room was stuffy, imprinted with years of denials and confessions.

Whelan repeated the formal warning and got started. 'Okay, Sunshine, what's your story?'

The shooter swallowed, then cocked his head. 'My lawyer?'

He'd looked snaky and dangerous in his bike leathers. In prison overalls, he was mild and forgettable, the washed-out shade of orange struggling to make it here in the glare of the fluorescent tubes. 'How about you tell us who you are, first,' Rigby said.

'No comment.'

'We're running your prints. You're in the system; I can smell it on you.'

'I want my lawyer,' the shooter said.

His gaze went around the room as if the smears on the walls might lead to doors and tunnels.

'She won't be getting you out any time soon,' Whelan said.

'You've got nothing on me. I want bail.'

Rigby laughed. 'You've been arrested on suspicion of a double homicide.'

'So charge me.'

'Oh we will, Sunshine, we will,' Whelan said. 'You'll go before a magistrate in the morning, bail will be denied, and you'll be taken to the Remand Centre in Spencer Street.'

Rigby wasn't interested in procedural ins and outs. 'All we want to do is clear up a few basic matters before your lawyer arrives, save some time, clear up any misunderstandings.'

A shrug.

'For the benefit of the tape, the prisoner has shrugged, indicating assent.'

'And the tooth fairy really exists.'

'Preliminary results of a GSR test indicate that you have fired a gun recently. Do you deny that?'

'No comment.'

'Do you have a firearm permit? Do you own a gun?'

'Did you find one on me? No. Where's my lawyer?'

'Two men were shot dead in Jacaranda Park at approximately seven o'clock this evening. You were seen leaving the park on a motorcycle shortly after that time. I put it to you that you were responsible for shooting those men.'

'No comment.'

'If it was self-defence,' Whelan said, 'it's in your best interests to say so for the record now. The resulting charges and sentencing will reflect that.'

'Like I said, I'll wait for my lawyer.'

Rigby ploughed on. 'Were you hired to kill these men?'

'No comment.'

'Was it a hold-up that got out of hand?'

'Like I said, no fucking comment.'

'A second motorcyclist was seen leaving the park shortly before you did. Can you give me the name of this person?'

'No comment.'

'It was your partner, right?' said Whelan. 'He ran out on you.'

'Go to hell.'

'Go to hell,' said Whelan. 'Good, our dialogue is progressing.'

Despite his tone, Rigby could tell that Whelan was bored and tired. He had no stake in the case. But she needed to get something concrete before the lawyer arrived. She leaned over the scratched and scored table top. 'The victims, Henri and Joseph Furneaux, were robbed in unusual circumstances yesterday morning. What was your involvement in that?'

'Like I said, kiss my arse.'

'Two Bank of England treasury bonds—to the value of a million pounds sterling—were found in your possession. I put it to you that these were also stolen.'

For the first time, he showed some emotion. He stiffened, clenched his fists and snarled in her face, 'You fucking cow.'

Whelan yawned. 'Watch your language, pal.'

'My language? Jesus Christ, the bitch is pulling a swiftie. I was carrying paper worth *twenty-five* million.'

Rigby felt the quizzical stare of the officer next to her. She shrugged, her features flattened and cynical as if to say, 'So a crook accuses a cop of dishonesty—what's new?' But she didn't want any kind of scrutiny. 'Can you account for these bonds? Did you steal them from the victims?'

'Fuck you,' said the guy, still disgusted.

Whelan answered a knock on the door, murmured thanks to the civilian clerk who slipped him a scrap of paper. 'Edward John Oberin,' he said, returning to the grimy little table, 'according to your prints.'

Oberin shrugged.

'You've got form—admittedly not much—for receiving stolen goods.'

'Really come up in the world, Edward,' said Rigby. 'Armed robbery, double homicide.'

'Bite me,' Oberin said.

Plenty of bravado but under it she could see a hunted look. Maybe Oberin was starting to realise he was looking at life in prison. She decided to work on that. 'Your partner got away free and clear, Edward, leaving you to face the music. Share the burden,' she said, leaning toward him. 'Who was it? Don't take it all on your own shoulders.'

His face screwed up in hate, and then it began to clear. 'Wyatt,' he said.

Whelan, slumped with his arms crossed, yawned again. 'Wyatt who?'

'Just Wyatt.'

'He was the other rider?'

'Yeah.'

'Was he the brains behind this?'

'Oh yeah.'

'Is he in the system?'

'Never been arrested.'

Rigby leaned forward until she was in his face. 'Where do we find him, Eddie?'

Oberin jerked back from her. 'That's not how it works.'

'How does it work?'

'I scratch your back, you scratch mine.'

He refused to say more. Whelan tried calling Oberin's lawyer, without result, so they returned him to the cells, but for a short period between interview room, corridor, phone call and lockup, Rigby found herself alone with the man. She could feel his scrutiny and contempt and tried to bluff it out. Finally he murmured, 'You're crooked.'

Rigby didn't respond.

'Make the charges go away,' he continued. 'In return, I'll tell you where Wyatt lives.'

She squirmed away from him. 'Tell me now.'

'No. I want something in writing.'

But what do *I* want? thought Rigby. *Two* hard men saying I ripped them off? Maybe she could shoot this Wyatt character in the line of duty and let Eddie Oberin rot in jail. When Oberin was taken to the cells, she started filling out paperwork for Whelan. It was not too late to make alterations—substitute 'twenty-five million pounds sterling' for 'two million pounds sterling'—or offer Oberin a deal and send an arrest team for the man named Wyatt, but she didn't, she packed up and drove back to her own cop shop, feeling light, as though her body didn't belong to her.

33

It had paid off for Le Page, hiding those extra transponders with the bearer bonds. The GPS receiver had come to life with a beep, the cursor winking, when he was staking out the park.

Not that it went smoothly after that. He'd factored in a double-cross during the handover—call it collateral damage— but the speed of it, the use of motorbikes, had surprised him. By the time he'd fishtailed the Subaru after the bikes, he was half a minute behind.

It was the traffic that foxed him, streaming along on the wrong side of the road. Then, as he crossed over onto the middle outbound lane, he'd been clipped by a taxi. Suddenly he was hemmed in, the highway choked and the commuters stopping to gawk. Tucking his knife beside his thigh, he watched the taxi driver get out. To his relief, the man didn't approach but began directing the traffic around the accident scene. A gap opened up, allowing access to the service lane at the side of the road. The taxi driver gestured, Le Page smiled his thanks, and followed the taxi. But he didn't stop. He whipped along the service lane and back onto the highway.

He was several minutes behind the bikes by then, the traffic too concentrated for sustained bursts of speed. He jerked along from intersection to intersection, checking the GPS signal, and that's when he noticed the cursor had almost stopped moving. He pulled into the slow lane, eventually spotting the unmarked police car and the bike. And the arrest. Two more police cars arrived and soon left again, one with the prisoner. By now Le Page had recognised the detective who'd been so interested in his cousins. Rigby disappeared behind a fast-food barn, then reappeared with a gym bag, got into her car and drove away. The GPS signal moved with her.

She pulled into a side street a short distance away. Before Le Page could work out how to approach her unseen, she moved off again.

He tailed her to a nearby police station, Outer Eastern, according to a blue and white sign. She parked outside the front door, and when she carried the gym bag into the building, he almost gave up. Instead, he waited, planning how he might break in overnight, when the station was undermanned.

Rigby emerged at 11 p.m., empty handed. She was dowdy and aroused a sour taste in Le Page's mouth. She drove away.

And the GPS signal travelled with her. Le Page wanted to sing. He followed her to a police station near Armadale, where she parked inside a cyclone and razor wire security fence. She got out, hovered by the unmarked car for a while, nodding hello as a handful of uniformed constables and plainclothed officers came and went. When there was a lull, she reached into the car. Le Page saw her remove both document wallets and transfer them to a silver Golf that gleamed under a security light. She entered the station.

Le Page waited, out of CCTV range, and watched the Golf. He thought about the woman. Was she chronically dishonest? Opportunistic? It didn't matter. What mattered was what she would do with the bonds now, and how quickly. Sell them, enter them into evidence, even destroy them? He couldn't risk breaking into her car. If she drove home with the bonds, he'd take her there. If she attempted to hide them en route, he'd interrupt. If her conscience got the better of her he'd take a chance and ambush her, right there at the side door of the police station.

She left at midnight. The GPS receiver led him to a house in an endless suburb in this endless city. The freeway was nearby. Parking on Burke Road, he ran to a little side street in time to see the Golf slip into a short driveway beside a nondescript house about halfway along. After fifteen minutes he entered the alley that ran behind the houses. Risking a peek through a crack in the fence he saw a patio with sliding doors and a faint spill of light on the floor within, indicating that the woman was nearby, maybe in the kitchen. He made one pass and when he came back the light was off. A new light showed, small, high on the wall. Bathroom. That light went off and he heard water in the pipes.

Soon there were no lights. After another thirty minutes he climbed over the back fence and circled the house. The woman's bedroom was at the front and through a gap in the curtains he saw her in her bed, illuminated by the kind of muted light that leaks into the corners of the night. The covers were half on the floor and she slept naked, in an attitude of turmoil and surrender, spreadeagled on her back amid tangled sheets.

Le Page crept around to the silver Golf and heaved up and down on it and she was out in a flash to cancel the alarm, one arm struggling with the sleeve of a dressing gown, her thin body turned whitish grey by the sodium lamps. House lights went on up and down the street. 'Sorry,' she said hoarsely, waving to her neighbours, 'sorry.' Silence restored, she returned shivering to her front door, where Le Page showed her his pistol and clamped a gloved hand over her mouth.

She bucked violently but he prodded her ahead of him into the house and kicked the door closed and turned off the hall light. 'To the bedroom,' he murmured in her ear.

There in her musty cave he said, 'I will now remove my hand. You will not cry out but get into bed. Do you understand?'

She nodded and did as he asked, recovering with gasps and whimpers, wiping her mouth and chin. She wanted to burrow beneath the covers so that he could not see her body through the gaps in the robe and she wanted to be upright so that she could fight. He solved it for her by stepping away from the bed and saying, 'Cover yourself.'

She pulled the sheet to her chin, her back against the wall. Courage returned to her eyes.

'The bonds,' Le Page said.

She didn't try to bluster or deny it. He saw her calculate the various odds. 'You followed me?'

'The bonds,' he said again, patiently.

She pointed. She'd thrown the day's clothes over a chair and partly over her briefcase. He edged towards it, keeping the gun on her, finally crouching and snapping open the lid. He found the document wallets and that day's newspaper and other scraps from her life. He thought of her miserable existence and expectations and debated the merits of shooting her. She had seen his face, but to shoot a police officer would bring extraordinary strife down upon his head.

Then she said, 'You're the French courier.'

Le Page gave her an amused look. 'You have been following Henri and Joseph?'

'Yes.'

'Both are dead. Your case is closed.'

They stared at each other. She began to tremble. 'Are you going to shoot me?'

'Perhaps.'

He jerked his jaw toward her bedside table, indicating a little Nikon digital camera sitting there with a glass of water, tissues and a fat paperback. 'The camera, if you please.'

She passed it to him with a twist of shame and outrage.

'It is not what you think,' Le Page said. He handed her a Bank of England treasury note redeemable for £100,000 sterling, together with the newspaper unfolded to reveal the front page. 'You will hold these beneath your chin,' he said.

Her mind was racing. She gave him a sour twist of the mouth. 'Arsehole.'

'You are alive, be thankful,' he said.

He took several photographs. 'You will close the file on me and the Furneaux brothers now.'

'Yes.'

'If you do not, if I receive unwelcome attention here or in Europe, then I shall inform your superiors.'

'I get it,' she said.

'I am finished here, but if I one day return and find myself in difficulties...'

'I get it.'

'The man you arrested.'

'Oberin,' the detective said.

'Did he give up any names?'

'One. Wyatt.'

'Good.'

Le Page gave Rigby his smile and leafed through one of the document wallets. 'Ah. Perfect.'

He handed her a bearer bond worth £25,000. She accepted it tensely, expecting a trap. There wasn't one. Le Page said, 'Spend it wisely,' and left her sitting there, eyes darting around the kitchen in search of somewhere to hide her windfall.

Le Page returned to the Sofitel. He was finished in this damn place; making contact with Henri's clients was risky now; time to go home.

His flight was not until 10 a.m. Saturday, Paris via Hong Kong and Frankfurt, but he used the hotel's lobby phone to reserve a next-day flight out of South Australia, the noon service to Auckland. After that he'd play it by ear, maybe a package tour to Fiji, but not leave Suva airport, take the next flight to Singapore instead, and from there fly to London, and finally Toulouse, using different identities for each stage.

He went upstairs, packed his bag and cleaned the room. No scraps of paper, no hairs in the basin or bathtub, no prints. The cleaners would come in and complete the task by scrubbing anything he'd missed and leaving behind an overlay of new traces. He never used hotel phones. His credit card and passport, while valid, were in a false name, another blind alley for the police.

Finally Le Page went downstairs, paid, and retrieved his car. He drove all night, his radio tuned to a news station. Police had released Oberin's name, but that's all they had to say. Reaching Adelaide at 8.30 a.m., Le Page took a room at the Hilton, where he napped, showered and ate breakfast. He was at the airport by eleven.

34

Friday morning, 8.55, and Wyatt was outside the Outer Eastern courthouse, carrying a briefcase and wearing a suit, a white shirt and a sombre tie. In the belief that a woman, a nun or a child was as capable of killing him as a man, he assessed everyone. There were some women around the building— lawyers, victims, mothers and wives of prisoners and victims— but no nuns or children. He didn't bother with the uniformed police, for they were clearly armed. He concentrated on anyone not in uniform—a woman wearing a jacket over slacks and two men in loose fitting suits. They were detectives armed with .38 revolvers and he'd have known they were detectives even if this wasn't a courthouse next to a police station. Perhaps they were waiting to appear in court, or guard a witness. They weren't expecting trouble, simply standing around yarning and smoking.

Finally Wyatt entered the courthouse. The building was cavernous, an echoing bluestone structure that dated from the

1920s and was the opposite of the dull new police station next door. Faced by a warren of corridors, staircases, shadowy corners and gloomy courtrooms, he stopped to get his bearings. The place thronged with magistrates, defence barristers, prosecution witnesses, jurors, clerks and the friends and family of victims and those on trial. Plenty of police coming and going, with prisoners or files and documents, but they looked busy and distracted.

He checked the security. A metal detector and a couple of armed attendants. This was a suburban courthouse, dealing mainly with bail hearings, intervention orders and minor crimes. No one had ever escaped from its custody, pulled a gun on a judge or done anything more violent than shout abuse at a witness. But security was ramping up everywhere, a factor Wyatt was forced to accommodate more often these days.

He thought about the metal detector as he checked a noticeboard in the foyer. Eddie Oberin was to face the magistrate in No. 3 court at 9.30 a.m.

Wyatt left the building and walked down a path between dying shrubs to the rear. He found a handful of furtive smokers standing around a sand tray, sliding doors, prison transport vans, expensive cars jostling for parking space and taxis pulling in and out of a drive-through, delivering magistrates and lawyers. Young law clerks hurried behind them, wheeling boxed files on small trolleys into a glass-walled foyer, the lino floor streaked black by tyres and shoes. Wyatt contrived to collide with a young woman as she approached one of the entrances, and his briefcase and papers went everywhere. She stopped, face flushed, teetering on high heels and inexperience, to help him gather the spill. When they entered the foyer, composed again, almost friends, no one pointed a quivering finger at him.

Wyatt found No. 3 court along an empty corridor on the first floor, accessed by a broad marble staircase, the steps worn and grimy, the light poor, the air full of tricky echoes. There was a bench against the wall outside the entrance to the courtroom. Wyatt sat there, a lawyer maybe, an expert witness. A mild guy waiting patiently with his briefcase in his lap and his shiny black shoes placed neatly together on the cold floor.

He heard footsteps and there was Eddie, in cuffs, struggling up the stairs flanked by a couple of uniformed constables. 'I'm telling you, she's crooked,' he shouted.

'Shut up, will ya?' said one guard in a weary cop's voice.

'My lawyer showed me the evidence list. It's bullshit. *Two* million? I was carrying bonds worth twenty-five million when that ugly bitch arrested me.'

Wyatt stood, the briefcase concealing the Steyr pistol, as Eddie went on, 'She pocketed twenty-three million quid and you bozos are going to let her get away with it.'

'Look, will you just shut your gob?' the other cop said.

Wyatt noted the words 'bonds' and 'evidence list' and filed them away for later. Right now, Eddie and his escort were nearing the top of the stairs.

'Rigby's the one should be facing a magistrate, not me.'

'Jesus Christ, shut your cakehole.'

'Fuck you.'

Their heads were level with the top step. Wyatt screwed plugs into his ears, stepped away from the bench and shot Eddie twice in the chest. The force threw Eddie back, but the reaction of the first constable was to protect him, grab his upper arms and manoeuvre Eddie out of the line of fire. The other did the opposite, trying to insert Eddie between himself and danger.

With all of that pushing and shoving, Eddie's chin jerked back, then slumped forward, giving Wyatt a perfect kill shot to the top of the skull.

It was quick. Too quick for the guards, who floundered, unable to take it in. They were splattered in blood and deafened, too stunned to draw their weapons.

It was later reported that Wyatt had said, 'Cop that, you bastard,' as he shot Oberin. In fact, he didn't say a word. Why waste words? This was revenge, but there was nothing heated about it. When he was working, his instructions to bank tellers, security guards, witnesses or the people working alongside him were calm and efficient. The words had a job to do and were not to be squandered.

He slipped into the courtroom itself, empty apart from the court reporter setting up her machine. Wearing earphones, and humming along to an MP3 player hooked to her belt, she seemed unaware of the drama in the corridor. She glanced once, saw a man dressed in a suit, and forgot about him.

Wyatt exited through a door behind the bench where the magistrates sat. He passed through rooms and along corridors, encountering no one who was a threat or looked at him twice, and strolled out of the building and across the street, dodging cars and a tram. He entered an alley between a lingerie shop and the branch of a community bank.

The alley hooked to the left, and when he was out of sight he stripped off his gloves, suit coat and shirt, knowing they would be engrained with gunshot residue. After stowing them in the pannier of a bicycle chained to a parking sign, he dismantled the pistol and concealed the barrel under a wooden pallet on the back of a delivery truck, the frame in a dump bin, the bullets amongst vegetable peelings behind a restaurant and the clip under a loose cobblestone.

Dressed now in a plain white T-shirt and trousers, he intended to leave the system of alleyways and take a cab to the main airport, where he could join newly arrived passengers who were queuing to take a cab back to the city. Too quickly, though, the air filled with the sounds of sirens and whistles. Then there were running footsteps and yelling. His options had shrunk. The police would be stopping buses and taxis and mounting a watch on bus stops and the local train station.

Coming to the intersection of two alleys, Wyatt risked a glance each way. Apart from a car parked hard against the wall and one or two garbage bins, the left-hand branch was empty. In the right were a couple of hard-core drinkers, a man and a woman. Wyatt took off the white T-shirt, rubbed it against the grimy walls and pulled it on again. He dirtied his hands in the mucky drain and rubbed them over his trousers, face and forearms. Now he looked dirty, lost and broken. Cities are full of men like him. But one thing was missing. He approached the drunks, who were squabbling piteously over the remaining few centimetres of sherry in their bottle, and said, 'Give you five bucks for it.'

They stopped bickering, the man with a days-old beard and scummy mouth, the woman with bloodshot eyes and wonky lipstick. They looked neat enough, but grubby and toxic. In comparison, Wyatt felt clean and wholesome and he needed to match them. 'Five bucks,' he said, showing them the money.

The woman narrowed her eyes. 'Ten.'

Wyatt could hear closer shouts and sirens. The police would be doing a sweep of the side streets and alleys soon. 'Fair enough,' he said, paying her.

He took the bottle and drained it, swallowing some but letting plenty of the sticky fluid dribble down his jaw and neck and into his T-shirt, too. He wanted the stink of the hardened boozer on his skin and clothing. The others were appalled at the waste and possibly because they'd expected him to share.

'Bastard,' said the man.

The woman reached for the bottle and tried to wrest it from Wyatt, who welcomed the tussle, for he could hear footsteps behind him.

'Fucking jacks,' the man said suddenly.

The woman released Wyatt. He knuckled his eyes to induce redness, scratched at his scalp with torn nails and, when the other two slid to the ground, muttering, he joined them.

'Piss off,' the woman hissed. 'This is our spot.'

Wyatt tilted the bottle again.

The police were young uniformed constables. 'Did any of you see a guy in a suit run past here?'

Wyatt tried to get them into focus. 'What?'

'Bloody deros,' muttered one of the cops. 'Come on, Marty, we're wasting our time.'

He turned to go, but his partner held back. Wyatt didn't want that. He burped, gave a gassy yawn then scraped at something on his ankle, hoping the cop named Marty would get the message. The drunks were staring mutinously at the empty bottle.

'Come on, Marty,' the policeman said again.

Marty ignored him. He stood over Wyatt and the others and said, 'You can't stay here. New regulations.'

Wyatt had no interest in the affairs of the city or the nation. He'd never voted and his name did not appear on electoral rolls. But he did know what was going on. He'd put together some of his biggest scores from studying the social and business pages of daily newspapers. Last month, when the Labor Premier ecstatically announced another Major Sporting Event for Melbourne, Wyatt's first thought was the money that would pour into the city. Now he remembered something else: the Premier had ordered a gradual eradication of street people in the lead-up to the event. So much for championing the downtrodden, he thought, about to see himself come unstuck on one man's glorious vision.

'So come on, get up,' the cop named Marty said, in this foetid alleyway in a well-heeled outer suburb.

'Jesus, Marty, leave it,' his partner said.

'Regulations.'

'Stuff regulations. They were never intended to—'

'I want to see them move along,' Marty said.

'Fuck you,' said the woman, still enraged with Wyatt. The bottle was empty and she didn't remember emptying it, but it was in Wyatt's hands now. That made her mad.

'I beg your pardon?'

'Fucking leave us alone.'

Please don't, Wyatt pleaded silently, closing his eyes.

'Maybe a day in the lockup will teach you some manners,' Marty told the woman.

'Marty, for Christ's sake. We've got a job to do.'

Meanwhile the woman had found ten dollars in her hand and wanted to spend it, but vaguely remembered being rolled by a copper once before, losing five bucks to him. 'Yeah, Marty,' she sneered, 'run along now.'

Marty stiffened. Wyatt tensed. This was bad for him. 'It's okay,' he slurred, looking up at Marty. 'I apologise for my friends. We'll move along.'

'The fuck we will,' the woman said.

'Yeah, fucking cops, always fucking hassling us,' her boyfriend said.

For some reason, that cracked them up. They nudged each other and chortled at the cops.

'I'm calling it in,' Marty said.

A police van was there in a couple of minutes. Wyatt and the drunks were arrested, thrown into a tight space of reinforced steel mesh, and taken to the lockup.

35

Wyatt found himself in a holding cell along with the man from the alleyway and four other drunks. Three were grimy, stinking wrecks. The fourth, asleep with his back to the wall, was about Wyatt's age, early forties, and about his size, tallish and lean. The same dark hair, but he wore glasses, trousers and a tweed jacket, and his hands were soft. His face told a different story, too. He was an accountant, a salesman or an office manager worn down by his job or home life, and he'd spent the night and early morning drinking and betting on horses that came in last. His story was in his face.

Wyatt watched the out-of-place drunk and let a plan gestate. More men arrived in dribs and drabs: a junkie caught purse snatching, two old vagrants and three TAFE students on a bender. Wyatt guessed that the police were also sweeping up possible shooters, but they'd be placed in another part of the lockup.

The morning wore on. Most of the other men looked harmless, but he was careful not to make eye contact with them.

He'd been locked up in an army stockade as a young man, and soon learnt how to handle it. You didn't smile; you kept your face neutral. You didn't accept the offer of a cigarette or anything else—it was never free. You never looked down—it indicated weakness. You didn't look hard or mean, either, for that was like a red rag to men who believed they were hard and mean and needed to prove it every day. And if a man did begin to get in your face, you needed to hit him immediately, put him down before he got very far with it.

And so Wyatt was left alone to doze and watch the tweed jacket, who remained deeply, drunkenly asleep.

At one point he saw furtive movements. Tweed jacket was reaching a hand into one sock, a thin, black businessman's sock, bunched around a spindly white lower leg and ankle.

Wyatt crossed the cell, dodging a restless schizo kid, who was pacing and muttering, and the vagrants, who were stretched out asleep on the floor. He perched beside the businessman and murmured, 'Don't let these guys see that.'

The man blinked behind his glasses. 'See what?'

Wyatt tapped a bony knuckle. 'That flask you've got hidden there.'

'Fuck you.'

'I don't want your booze,' Wyatt murmured. He indicated the other men in the cell. 'But these guys will take it off you in a heartbeat and kick your teeth in for the hell of it.'

The man blinked again. 'Thanks,' he said, and between them they worked out a way for him to drain his flask unobserved. It was scotch, he said. Almost full. The cops had got him to empty his pockets but hadn't thought to search his socks. 'Want a swig?'

Wyatt shook his head. 'What are you in for?'

'I was having a quiet drink in the pub and the landlord called the police, said I was being rowdy, which is total rubbish, I was simply minding my own business.'

Wyatt knew there was probably more to that story, but it didn't concern him. The jacket did. The glasses. The guy's name.

'Parker,' the guy said, shoving a frail white hand at Wyatt.

'Pleased to meet you,' Wyatt said.

Time passed and Parker drained his flask of scotch and soon Wyatt was aware that they were being observed from the other side of the cell. The drunk from the alley wandered across, his face elaborately innocent. 'Hi, guys,' he said, his gaze flashing up and down Parker's prone body. He sat close by on the other side of Parker. Wyatt breathed shallowly: their combined odours were of alcohol, cigarette smoke, grime, sweat and stale aftershave.

'Got a drink?'

Wyatt said levelly, 'Piss off.'

Ignoring him, the drunk got into a crouch and reached for Parker's flask. A moment later he was crumpled on the floor, unconscious, and Wyatt was flexing his fingers to ease the temporary numbness.

Parker mumbled and Wyatt said, 'The bastard was trying to rob you.'

Parker smiled and went to sleep. After a while, Wyatt began to swap clothes with the guy, all of his movements gentle and economical, and he finished by stretching Parker out on his side so that he wouldn't choke if he vomited. The other men watched. Their instincts told them to leave Wyatt alone. They'd seen the cold purpose. They went back to what they were doing—pacing, sleeping, bickering—and Wyatt washed his hands and face with spit and a handkerchief, finger-combed his hair, thumbed Parker's glasses onto his nose.

When he felt that no one was watching, Wyatt fished $200 from his shoe and pocketed it. Carrying a concealed wad of cash was instinctive to Wyatt, as familiar as breathing. He waited, intent on his surroundings. Passivity had set in among the other men, and little was happening outside the cell, which was part-way down a long corridor. Now and then a constable wandered by, checking that no one had died, choked or attacked another prisoner. A couple more men were delivered to the cell, a sullen teenage dealer and a middle-aged man in tears. Wyatt, standing next to the corridor, heard them being booked. The station was understaffed; arresting and holding a few drunks was an irritation. It wasn't proper police work, not when a killer was loose. The drunks would be released after four hours, and the small-time dealers and thieves brought before a magistrate, but the whole process would be repeated the next day, and the day after that.

In the early afternoon the custody sergeant came by with a doctor and they took the schizoid kid away. Later still the students were told their parents were outside. 'We're releasing you into their custody,' the sergeant said.

Twenty minutes after that he came back and called the name that Wyatt had supplied when he was booked.

Wyatt didn't respond.

'Warner,' said the custody sergeant again.

Wyatt uncoiled from the wall and said, 'I think it's one of those guys.' He pointed to Parker and the man from the alley.

The sergeant nudged each man with his boot. 'Come on, get up.'

They didn't stir. Cursing, the sergeant called out the next name on his clipboard. 'Parker.'

'That's me,' Wyatt said.

The sergeant was escorting him up to the front desk when they were forced to give way to a couple of hard men in suits, heading down the corridor towards the cells.

'What's up?' said the sergeant, his hand on Wyatt's elbow.

'Don't know,' said the file clerk. She looked to the desk constable for an answer.

'They think one of our drunks might be the shooter from this morning,' he said.

Wyatt tensed. The arresting officers hadn't taken his fingerprints before throwing him into the cell. He was only a drunk, after all, obliged to sleep it off for a few hours. But what if the police decided to start printing every man in the drunk tank? Wyatt had never been arrested but didn't doubt that his prints had been collected and stored in some national database. Now and then over the years he'd been forced to go on the run, obliged to leave behind a bolthole, a bank vault or a body. If the police ran his prints and got a match, they'd arrest him for past armed robbery and murder offences. Not to mention looking at him very closely for the hit on Eddie Oberin.

'You're kidding,' the sergeant was saying.

The constable peered over the desk at Wyatt. 'So what's this guy's story?'

The sergeant laughed. 'He's a pisspot. We picked him up before the shooting.' He leaned over the counter. 'Check for a Parker.'

The constable ran his finger down a list, said, 'Got it,' and handed over a large envelope.

The sergeant nudged Wyatt through glass doors to the footpath. A service road bisected the space between the police station and the courthouse. Parked cars, a few plane trees, police officers running errands between the two buildings.

'What will happen to me?' Wyatt said. He guessed he was no more than a couple of minutes ahead of a permanent place in the system.

'Depends. Plead guilty to being drunk in a public place and we can take care of the paperwork in about, oh, a couple of hours? Plead not guilty and it will be a fucking hassle for you and for me.'

'Guilty,' said Wyatt, eyeing escape routes and obstructions. There was tension in him.

The custody sergeant laughed, then nudged him. 'Nah, just joking. You're free to go. Just lay off the sauce, okay?'

He handed Wyatt the envelope. Parker's wristwatch, wallet, keys and handkerchief. 'Thank you,' Wyatt said, abject, like a man of good character.

36

First he put plenty of distance between himself and the lockup. Using Parker's money, he bought a train ticket to Box Hill. Parker's keys told Wyatt he drove a Toyota fitted with remote locking, but there was no way of telling where he'd left the car. The wallet held $160 and plenty of cards: Visa, Medicare, driver's licence, Blockbuster Video, HBA and the ambulance service. Parker had also listed himself as an organ donor, had a bewildered-looking wife and two toothy blond boys, and had ignored his bank's warning not to store his PIN with his cards. According to a credit slip with the cash, Parker had withdrawn $500 earlier in the day. With any luck his daily limit was $1000.

At Box Hill Wyatt disappeared into the shopping centre and found a cheap department store where he bought jeans, a white T-shirt, a cotton jacket, a baseball cap and wraparound sunglasses. He changed in a public men's room and donated Parker's jacket and trousers to a Red Cross opportunity shop. After that he went looking for an ATM. There were several; he knew he'd be filmed at all of them. Choosing one at a bank near the highway, he pulled the cap down over his face, keyed in Parker's PIN and withdrew $500.

Then he set out to spend it. First he took a taxi to Melbourne airport, which was hectic, the queues long. He bought a Virgin Blue ticket to Sydney using Parker's ID, then in the shelter of a men's cubicle he tore up the ticket and tossed the pieces into a bin. All he wanted was for Parker's name to show up on a computer. Then he queued with newly arrived passengers at the Skyways bus. By late afternoon he was back in the centre of the city.

Now it was time to alter his face again. It was all about suggestion. This time he suggested the great outdoors, buying sale items in a camping store: walking boots, cargo pants and a jacket overloaded with pockets and patches. To Wyatt, camping and hiking were ludicrous activities, he couldn't imagine engaging in them unless he was on the run from the law, and amused himself by calculating how he might rob the store.

He finished with a cheap MP3 player and headphones from a discount store. The device was empty and switched off, but that wasn't the point: he didn't want anyone to talk to him. He walked across town to the station and boarded a train for Frankston. The carriage filled with office workers and schoolkids, their lives pointless and unimaginable. As always, he watched, gauging who might help or hinder him if things fell apart.

The doors closed, the train pulled out. Wyatt swayed with the motions of the carriage and worked out what would happen next.

First, he needed to know the full story behind Wednesday morning's hijack. Eddie Oberin had been raving about bonds worth millions of pounds: was that the real target all along? He remembered how light the titanium cases had felt, with no hint of any metal objects shifting around inside them. If Eddie could be believed, the cases held bearer bonds and most were pocketed by the arresting officer, female, name of Rigby. Wyatt needed to learn her story.

Then Lydia Stark. Recuperation in a private clinic under the doctor's care, after which she'd need to lie low and maybe disappear.

That left Eddie Oberin's girlfriend, and only old ground to go over. He'd search the North Melbourne house again, question Lydia again, spread money around inside Blue Poles again.

The spring racing carnival was on. At Caulfield station the doors opened and a horde of racegoers stumbled aboard the train. They were young, raucous, the women underdressed and hanging on to mouth-breathing boys unused to wearing suits. They were mindlessly having fun and would mindlessly marry, raise families and vote. It was not contempt that Wyatt felt. He was barely curious about them. Some of them would have money one day, that was all, and he'd take it away from them.

He rode with them all the way to Frankston. A few of the young women glanced sidelong at him, momentarily calmer and less shrill. In the minute flexing of their arms and thighs, the tiny motions of their throats, they betrayed their awareness of him. Their friends and boyfriends retreated from their minds. Wyatt rode in a cocoon of their longing and felt safe.

The spell broke at the end of the line. He saw them blink awake and shriek again and stumble away on their high heels, in their cheap, flimsy, tasteless dresses. He followed them out and then he cut down a side street to the lane where a few days ago he'd made his escape after robbing the harbourmaster. The .32 automatic was still on the roof of the clothing shop. When evening settled he retrieved it and headed back to the Southbank apartment.

37

Khandi Cane slept through Friday and found herself waking in a big bed in a little room full of sweetness: scarves draped over photo frames, Body Shop cosmetics, books on massage, aromatherapy oils in dark vials. Repulsed, she turned her head and there was the pub waitress beaming at her from the other pillow.

'Hi.'

Her voice was loaded with desire. Khandi felt vaguely ill. 'What's the time?' she croaked.

'After four.'

Khandi was confused. 'Morning?'

'Silly!' said the girl. 'Afternoon.'

'Oh, god.'

'I'm all sore,' the girl said, wriggling close.

Khandi remembered a tight, appreciative, squirming little body, wrists manacled to the bedposts with silk scarves. She groaned and reached for her cigarettes. 'Don't you have to go to work soon?'

'An hour.'

What the fuck was her name? Theresa? Tina. Khandi reached for and knocked over the glass of water beside the bed. 'Shit.'

'I'll get it, don't worry,' Tina said, springing out and running to the kitchen for a cloth. Desire flickered; Tina was slim and firm and soft and round all at once.

Tina returned from the kitchen and there was some dabbing and mopping that turned into other things, and sometime later—languid, but ready to face the world—Khandi rolled a joint.

Tina gave a little cough, opened a window and fanned out the smoke. 'I'm having a shower.'

'You do that,' Khandi said. She flipped open her mobile phone and called Mindi at Blue Poles. 'Anyone looking for me?'

'Where have you been? The boss is going mental.'

'Fuck him. I want to know if anyone's after me.'

'Like who?'

'I don't know,' yelled Khandi, swinging her long legs off the bed and planting her feet on a thick, ethnic-looking rug that somehow fanned her irritation.

'Well...'

'Well, what?'

'Don't yell at me. No cops, but there was this one guy.'

Mindi described a thin, calm guy. Pitiless, she said, uncharacteristically. Khandi churned. It sounded like Wyatt, the guy she'd shot in the park. How was she to know he'd been wearing a bullet-proof vest? Eddie's fault for not warning her, the treacherous, cuntfaced moron. A chink of something that might have been doubt surfaced in her mind. She'd failed to put Wyatt down and now he was hunting her.

Maybe. On the other hand, Eddie had told her where he lived.

But could she be bothered? She thought about it as she pulled her clothes on. Why not lay some rubber down and head for Sydney, where she was unknown. Find corners in which she could truly express herself. Tina wandered in, pink, rubbery and self-conscious, crossing Khandi's field of vision and turning on the TV set. 'Five o'clock news,' she said. 'The world at peace.'

It was said wryly and Khandi wanted to smack her. She bit her tongue and watched the screen. First up was a local story, a prisoner shot dead inside the Outer Eastern magistrates' court that morning. They showed his face, an old arrest photo.

Khandi tried to swallow. She couldn't name the heartache and desolation that swamped her. Her dear sweet man gunned down in chains, unable to protect himself. She'd never known a love but one—and he'd been taken from her. She wept, gulped and felt entirely alone in the world.

'Honey?' said Tina.

She was towelling her hair. In other circumstances it might have been appealing, even arousing. 'Nothing,' Khandi said.

Tina followed the direction of Khandi's gaze, craned her neck to see the screen. 'Another gangland shooting.'

'Looks like it,' Khandi whispered, knowing her voice might not hold.

They were showing footage taken at various times last night and throughout the morning. First the footbridge in the park, floodlit by a helicopter, cop cars strobing blue and red, shadowy figures and a body on the bridge. Crime-scene tape around Henri Furneaux's sports car. Then the courthouse this morning, more tape flapping in the breeze, armed response cops in helmets and flak jackets milling around, the newsreader connecting Eddie to the shooting of two men in Jacaranda Park the previous evening. 'Police carried out a thorough sweep of the area,' the on-scene reporter said, and the screen showed divisional vans arriving at the cop shop next to the courthouse and unloading a fair cross-section of humanity. Mostly men, mostly young, mostly black, Asian or otherwise foreign looking.

Khandi gave Tina a glitter of eyes and teeth. 'Spot the Aussie, eh?'

Tina stiffened and her face shut down. 'I don't fuck racists.'

Khandi sprang off the bed and slapped her hard enough to rattle her teeth. 'I don't fuck dykes.'

Without a further thought, Khandi left Tina's poky room, straddled and fired up her bike—twisting the throttle until the motor red-lined and the birds fled from the sky—and shot down the road and across the valley. She was filled with emotions, some of them unfamiliar and all of them exalted. Eddie was dead, bless his tight bum, and Wyatt was responsible.

Now he's coming for me, she thought. Am I scared? Am I, fuck.

Wyatt wouldn't expect her to go on the offensive.

She stopped short of the cabin and checked it in the waning light of late afternoon. Satisfied that the cops didn't know about the place—otherwise they'd have searched it by now—she stowed the money inside the woodheap and shot back down the highway in search of the man who wanted to kill her.

First things first. She detoured into the Chadstone shopping centre, which was going great guns at that hour of a Friday evening, and splashed some money around. Leaving her fishnets on the floor of a changing room, together with her crotch-length micro skirt, high-heeled boots and tit-flashing T-shirt, she headed off again dressed in sensible bone-coloured pants and a pale blue cotton shirt, with the Beretta automatic inside the most boring shoulder bag ever made, $8.95 from Target. Then she checked into a fleapit on Spencer Street where she cropped her hair and dyed it mousy brown. Checking the effect in the fly-spotted mirror, she almost gagged. These were the sacrifices she would make to avenge her man.

38

Before entering the Westlake Towers complex, Wyatt stepped into the laundromat on the other side of the street. It was empty but machines churned; jeans and underwear flapped inside a lonely dryer. He sat as if waiting for his load to finish and watched his building. It dozed in the evening light but he wasn't ready to walk across the road and enter it.

He heard a metallic squeak. The manager hip-bumping through the swing door in the back wall, carrying a plastic basket piled with sheets. He nodded. 'Long day?'

The manager grunted. She was rake-thin, bitter, hostile, wreathed in cigarette smoke.

'Me too,' Wyatt said.

She didn't give a damn about that.

After a while Wyatt said, 'I hear there was some excitement today, over at the flats. Cop cars, the whole works.'

The voice came sourly from her stove-in face. 'You're dreaming. I was here all damn day and nothing happened.'

She dumped the washing and went back through the swing door. Wyatt slipped across the road and up the stairs to his bolthole. Lydia's bedroom door was closed. He walked past it to the bathroom, stripped off, adjusted the water temperature and drew the shower curtain. He'd never noticed before but the curtain was patterned, a dolphin leaping across it in a subtle mix of shiny and matt plastic. He began to wash away the alley and lockup grime.

Lydia's voice sounded on the other side of the curtain, 'Where were you today?'

He poked his head out, hair water-pasted to his skull. She stood wreathed in steam, looking better. Some natural colour in her cheeks, some natural fire in her eyes.

But aggrieved. 'I woke early, but you were already gone, and there's a note on the kitchen table telling me to keep an eye out for the cops because Eddie's been arrested. How do you think that made me feel?'

'Give me five minutes.'

'Fuck that,' she said, wincing in pain. 'I spent all day not knowing what was going on. Eddie's arrest was all over the news, and suddenly he's all over the news again because someone murdered him inside the courthouse.'

Wyatt met her gaze, saying nothing. Watching the race of thoughts behind her eyes until at last he saw that she understood. She nodded once and left the room, the steam eddying with the motions of her body and the door.

Wyatt closed the curtain and rinsed off. He shaved, dressed in his room, and found Lydia in the kitchen. A glass of water sat at her elbow, together with a bottle of Lowe's painkillers. She didn't look at him as he entered. 'I'm supposed to take one every few hours, but they make me drowsy. I took one last night and it knocked me out. When I woke this morning, you were gone.' Her tone was flat, as if she had no control over anything. 'All day I was tense. In pain.' She paused, glanced at him. 'You're a pain.'

It was a weak joke but he smiled and then so did she. Wyatt said, 'Take it if you need it.'

'No. I need a clear head.'

Her tone was a warning, and he gazed at her and waited.

'Eddie and his woman tried to kill us.'

'Yes.'

'They killed Henri and Joe.'

'Yes.'

She gazed at him now. 'For you, everything changed when they tried to kill us.'

Wyatt shook his head. 'Nothing changed.'

He was going to elaborate, but saw the frown and the puzzlement clear from her face. 'Betrayal's always on the cards,' she said. 'You expect it, right? If it happens, you act on it.'

'Yes.'

She hugged herself and stared at the floor. 'Poor Eddie.'

Wyatt saw that it wasn't grief. She was letting go of Oberin, and accepting a buried aspect of herself. In this game, there was no shrugging your shoulders and walking away. Her eyes, when she lifted her head, were clear. She understood what Wyatt had done and who he was, because the ground she walked on overlapped with his.

'Are you hungry?' she asked. 'We could go out. I'll wear a scarf and sit in a corner. You do know how to go out on a date, don't you?'

'We have scrambled eggs or scrambled eggs,' Wyatt said, taking out eggs and milk.

Lydia slumped in her chair as if the strain had leaked away and watched Wyatt melt a dab of butter in a frypan. 'You do know about cholesterol?'

Wyatt shrugged. There were unimaginable reaches in the habits and beliefs of people. 'All I know,' he said, 'is there never was any jewellery, we've got people after us, and tomorrow we get out of here.'

Lydia stared at him in frustration. 'That's tomorrow. Take a break. Tell me about yourself. Chill out.'

'More chills than chilling out in my life,' Wyatt muttered. He hated being questioned. There was no point to it. He never looked inwards, and there was nothing he wanted to impart to anyone.

'*Fine*,' she said, putting a hand to her face, eyes tight with pain. 'So what were Henri and Joe carrying?'

Wyatt told her what he'd overheard in the courthouse.

'Treasury bonds? That's not Eddie's style.'

'His girlfriend's style?'

Lydia looked doubtful. 'Maybe.' She paused. 'You think it was Eddie bullshit, accusing the cop of ripping him off?'

'He sounded genuine.'

'He would.'

They brooded on it. 'The thing is, Eddie and his stripper stuck around afterwards. Why would they do that? Why not disappear? Something else was going on.'

Wyatt watched her think it through.

She gave him a twisted smile as it hit her. 'They were *expecting* jewellery, same as us, got bonds instead. Didn't know what to do with them, decided to ransom them back to Henri Furneaux.'

Wyatt nodded. 'Something went wrong and Eddie got himself arrested.'

Lydia was looking into the distance. 'Do you think he talked?'

'He knew where I lived. The police would have swooped by now.'

Butter was spitting in the frypan. Wyatt beat, added and stirred the eggs. 'But we do need to leave here.'

'Do the police know about Le Page?'

'Damn,' muttered Wyatt. He hadn't thought of everything. He unhooked the wall phone and dialled the Sofitel.

'I'm sorry, sir,' the desk clerk said, 'we have no guest here of that name.'

A false name, Wyatt thought, or Le Page was gone.

39

Across town, two suits from Ethical Standards were sitting across from Lyn Rigby in one of the station's interview rooms. Last night everyone had said, 'Good result, Lyn,' but now the whispers were flying.

'The shooter's been described as tallish, thinnish, tanned or olive skin, wearing a suit. Ring any bells, sergeant?'

'Why should it?' Rigby demanded. She was tired; the air was stale and sweaty. 'I wasn't there. It's Outer Eastern's case.'

Friday, early evening, and all Rigby wanted to do was go home. She contemplated her job, her mortgage and the men who ran her life. When you happen upon treasure worth millions, you dream in the millions. It would be hard going back to the reality of her paycheck, only the passing of the years and a stingy pension ahead, and one measly bearer bond for £25,000 to pad it out. That's if she managed to avoid the sack— or prison. No one was saying 'good result' any more.

'You don't know anyone like that?'

'Everyone knows someone like that.'

'You put away a hitman two years ago.'

'Hitman? The guy was a drunk, hired by another drunk to shoot his wife. That's the extent of my knowledge of hired killers.'

'You'd want Edward Oberin dead, wouldn't you, sergeant?'

Rigby supposed it was an angle she'd investigate if she were one of the dogs in Ethical Standards. She'd been the arresting officer, running her own operation, wanting to interrogate Oberin without a lawyer present. A lawyer who didn't exist. They'd have listened to the interview tape, leaned on Whelan.

'Why would I want to kill Outer Eastern's prisoner?'

'Oberin implicated you in the theft of treasury bonds worth millions of pounds sterling.'

Rigby knew that your body could betray you, but couldn't recall what the indication of a lie was—something about glancing off to the left, or was it the right? She looked straight ahead.

'Absolute bullshit,' she said. 'Sir.'

'Why did you arrest him?'

'I told you already: the Furneaux shootings.'

'You believed he was the gunman?'

'Yes.'

'But you didn't at that stage have GSR or ballistics results.'

'Yeah, like heaps of people walk around carrying freshly-fired guns every day.'

'Careful, sergeant.'

She gave them a blank face and tried not to swallow. 'Plus he was in possession of stolen goods.'

'Found *after* you arrested him.'

'His prints were on the bag and the bonds inside it.'

'What were you doing there in the first place?'

Rigby figured that outrage was her best tactic. 'Didn't you ever operate solo sometimes? Back when you were a proper cop?'

The suits didn't flinch. 'According to your statement, you saw Henri Furneaux clearing out various bank accounts—'

Rigby tensed over the desk top between them. 'The day *after* his delivery vehicle's stolen and torched. What does that tell you?'

'We ask the questions. So, prompted by your suspicions, you followed the brothers out to Jacaranda Park and witnessed an exchange and a doublecross.'

'Not exactly. I couldn't see—'

'You saw two suspects on motorbikes.'

'One left the scene. Then I heard a couple of shots and was in time to see the second rider drive up to the Mercedes and shoot Joseph Furneaux. Only I didn't know it was Joseph and I didn't know Henri was dead on the bridge. All I wanted to do was go in pursuit of the second bike.' She paused, gave the suits a snooty look. 'Just as well I did, really.'

'We've heard the radio logs. You weren't very forthcoming to the dispatcher.'

'I had a job to do, and I could see witnesses calling it in.'

'When you arrested Oberin he had nothing in his possession—no gun, cash, drugs, jewellery. No gym bag.'

'Before he legged it behind the burger place I saw him remove the bag from his bike.'

'He dumped it in a bin.'

'Correct.'

'And when you recovered it from the bin it contained two Bank of England bearer bonds.'

'Yes.'

'Oberin claimed there were more than that, a lot more.'

'Well, he would,' Rigby said.

'I put it to you, sergeant, that you accompanied the Furneaux brothers to the park to protect an investment and it went pear-shaped.'

Rigby was shocked. She hadn't expected this tack. 'No way. Absolutely not.' She stabbed her chest. 'I'm the only one who showed any gumption in this case. And you can tell my boss I said that.'

'All right, how about this. You were running an investigation that no one sanctioned or believed in and when you found a gym bag crammed with bearer bonds worth millions of dollars you thought you'd reward yourself.'

Well, that was spot on. Rigby settled her shoulders, jaw and chin against the Ethical Standards officers and said, 'With respect, this is glass-ceiling bullshit. You guys hate serving alongside female officers, especially those who show initiative and get results.'

'Nice try, sergeant. According to the paperwork, Henri Furneaux met with a courier from Europe several times a year.'

She kept her face empty. 'Yes.'

'Is he presently in this country?'

'I've no idea.'

'Was it this man who shot Oberin this morning?'

'I have no idea. Look, it's late, I need sleep. Can I go?'

'I don't think so, do you?' More sheets of paper were turned and scrutinised. 'According to the computer logs, you accessed various data bases today.'

'Yes.'

'Why?'

'You know why.'

'Why don't you tell me?'

'Oberin told me his partner's name: Wyatt. I thought I'd see what we had on him.'

'And?'

'Whispers. Nothing concrete.'

It went on like that. An hour later she was letting the Ethical officers and a couple of uniforms into her house, insisting, 'There's nothing here, I'm telling you that now.'

The inspector cocked his head at her. 'Are you sure, Lyn? You sound a bit tense to me.'

She checked her agitation. 'I just think it's bullshit.'

The inspector relented. 'Look, you know the drill: if there's a complaint or an accusation, we're obliged to follow it up. Otherwise this could come back and bite us on the bum.'

'You won't find anything.'

'In that case, you're in the clear.'

'Who's to say you won't plant something on me?'

The inspector leaned his bulk over her. 'Fair warning, sergeant—the more you mouth off, the more inclined I'll be to dig my heels in.'

'Sir.'

'You can wait in the kitchen.'

'No thanks.'

'Suit yourself.'

She followed them from room to room, edgy, on the verge of cracking. To cover it, she sniped at their hamfistedness and amped up the victim routine. 'It's obvious Oberin wanted to get at me,' she said, to whoever would listen.

Four men searching her house. She couldn't cover them all. And then the inspector got to the kitchen ahead of her and said, 'Well, well, well, what have we here?'

For a moment, she could scarcely move or breathe. She found him standing by the table.

'Sergeant Rigby?' he said.

Thank God. It was the Furneaux paperwork he'd found. Don't fold now, she told herself. Keep up the stance. 'So what?' she demanded. 'I've been working the case in my own time. My other work doesn't suffer.'

'Lyn, Lyn, Lyn...'

'What, what, what? Everyone takes files home.'

'Not everyone.'

'So sue me. Anyway, it's a year's work down the gurgler and I still don't know what they were up to.'

The Ethical officer put the files to one side and began to sift through her e-mail and Internet printouts. 'You have been busy.'

'So?'

He waved a newspaper story at her. 'You think the bonds came from a street robbery in London?'

'Maybe.'

'You think the courier brought them in?'

'Maybe.'

'You're full of maybes. Okay, back to the station,' the inspector said.

Rigby folded her arms. 'Not me. Tomorrow's a work day and I'm going to bed.' She paused. 'Soon as I clean up after you lot.'

'Knock it off, Lyn. We had to investigate, you know that.'

'Yeah, but this kind of thing sticks to you. Always there on your record.'

She was fishing. The inspector sighed. 'Yeah, all right, Lyn, we'll mark it "cleared, no further action".'

40

Saturday morning. Wyatt woke to find Lydia lying beside him, asleep. There was a little dried blood on the pillow, but her colour was good. He watched her and he touched her upper arm. He couldn't believe he hadn't snapped awake the moment she'd crept into his bed. How long had she been there?

Why was she there? Desire? Insecurity? Maybe it was a simple longing for closeness, one of those feelings he wanted to act on but rarely did because he didn't understand its meaning. It was unnerving. He found himself leaning over her. She was breathing steadily and all of the strain was gone from her face. He stroked back a comma of hair caught in her mouth, revealing the down on her cheek and shapely lips, the corners tipped up as if in a smile. Thinking the tiny, chocolate-brown spot beside her earlobe was an imperfection that perfected her, he put his lips to it, and, after that, didn't know what to do.

Flustered, he eased out of the bed and left the room. Using the kitchen phone he said, 'Doc, she needs to be moved today.'

'The private hospital we talked about?'

'And her bandage needs changing,' Wyatt said.

'I'll be there at lunchtime.'

'You know the drill.'

'I know the drill,' said the doctor testily. 'I call her mobile if the coast is clear, the apartment phone if it's not.' He paused. 'You owe me now, Wyatt.'

Wyatt terminated the call before Lowe could ask him to steal the John Brack that was hanging on his wife's bedroom wall.

Lydia entered the kitchen with a sweet, sleepyhead look hinting at embarrassment. She touched his wrist as she passed on her way to the sink, where she filled a glass from the tap. 'Sleep well? I slept like a log—no painkiller, either.'

Wyatt nodded, his mind racing. There were proprieties he didn't understand, and had never been taught, but his instincts kicked in. It seemed unfair to say nothing; besides, he liked finding her next to him. He should be so brave.

'I'm sorry I didn't wake up when you came in. In other circumstances...'

She went red. 'It's okay.'

Wyatt shifted on his feet. 'The doctor's coming later this morning. He'll take you to a private hospital.'

'Where are you going?'

He stared at her for a beat of time. 'To see the cop.'

'Take me with you.'

'No.'

There was a pause in which Lydia stared at Wyatt as if realising he couldn't offer her any satisfactory resolutions. 'I want to...When I'm better, maybe we could hook up together.'

Wyatt knew they'd recognised each other's aptitudes. Complementary ones, especially for the kinds of heists that needed a woman's face and touch. But she was ill. He needed to find another base, and this current job hadn't yet run its course.

Only seconds elapsed but they were seconds too long. Lydia looked past him at the window and the city glistening beyond the cold glass. She was looking into the future, Wyatt guessed, and back at all that had been lost. It unmoored her. He wondered what he could do about that. He saw the inescapable truth in the old saying that you're bound forever to those you save. She came close, reached up and kissed him quickly, soft lips on his mouth. Then she walked to her room and shut the door with a click so quiet and final it was like a slam.

Wyatt swallowed. He gathered the .32 and his remaining cash, sets of false ID and the deeds to both of his apartments. He pocketed the pistol and the cash, but addressed the ID to himself care of *poste restante* at the GPO in Sydney, and wrote brief letters of instruction to the firms that would broker the sale of the apartments. Then he drove away in his old car and posted the letters at a box on a side street before heading away from the river.

He parked near the Outer Eastern police station and used the payphone of a nearby 7-Eleven, asking for Sergeant Rigby, not knowing her first name. He watched the front and side doors of the police station as the officer on the other end of the phone shouted to someone, who shouted to someone else, and the receiver was apparently bashed and knocked flying. Then the voice said, 'Putting you on hold.'

Wyatt waited, hoping that Rigby worked on Saturday mornings, and was in the station. He thought about the detective, not surprised that she was a thief. As he saw it, incompetence and corruption were the main forces that drove humankind. All that interested him was what Rigby might do in the next little while. If she still had the bonds, she had four choices: hold onto them, sell them, destroy them or enter them into evidence.

The voice came back to Wyatt: 'Transferring you now.'

Rigby had the voice of a woman habitually suspicious and offended. 'Who is this?'

'Jeff Grofield, *Herald Sun*,' Wyatt said. 'I wondered if I could ask a few questions regarding Thursday night's shooting.'

'How did you get my name?'

'Your neighbours said you'd be difficult.'

'My neighbours? Fuck—' and the line went dead.

Wyatt was in his car with the motor running when the detective came running from the building. He stayed a few car lengths behind her silver Golf, but she was intent on what was ahead of her, not behind. Struggling to keep up, he tailed Rigby to a street in Glen Iris. Running from Burke Road, it was no more than one hundred metres from end to end. This part of the suburb consisted of small, older-style brick houses along narrow streets, backed by alleyways. The uniform colours were green and terracotta—the gardens, the tiled roofs—but among the old cottages were boxy new cement and glass houses showing a rolladoor garage to the world like a blinded eye. A world of glum professionals jealous of their modest wealth, thought Wyatt, slowing at the entrance to the street, noting where the Golf came to rest. There would be security systems on every door and window.

He U-turned and parked on the other side of Burke Road. If he had to make a run for the freeway, this would save him a few seconds. He got out and crossed the road, hovering at a bus stop to watch Rigby's movements. The detective's house was the shabbiest. Rigby stood in the weedy driveway, glaring at her own front door, then both ways along the street, hands on her hips. Finally she tried raising the neighbours, but no one was at home. She accosted a couple of builders; they shook their heads.

Wyatt watched, and when she climbed back into the Golf and drove away, he walked to the bottom end of her little street. There was a whiff of renovation in the air, the dump bins crammed with builders' rubble. No dogs threw themselves at him as he passed by. The only sounds were the distant freeway, a tram on Burke Road and the blaring radios of the carpenters and bricklayers. At the end he saw, past a couple of iron bollards, the intersection of two alleyways. A short distance along one of them was the entrance to another street. Here was an alternative way out, should he be cut off from his car.

Then he prowled along the alley that ran behind the woman's house. Cat piss. Garbage. Stopping at Rigby's back fence he peered through a gap between planks and saw patio doors, curtains drawn across the glass. Checking that he couldn't be seen, Wyatt climbed over the fence and dropped onto rock-hard dirt. She'd been trying to grow a creeper. The creeper was dead; the soil was dead. That was her life right there, Wyatt thought dispassionately: long hours, overtime, fatigue and miserable expectations. No wonder she'd been quick to pocket the bonds.

He eased himself onto the decking. The boards were rotting but didn't shift or creak. The only furniture was a deck chair, the torn, sun-faded canvas patterned with palm trees, cocktails and sunglasses. If Rigby had dreams, they were weathering to nothing on this forlorn patio.

Brick walls, tiled roof, overgrown bushes and the drooping branches of demoralised suburban eucalypts. Wyatt skirted the place once, keeping close to the walls and the whispery touch of a few ferns, examining the doors and windows. The burglar alarms were basic but effective, arming entrance and exit points rather than the rooms within. Siren box high on the side wall. He crept around to the back yard, where he was screened by the high fence and oleander bushes, and glanced up at the roof. Fixed to the wall just under the peak was a dark shape: an air vent into the attic. He doubted it would be alarmed; he doubted there'd be sensors in the attic.

Time to go in.

41

Tyler Gadd, a nice little buzz on, was also contemplating a break-in.

He rejected the roof of Wyatt's apartment building, not having a helicopter to hand; also the various balconies and windows, not having a ladder, a rope, or drain-pipe skills. As far as Tyler could see, entry was only via the underground car park, for which he didn't have an electronic gizmo, or the front door, for which he'd need the keypad code.

Maybe he could walk in behind one of the residents. He sat in the courtyard common to the four apartment blocks and waited. Ten a.m. Eleven. No one went in or out. Then a woman returned from walking her dog. Instead of keying in her access code, she stood there foursquare with the dog, watching him.

'Do you live here?' she demanded.

'Yeah. I—' said Tyler.

'No, you don't,' the woman said. 'Piss off.'

She knelt and unclipped the dog, which had short hair, a ropy spine, and teeth.

'Bitch,' muttered Tyler, moving off toward the street.

He returned ten minutes later. A young chick with a daypack came along, Chinese, some kind of slanteye anyway, wearing glasses with black frames, fine black hair that reached down to her tiny butt, discreet gold here and there on her fingers, ears and neck. Where did these Asian kids get the money? Tyler wanted to know. This chick with her swanky apartment, designer jeans, leather pack and iPod. It made him mad. He wondered, as he strolled over, whether it was true, the slit on your oriental female ran east-west, not north-south.

He was behind her as she reached the keypad and then there was an explosive jabber behind him, some guy, boyfriend, brother, waving his arms around. Tyler veered right, heading down the side of the building as if he'd been going in that direction all along.

At the rear of the apartment block he found a small fenced area for garbage and recycling bins. The gate was locked. Tyler moped about for a while, then scouted around for a way in. He tried standing on a water meter at the intersection of the fence and the wall, but it wasn't high enough. Fed up, he went out into the street to walk around and think it through.

Someone had abandoned a supermarket trolley in the alley beside the laundromat. He wheeled it to the rear of Wyatt's building, hopped on and hauled himself over the fence.

So far, so good. And there was a rear door—but heavy steel, mounted flush to the wall, and dead-locked.

Tyler thought again. Hoping that he was unobserved, he opened the nearest garbage bin and took out a stinking bundle of rubbish crammed into a black bin liner and fastened with a bright yellow tie. He set it on the ground, untwisted the tie and scattered fists of sodden tissues and a couple of egg shells across the concrete paving, then rested on his heels to wait.

Late morning the door opened and a young guy emerged, cell phone clamped to his ear, two empty milk cartons hooked on the ends of his fingers. He scarcely noticed Tyler, moving in a smooth dance through the door, dumping his milk cartons into his recycle bin, returning to the door, all the while yapping away on his phone in the argot of the middle-class cokehead surfer dude.

'The bag split,' interrupted Tyler, indicating the mess at his feet, holding both hands away from his body as if they might be soiled. 'Need to grab a broom. Hold the door for us?'

The guy complied, straight-arming the door and continuing to speak on his phone. Tyler ducked past, into the building. 'Thanks, pal.'

'Awesome,' the guy said.

Tyler didn't know what was awesome, his ruse to get inside the building, saying thanks or calling the guy a pal. He ran up an echoing stairwell to the fifth floor before the guy could take stock and wonder who Tyler was and where he lived. He lurked for a few minutes, waiting for silence to settle, then walked down to the first floor and Wyatt's apartment.

Tyler ran his gaze around the edges, lock, handle and hinges. A guy like Wyatt might spit-paste a hair or a thread on his door to warn of unwanted visitors. Nothing. He took out his picks and one minute later was inside the apartment.

He didn't know what he'd been expecting, but not this. Four walls full of paintings lit by spots. He squinted at the signatures: John Brack, Mike Brown, John Olsen, Lloyd Rees, Margaret

Preston. Nobody he'd heard of. Only one of the paintings made sense, some fucking cups and saucers.

Plus books, CDs, shelves of them. Quality furniture, rugs and lights. Tyler felt weird, standing there in the quiet and calm. He felt obscurely uncool; wrong-footed by Wyatt's apartment. He was moved to trash the place as he searched. There was little other satisfaction to be had, no footie poster on the wall, no beers in the fridge.

Nothing but an unlocked safe. No bills or other paperwork, no photos, birth certificate, letters or postcards. Wyatt was a man without a history, a disquieting image in the corner of Tyler's eye.

He settled down to wait. Took out one of Ma's pistols and snapped the safety off.

An hour passed. Two. Tyler fixed a snack, sank half a bottle of vodka, tried to be patient. Jerked off half-heartedly; snoozed for a while.

When he wasn't doing those things he collated his grievances. One, Wyatt warning him off. Two, Ma warning him off. Three, Wyatt and his pals dropping out of sight. Four, the jeweller guys getting topped before he could squeeze a reward out of them.

Fuckwad losers, the lot of them. Whereas he, Tyler Gadd, was going to be the guy who got the guy who shot Eddie Oberin inside a courthouse.

There was a knock on the door. Tyler jumped. He crept down the hallway, put his eye to the peephole and saw the chick.

42

On the side street in Glen Iris, Wyatt stood on the low-pitched veranda roof and prised off Rigby's attic air vent. He ducked, expecting trouble, when the rusty screws screeched free of the rotting frame, but the street was tomblike. Saturday morning. The inhabitants were at Ikea and Mitre 10.

He slipped into the ceiling cavity. Stale, dusty, and the joists creaked. He crept with a small torch between his teeth to the trapdoor and opened it. This was an old, high-ceilinged house and he knew that once he'd lowered himself out of the attic there'd be no easy way back up again.

He landed with a thud that reverberated through the floor and walls, and froze. Nothing stirred. Rigby would have set the door and window alarms when she left the house, so he went searching for the terminal box, finding it beside the main junction box in the hallway. The alarm system was wired into the phone system, and there was also a battery backup in case of a power failure, so he couldn't risk turning the power off to disarm it. But he could trick the unit by flattening the battery. He identified the battery circuit and then scouted around for something to wire into it. In the end he used a cordless razor from the bathroom. When the battery was flat, he closed the main circuit breaker then disconnected the phone wires. Now, if it came to it, he'd be able to walk out of the front or back doors without setting off the alarm.

Time to hunt. He checked drawers and cupboards first, then moved on to common hiding places. There were no hidden skirting-board compartments, nothing under the cistern lid or in the freezer, and the curtain rods were solid wood, not hollow. The house was exactly what it seemed to be, the home of a woman with no life beyond her work.

But she was a cop. She would know the concept of hiding in plain sight. Also, he realised he'd gone about his search as though looking for something bulky, like wads of cash or bunched jewellery. Paper was flat. He refined his search, lifting rugs and carpets, checking files, riffling through the reams of printer paper on her desk.

Then he told himself that bonds can be rolled into tubes— and there it was, inside the rubber-stoppered chrome leg of her retro kitchen table. A bond with a face value of £25,000. If she'd hidden others in the house, he couldn't find them. He slipped it inside his sleeve and sat down to wait. She would still be thinking about that phone call from the *Herald Sun*. There was a good chance she'd be back.

Twenty minutes later he heard the front door and she was hurrying into the kitchen. He observed the usual little jerk of shock and waited while she said what everyone said: 'Who the hell are you? How did you get in here?'

Her gaze went to the hallway, the keypad and the table. She looked tense and addled, her hair scraped back, her pants and jacket wrinkled. There was a file under her left arm, a briefcase in the other hand. Wyatt showed her the pistol. 'I want you to sit. I want you to concentrate.'

She sat.

'I came for the bonds,' Wyatt said, to get that out of the way.

'What bonds? Who are you?'

'You know exactly who I am. Eddie would have told you.'

Her eyes slid a little. 'Maybe.'

'The bonds?'

Contradictory emotions played across Rigby's face. 'I don't have any bonds. Everyone's been saying I do but I don't.'

Wyatt fished the bond from his sleeve. She closed her eyes.

'Let's start again.'

'What do you want?'

'Where are the other bonds?'

'I've no idea.'

Wyatt let it pass. 'What happened on Thursday night?'

Rigby examined the worn linoleum floor. Wyatt racked the pistol and it sounded loud and final in the little room. Rigby jerked. She swallowed. 'I was following Henri Furneaux and his brother.'

'And?'

She sighed. 'There were two bikes, two riders. One got away with the ransom money. Eddie killed the jewellers and would have got away with the bonds if he hadn't fucked up.'

'Was the other rider a woman?'

'No idea.'

'Have you heard the name Khandi Cane?'

Rigby snorted. 'Some name. No.'

'Alain Le Page?'

'The courier? What about him?'

Her tone was indifferent but her fingers, resting on the file in front of her, went tense. Wyatt reached over and slid the file towards him across the table. He opened it and there was a photograph of Le Page's bony features, together with an e-mail from Interpol and printouts from Web editions of *The Times*, the *Evening Standard* and the *Herald Tribune*. Wyatt checked the e-mail date: Rigby had received it that morning. He scanned it: Le Page's address in France, and a note to say that he'd been seen in the company of members of the Russian mafia.

Pocketing the e-mail, Wyatt said, 'Tell me about him.'

'Are you going after him?'

'I'm asking the questions. Tell me about Le Page.'

'He shows up a few times a year, couriering legitimate precious stones and settings, but we think he also brings in stolen gear.'

Wyatt scanned the newspaper clippings, one hand on the pistol aimed at her chest. 'You think Le Page knifed the courier?'

She shrugged.

'Explain the bond hidden in your table leg.'

'So I stole it. So what?'

Wyatt's heart skipped and his mind raced. 'Are you under investigation?'

'No.'

Wondering how much time he had, he said, 'Where are the other bonds?'

'There were no others.'

The way she was slumped, one wing of her jacket was open. Wyatt fired, the pistol bullet plucking through the fabric and she shrieked and pushed back in the chair and fell to the floor, holding herself tightly. He tracked her with the gun, rising from his chair and leaning across the table. She was white and shocked. 'I'll ask again,' he said. 'Where are the other bonds?'

43

It wasn't until lunchtime that Khandi got to Wyatt's apartment complex in Southbank, there on some back street that had once been warehouses and light industry. According to Eddie, Wyatt lived on the first floor of Building D, apartment 6, blue door. Three other buildings just like it faced a courtyard, and that's where Khandi headed, feeling like shit, even if she was dressed like a fucking Sunday School teacher. A new look but old habits: last night she'd scored outside the King Street clubs and hadn't got to bed until four in the morning.

Stationed on a courtyard bench with a fat paperback and Fanta in a plastic bottle, sandals off, bare legs in the warm air, toes wriggling on the cool grass, she saw Eddie in her mind's eye, mouldering in the morgue. He'd thrown it all away, the sweet, deceitful, knucklehead. But gunned down in cold blood? He didn't deserve that. Khandi's grief was boundless. The love she'd shared with Eddie had been a wondrous thing. And cocksucking, motherfucking, retro hood Wyatt had stolen it away from her.

The lunch hour passed. Khandi was all but invisible. People assumed she lived in one of the buildings facing the courtyard, or worked in a nearby office. She was joined for a while by a young woman with a phone clamped to her ear. 'Where are you? I'm outside. Can you see me? By one of the benches.' Who fucking cares? thought Khandi, watching the woman wave and cross to one of the other buildings.

Later a young guy walked past with a dog, let it crap on the path near Khandi's foot, and walked on. 'Aren't you going to clean that up?' said Khandi, incandescent with rage.

'Fuck off,' the guy said.

Khandi fingered the Beretta and counted to fifty. Then a couple of students sat for a while on a nearby bench, clutching hands, full of angst. Apparently their situation was complicated: there was another person involved, and this person would feel hurt if she found out. Khandi shook her head. The solution was simple: either they got up a threesome or went at it guilt-free.

An old geezer came tapping along with a stick, weighed down by Safeway groceries. She watched him lift his gammy leg up the shallow steps to the front entrance of Wyatt's apartment building and pause at the keypad. Both of his hands were occupied. Khandi read his thoughts: first he'd have to place his shopping on the ground in order to enter the access code, then pick up his shopping again, but that would mean bending down twice, and could his stiff and crumbling spine and hips stand the pain?

Khandi slipped her sunnies to the top of her head and materialised at his side, carrying her Fanta, keys jangling reassuringly in her fist. 'May I help you?'

He turned to her and saw a young woman with a beautiful

smile. Beautiful eyes, too. Was she the one from the fifth floor? They came and went, these young women. Someone would snap this one up sooner or later: she was delightful, rather like his daughter, his daughters-in-law, even his late wife in her early years. And then an extraordinary thing happened. A sultry light came on in her eyes, her breasts appeared to swell and her whole being seemed to lap at him.

'Thank you,' he whispered, letting her take the shopping from his gnarled hands. Dazed, he entered the access code. She watched with a smile of encouragement and he was disconcerted to see that she was a pleasant young woman again. The siren call was gone. Had it ever been there?

'Let me help you into the lift,' she murmured.

'Thank you.'

He pressed the button for the third floor, so Khandi pressed four. When he got out, she stayed on, smiling at him as the doors closed. She exited on the fourth floor and walked back down the stairs to the first floor.

She encountered no one in the corridor. Apartment 6, blue door. She examined the door, using all of her senses. No sounds, no smells, but the eye-level peephole was lit from within. Wouldn't Wyatt switch off lights and draw curtains if he went out?

Some kind of animal awareness crept over Khandi. Checking both ways along the corridor, she drew the Beretta and clamped the barrel inside the empty Fanta bottle. Then she knocked, the makeshift silencer pressed beside the peephole, where it couldn't be seen. Presently she heard the faint susurrations of someone walking to the door and pausing to see who'd knocked. The peephole went dark, a head, an eye, blocking the light. Khandi fired through the door. She heard Wyatt drop with a slack, bony thump.

She dismantled the silencer, shoved bottle and Beretta into her bag, and strolled out of the building. It was over now. Time to retrieve the money and start again. As she was thinking these things, she collided with an older guy in a suit. Carrying a black bag, he was one of those brisk, clipped and combed doctor/lawyer/CEO types who paid to have sex with her. He was saying into his cell phone, 'Lydia? Doctor Lowe. I'm here to change your dressing.'

Another pointless mobile phone call. Khandi was about to curse him for bad manners when he said, 'And when Wyatt comes back we'll move you.'

Khandi went still. She tried to join the dots: 'Lydia' and 'dressing'. 'Wyatt'. The bitch hadn't died in her car; Wyatt had her stashed in his apartment. So who was lying behind the blue door? Maybe I only winged her just now, Khandi thought, the titless fucking dried-up ice-queen cunt. In which case she'd have warned the doctor guy, except he didn't look worried.

Khandi shrugged. Wrong door, civilian casualty. Swift and fluid, she pushed in hard behind the doctor as he finished keying in the access code. 'It's a gun,' she murmured.

He froze, halfway through the door.

'Take me up to Lydia.'

'Don't know what you're talking about.'

'And we'll wait for Wyatt to come home.'

'Who are you? What on earth are you talking about? You want money? Drugs? I have about fifty dollars in my wallet and a few painkillers in my bag.'

'Tempting,' said Khandi, 'but no.'

She could feel his fear through the pistol barrel hard against his spine. 'If you do what I say,' she said, 'you won't get hurt. You always call before you enter the building?'

'Why should I—'

A tiny resurgence of courage in his voice. To cancel it she ran the barrel down the crack of his arse and poked it in under the base of his balls. He gasped and began a jerky dance of fear. 'This is why,' she answered.

'Okay, okay.'

'Let's start again. You call before entering the building. Then what?'

'Er, I call again when I'm inside, to reassure them that no one followed me in.'

'Okay, do it, but tricks or tough-guy bullshit will get you nowhere. I'll shoot you in the spine and cripple you for life, then shoot my way into the apartment.'

The doctor was trembling again. His fingers shook as he worked the keys of his phone. 'Lydia?' he said. 'All clear, coming up now.'

They entered the lift. 'Push the button,' Khandi said, teasing the guy's hole with her pistol.

He pressed eight. *Eight?* Was he trying something on? Her mind raced. No, the little shit was way too scared. Wyatt must have two boltholes in the same building. The neatness and simplicity incensed her. She smacked the pistol against the doctor's skull for a while. So who the fuck had she just shot?

Wyatt. Had to be. She felt a surge of emotion. She'd plug old Lydia, then check it out.

44

Lydia had stuck to Wyatt's plan, stashing the mobile phone beside the bed when she rested, in the pocket of his thick robe whenever she moved around the apartment in the mornings and evenings, and in the pocket of her Levi jacket during the day. She was weaning herself off the robe. It made her feel like an invalid and that would delay her recovery. Besides, it aroused troubling sensations, the friction of the thick cotton pleasing, as though Wyatt was wrapping himself around her. She wanted him. It was more than attraction: she was like him in fundamental ways. Which was why she didn't want to be involved with him. A simple fear trumped everything: he'd get himself killed one day.

When the doctor called on the mobile, she uncoiled from the sofa and crossed to the window. She looked down. There he was, in the courtyard, short and misshapen in the angled perspective. A woman was standing near him, and, as Lydia watched, the woman swung around and stared at Lowe's back.

That bothered Lydia. She watched the woman follow Lowe to the entrance. Eddie's girlfriend? Lydia felt afraid and her eyes darted around the apartment. All of that fear was confirmed when the phone rang, the *landline* phone. The signal to run.

Lydia dithered, her heart hammering. She should warn Wyatt. She should get out.

Self first, Wyatt later. She couldn't risk the corridor, the stairs or the lift. That left the balcony, and Lydia slipped through a gap in the sliding door. A quick glance told her she couldn't climb down, and the adjacent balconies were at least three metres away, well beyond jumping distance.

But there was no other way out. She looked again. The balcony on the left was cluttered with pot plants and someone was at home, she could see a net curtain wisping in and out of the doorway, stirred by a breeze. The balcony on the right was empty and the sliding glass door had the implacable look of locked doors everywhere.

Panicked, she ran inside, racing from room to room. She lifted each mattress, but the bed bases were bolted to the frames and would be difficult to manoeuvre.

She discounted the chairs, the tables, the desk. There was nothing else. Maybe a broom handle?

That's how she found the ladder.

Stacked with the vacuum cleaner, mops and brooms was an extendable ladder in lightweight aluminium. Two metres long, it would extend to four, and she ran with it to the balcony, closing the curtain and the sliding door behind her. Now she was alone in the breeze from the river, eight storeys above the hard ground.

Wyatt, being a minimalist, had left nothing on his balcony to impede her movements. She extended the ladder, rested it against the railing and then slid it out until she'd bridged the gap between her balcony and the one with the plants and open door. She'd crawl across, slip inside and call Wyatt.

That's if the rungs and rivets held her weight. They seemed to protest. The metal flexed beneath her, bit into her knees and hands. Her wound throbbed and flared into an acute ache behind her eyes. Then she felt movement in one swaying wing of her Levi jacket, the breast pocket, and, reaching around with her right hand while balancing with her left, was too late to save her mobile phone. It plummeted to the ground, splitting open on the footpath, scattering fragments of plastic.

Panic washed through her. Her only record of Wyatt's number was on that phone. Now she couldn't warn him, he couldn't call her, they couldn't find each other.

Lydia scrambled across wanting to kick and weep, and when she reached the other balcony, and stood, her head rushed with stars. She reeled, clasped the railing. Controlled breathing, she told herself. The stars receded.

She recovered the ladder, restored it to its original length, and carried it with her into the apartment. She was in a living room. Seeing that it was empty, she concealed the ladder behind a sofa.

A student pad? She could smell incense and marijuana. Plenty of other clues, too, such as textbooks and folders scattered over a table, an open laptop with a Chinese boy's face for a screensaver, a pair of knickers on the floor, some bright cushions and scarves, and photographs of a smiling Chinese family posed before the towers of Hong Kong city.

But no one in the open-plan main room and adjacent kitchen. Whoever lived here was in the bathroom or the bedroom. Pausing to grab one of the scarves and pocket a pink mobile phone and $3.75 in coins, Lydia crept down a short hallway to an open door. She peeked and saw a Chinese girl lying on a bed, headphones clamped to her ears, eyes closed. The room was hazy; Lydia hoped the girl was stoned.

She pulled the door until it was almost closed. If fully closed, it might puzzle and alert the girl. If open too far, she might be seen, a movement, a shape flickering in the light.

Then Lydia stationed herself at the front door and looked through the peephole. By angling her head she was able to see a short distance in each direction. She saw the woman from the courtyard pass the door, prodding the doctor towards Wyatt's apartment, a gun at his spine.

45

Khandi shot out the lock and pushed the doctor in ahead of her. She raced through the apartment, using the guy as a shield, but it was clear that bitchface had skipped. Right apartment, though: the clothes in the bedroom, the cloying perfume hanging in the air, fine auburn hairs in the bathroom, bandages in the trash bin.

'Where is she?'

'Don't hit me,' croaked the doctor.

Khandi hit him. 'Where is she?'

'Don't know. I called her, you heard me.'

'You warned her with that second call.'

'No!'

Khandi pistol-whipped the doctor for a while. When the guy was on his hands and knees, spraying blood, mucous and teeth, Khandi nudged him with her toe. 'You're pathetic. What are you?'

The doctor spat again.

'Pathetic,' said Khandi. 'Say it: "I'm pathetic".'

'You're pathetic.'

Khandi was shocked. She began a battery of kicks, wallops and froth-flecked denunciations until the doctor was begging for mercy and the phone rang.

Wyatt was puzzled when Lydia failed to answer her mobile. He pressed redial, with the same result.

He ran through the explanations. She was separated from the phone. Someone had a gun to her head. She was unconscious. She was dead.

A knot of unfamiliar emotions started inside him. He stood in the shadows outside his building, trying to name the feelings. It was more than dread—dread tinged with grief. If she wasn't answering, someone had come for her. He should have waited with her, tackled Rigby later.

He shook off the regret. Regret was useless. Whatever had transpired in the apartment was less important than what happened next. Before going up, he dialled the landline number. If someone answered, he'd know more than he knew now. The apartment phone rang and rang.

Khandi stared at the phone, a black cordless on a small bureau pushed against the sitting room wall. She prodded the doctor. 'Answer it.'

He complied. 'Hello.'

Khandi tried to listen as the doctor grunted 'uh huh' a couple of times and said, 'Sorry, not interested.'

He replaced the handset and said, 'I think he was calling from India, something about phone plans.'

Khandi was a patriot. She didn't see why the country's banks, department stores and phone companies had to use overseas call centres, and she didn't like cold callers anyway. She shot the phone dead centre. Amid the smoke and racket the doctor crouched on the floor and whimpered.

Then one of Khandi's instincts kicked in. 'That was Wyatt, wasn't it?'

The doctor hawked and spat, and out popped a red tooth.

Wyatt ran down the incline to the underground car park and across the shadows, touching a handful of car bonnets out of habit. One, an elderly Holden, was still warm, the engine ticking as it cooled. Behind a security door in the far corner was a small, enclosed stairwell, with concrete steps that made one turn and ended at a metal door beside a storeroom in the foyer above. It was not continuous with the building's main stairwell and so Wyatt didn't know he had company until Khandi and Lowe appeared on the landing above him.

Nothing was said: he halted, the woman and the doctor halted.

He aimed the .32 at the woman. It was a difficult shot, on two counts: it was uphill, and she'd shielded herself behind Lowe. The doctor was irrelevant to Wyatt, but the woman didn't know that. Lowe made an effective shield, however. Only a corner of the woman's head was visible behind his left ear. Wyatt ran his gaze down the doctor, ignoring the dishevelled clothes and clots of blood. He could see the woman's left ankle and foot.

Wyatt weighed the options. It's more difficult to fire accurately up a flight of steps than down. On the other hand, he was ready to make his shot, whereas the woman's gun was still in Lowe's back. He had the advantage, but only for a second or so.

He studied her face. Plenty of hyped-up rage there, her mouth and eyes stoking the anger. Something personal here, Wyatt thought, and knew where his advantage lay.

'You shot Eddie,' she screamed.

'Like a fish in a barrel,' Wyatt said. 'He died calling for Lydia.'

It was inspired. The woman flung the doctor aside and crouched, swinging up her gun arm, and Wyatt shot her through the throat. He'd gone for a groin shot, but she'd ducked too quickly, surprising him, and the bullet tore through her gullet. She fired too, but twenty minutes of carrying a heavy pistol and beating it over the doctor's head had strained her gun arm. Her shot went low and wild, buzzing off concrete and over Wyatt's skull.

He stood. Lowe had scooted away from the woman, his eyes wild in their cut and swollen sockets. 'Is she dead?'

'You're the doctor.'

Lowe looked. 'She's dead.'

Wyatt hauled Lowe to his feet. 'We have to get her out of here.'

'What about Lydia?'

'Isn't she dead? In the apartment?'

Lowe shook his head. 'I warned her, using our phone signal. She got out.'

So why wasn't she answering her mobile? Wyatt didn't have time to think about the implications. He doubted that anyone had heard the shots—a small, enclosed location under the ground—but the stairwell was a convenient shortcut to the car park. Tearing off his jacket, telling Lowe to mop up the blood with it, he shouldered Eddie's woman down the steps and through the metal door. The tenants' cars sat in their bays like patient beasts in a barn, the air hung motionless and toxic. Wyatt hurried to the recently-parked Holden. It was an easy car to break into, the trunk was roomy, and the owner might have finished with it for the day.

He tumbled the dead woman into the trunk, and was returning to help Lowe when he noticed dry mud caught in the tyres of a nearby Land Rover. He gathered some of the mud and entered the stairwell. Lowe sat on a step, shocked, swiping uselessly at Khandi's spill of blood.

'Get up,' Wyatt said.

There was less blood than he'd thought, but he finished mopping and then crumpled the mud clods into dust and powdered the steps with it. It was makeshift, but would fool the eye. That was something Wyatt knew how to do.

He got Lowe into the car and away from the building. Out on St Kilda Road, he said, 'Are you going to be okay?'

'I didn't sign up for this.'

'Are you going to be okay?'

Lowe brightened. 'The wife's Bill Henson.'

Wyatt gave a twist of the mouth. 'Full recovery,' he said, stopping the car. 'This is where you get out. Go straight home. If Lydia contacts you, look after her. I've got things to do.'

'What things?'

Wyatt didn't answer but steered the Holden through the streets. Saturday afternoon, cars streaming to DIY stores and sports grounds, no one to notice him enter the forgotten corners where Abbotsford abutted the river. Seven minutes later he was wiping the car and setting it alight and walking away from another death.

Now he allowed himself to think about Lydia Stark. He didn't expect to see her again, but she'd rub against his thoughts like a pebble in a shoe.

46

Lydia had remained at the peephole, not daring to leave the Chinese girl's apartment. She heard shrieks of rage next door, and then Dr Lowe was being prodded back along the corridor, Eddie's woman screaming, 'Where was he calling from? Foyer? Car park?'

Wyatt, Lydia thought. She caught herself wringing her hands and stepping from one foot to the other. She didn't know how to warn him, she didn't know how to save the doctor, and she'd be going head to head with Khandi if she tried. She stayed put. Heard the soft boom of the heavy stairwell door, and then silence, as if all sounds were trapped. Five minutes passed, and in the bedroom behind her the Chinese girl coughed and yawned.

Lydia fled. Khandi had gone down the stairs, so she chose the lift. At ground level she poked her head out, half expecting to find a couple of bodies sprawled there. She felt claustrophobic, the entire building a trap. Breaking cover was her only choice.

Pausing at the front door to wrap the stolen scarf over her crown and ears, she stepped into sunlight. People would notice the scarf, nothing else, not her poor, bandaged, shot-up scalp. She didn't know where she was going or where she should go. Not that she'd get very far with only the Chinese girl's pink mobile and $3.75 to her name.

Hang on: if the SIM card from her damaged phone worked in the pink phone, she'd be able to call Wyatt. Head down, she skirted the courtyard and headed along the footpath below Wyatt's window, searching for the wreckage. On the path, and in the grass border, she found bottles, wrappers, shards of plastic and tiny scraps of soldered electronics. No SIM card.

Mid afternoon now. Lydia hurried away from Southbank, still with her head down. She couldn't risk making eye contact with anybody. They'd see the fear, and they'd want to help, or interfere, or at least remember. She had to be invisible now. Eddie was dead, Lowe probably dead, and although Wyatt didn't *feel* dead in the corner of her being that registered these things—he remained an unstoppable force going about his business—she didn't know for sure. The realisation broke her a little. Her eyes watered, she gulped and stumbled. She was on her own. She had no resources. She couldn't go home again.

Get a grip, she told herself. She knuckled her eyes and walked on, taking stock. Find money, then friends. A bolthole. Start with what you've got, even if it's only a handful of coins, the clothes on your back and a stolen mobile.

Recalling Eddie's nod-and-wink relationship with men in certain pubs around the city, pubs where no one asked questions, Lydia altered direction, heading northeast now, over St. Kilda Road and across the park to the Swan Street Bridge. She followed Swan Street into Richmond, the setting sun at her back. Wandered until she found a depressed pocket of greasy potholes, Housing Commission flats, pockmarked workers' cottages and the kind of corner pub that a woman down on her luck can fade into.

She bought a Coke poured over ice and wandered through the pub, stopping at a chokingly small side bar, the walls painted with decades of cigarette smoke and hopelessness. The sole occupant wore day-old stubble, an anachronistic ponytail and plenty of chunky gold. She watched for a while, and knew he was a guy who makes a living by sitting at a corner table and letting people come to him. So that's what she did. Seating herself across the grimy table, she murmured, 'I've got a mobile phone.'

He ran his gaze over her. 'Gis a look.'

She took it from her pocket and pushed it across the table. A milli-second later, the pink phone was in his lap and she could hear the beeps as he ran through the functions. 'You've got a bandage above your ear,' he announced, as if she mightn't have noticed.

Lydia tightened the scarf. 'Got shot,' she said, amusing herself.

His snort was derisive. 'Give you ten bucks.'

'Twenty.'

'Ten.'

She shoved out her hand. The guy wet his fingers and peeled a ten from a fat, dampish roll of notes, taking his time as if to underscore his contempt. Lydia got to her feet and returned to the streets of Richmond.

She almost gave up then. Having only ten dollars in her pocket was somehow worse than having nothing at all. Ten dollars was all she was worth, all she was capable of raising. Shoulders slumped, she wanted to weep.

Then she recalled her escape from Wyatt's apartment. Had she really done that? Done it alone? It had been a Wyatt kind of move.

Think like Wyatt. That would save her.

And so Lydia Stark began to map out the next few hours of her life. Planning, anticipating hazards and making decisions that took her to South Yarra, to a house she knew from tailing Henri Furneaux.

Furneaux had been dead since Thursday: surely the police would have finished searching his place by now? She watched and waited in the evening light for any sign of a surveillance team on the street or in a nearby house, but this corner of Melbourne slumbered, dense with shadows and sedated by expensive goods and old, hard-to-get-at money.

She darted into the front garden and skirted shrubbery to the main door. No key under the nearby rocks and pot plants, so she headed around the side of the house and found the laundry. She eyed the window beside the door. The street was unbearably silent; the whole world would hear it if she broke the glass. She began to edge back into the shadows.

But sometimes you just got lucky—did luck come Wyatt's way, too?—for at that moment a racket erupted from a shed on the other side of the fence. Drums, cymbals, guitars, tormented voices: teenagers, she guessed, a garage band. Lydia smashed the laundry window, reached through to unlatch the door, and entered the house. She wasn't worried about the alarm: the police would have turned it off and not reset it, knowing they might need to visit the house again.

First she searched the laundry itself. Still lucky. In a cupboard beside the sink she found a torch, masking tape and rubber gloves. Stepping through into the main part of the house, she moved from room to room, closing the blinds with her gloved hands and taping the edges hard against the frames. She knew that the windows wouldn't be entirely light proof so she kept the torch beam trained on the floor as she prowled through the rooms again, familiarising herself with the layout. Furneaux had struck her as a man who needed pampering, but the house was a newish box, barely furnished, with expanses of white walls and polished floorboards. A cold house, an unstamped house, not loved or lived in. At the rear she came upon glass, cold, uncurtained walls of it overlooking a terraced garden. She kept to the front rooms after that. She walked in Wyatt's skin—or maybe he walked in hers, with nerve, containment and a sense of focus.

There was plenty to indicate that the police had searched the place. Furneaux wasn't coming back to chide them, so she was obliged to wade through upended drawers, overturned mattresses and split-open packets of pasta and biscuits. Furneaux's computer had been confiscated and his desk and filing cabinet stripped of every sheet of paper. They'd ransacked the freezer and dumped the lid of the toilet cistern in the bath. The manhole cover in the hallway was still open, the laundry sink was full of detergent and the guts of the TV set were laid bare.

Lydia checked the garden shed and the garage: same story.

Maybe the police had already found Furneaux's escape stash. Lydia believed there had to be one: money, and passports, credit cards and drivers' licences in false names. She returned to the house and searched every room, drawn to the kinds of small, overlooked spaces found in any domestic setting.

All she found was dust and air.

There was something about the bathroom though. She tapped the tiles around the bath. Hollow. Everything inside her lifted in hope. She smashed her way in—more dust and air—and stood glumly. A moment later it occurred to her that Furneaux had fitted the room with a cluster of heat-demist lights above the mirror and heating rails for the fat towels. So why was there also a panel radiator bolted to the wall?

She returned to the garage and came back with a toolbox. The radiator lid was removable. Beneath it was a small hollow and $2500 in a rubber band, together with a credit card in the name of Leslie Shirlow.

Someone rapped on the front door.

Lydia ducked into Furneaux's bedroom. The wardrobe was crammed with suits. She adjusted the scarf around her head, then draped the darkest suit over her arm, together with a white shirt and a sombre tie, and made for the front of the house, working an expression of sadness onto her face.

'Yes?' she said to the elderly man on Furneaux's front step. He was bisected by the crime-scene tape.

He peered at her in the poor light. 'I live across the road. I saw lights on and thought I'd better check.'

Good thing he didn't call the cops, Lydia thought. Her voice loaded with grief, she said, 'Henri is—was—my brother-in-law. I just called in to collect a suit for his ... you know ... his coffin.'

The man was appalled to think that he'd been insensitive. 'Yes, of course,' he said, backing away, almost scuttling.

'Thanks for your concern,' Lydia said.

Sooner or later he'd think again about what he'd seen. Lydia ducked back inside, found a handful of shirts, T-shirts, pullovers, shorts and even jeans that might fit her, crammed them into a small pull-along suitcase, and left the house.

As she rode the last bus of the evening out into the Yarra Valley, Lydia thought about the name on the credit card: 'Leslie Shirlow'. Leslie was a name used by men and women. She practised writing the signature on a scrap of paper and began to think her way into the skin of Leslie Shirlow.

Ten at night and Yarra Junction was dead. Lydia walked into a motel and said, 'My car died.'

'You poor thing,' the woman on reception said, handing her a room key.

In the morning she set about finding Eddie Oberin's aunt's cottage. She'd been there only once, early in her marriage, about fifteen years ago, and the area had altered a lot. She didn't want to set tongues wagging or be bounced from pillar to post, her face registering with the town's busybodies, so she went straight to the priest. A strict Catholic, his aunt, Eddie had said.

The priest was old, frail, but remembered Eddie's aunt well. 'Dear old soul,' he said, drawing a spidery map for Lydia.

She shoved $50 into the poor box and returned to the highway, where she used some more of Henri Furneaux's $2500. Years since she'd ridden a bicycle, and the road beyond the town was winding and steep, petering out to a strip of degraded dirt and gravel. But at the end of it she spotted the cottage and dismounted. Tucking the bike behind bracken, she darted from tree to tree until she had good sightlines to the only doors, one at the rear, and a side door to the kitchen. She watched for an hour. She tossed pebbles onto the roof and against a window. No reaction.

Lydia went in. Eddie and his woman had marked the place: sex and other odours, empty bottles, food scraps, the stubs of a few joints. But it would do for a couple of days. She cleaned away the crap, swept, dusted, scrubbed. Then, knowing the temperature would plummet by evening, she set a fire. And found $120,000 stowed in a backpack under a pile of kindling, bark, twigs and pinecones. As though someone expected to come back for it pretty soon.

Clearly not Eddie, but a mad woman with a gun. Lydia shrugged the pack onto her back and returned to the bike. Fatigue ran deeply in her now, but she was alert for cars as she rode down into the valley again. Here a taxi took her to another town and a choice of three used-car yards. Wyatt was in her thoughts the whole way. She looked for a set of wheels that wouldn't attract attention, knowing that's what he'd do. Nothing fast, fussy or old. She almost selected a silver Corolla, until she realised the white Holden coupe gave her a dimension far removed from getaway driver, robber or fugitive. Farmer's wife, perhaps. Gardener. Someone into horses. Curiously, she began to feel a kind of release from Wyatt, knowing she was able to operate as he did. Their paths would cross again, or they wouldn't. He'd track her down, or he wouldn't. She didn't hope for it, wouldn't seek it, but wouldn't knock it, either. In the meantime, she'd be fine on her own. She'd been doing that for a long time.

She headed north in the coupe, picturing Wyatt's thin, watchful face, and gave a crooked grin as she saw him acknowledge, in some distant time and place, why she'd had to spend $9995 of their hundred and twenty grand.

47

Still the Westlake Towers slumbered. Wyatt crossed the road and went in, all of his senses tuned. Nothing tugged at him. He climbed to the eighth floor. Still nothing. A matter of time, he thought. The torched Holden would be traced back to his building, Rigby was ambitious, and other players might have talked.

He wiped down the apartment and made a final run-through of his possessions. A corner of him hoped to find Lydia Stark, hiding where Khandi and Lowe had failed to spot her, but she was gone.

And so was the ladder from the broom cupboard. He knew at once how she'd used it, and found the proof on his balcony, fresh scratch marks on the railing and the gentle exhalations of a curtain on an adjacent balcony. Wyatt kept tabs on everyone in the building. His neighbour was a student from Hong Kong and unlikely to have gone out leaving her balcony open.

So why hadn't she reported an intruder? Had Lydia hurt her? Lydia was like him in unwitting ways, and she'd have recognised two options: remain next door, hoping Khandi would think she was in the wind, or break cover, knowing there might be other shooters on the street.

Wyatt left his apartment for the last time and knocked on the neighbour's door.

He knocked again.

The security chain rattled into place on the other side, the door cracked open, and he was examined by a nervy eye and a wing of dark hair. 'My electricity's off,' Wyatt said. 'Is yours?'

The girl's head jerked back. He heard a light switch, and then she was opening the door, smiling shyly and demonstrating that she had power to her hallway light. She'd been asleep, her T-shirt rucked, her cheeks pillow-creased. 'Thank you,' Wyatt said, projecting his voice into her apartment. 'Sorry to have bothered you.'

She smiled again, and began to close her door. Lydia didn't come rushing out.

Then Wyatt realised that Lydia had a third option: his first-floor apartment. If she reasoned that Eddie's sweetheart had already searched it, she might go there. She might reason that he would, too.

He walked down the stairs, entered the corridor, and stopped. The gunshot odour was acrid and recent.

He crept to the blue door and saw the hole, the wood splintered, stippled with gunshot residue, and believed then that Lydia was dead. He didn't allow himself to feel anything but keyed the lock and pushed on the door, meeting the resistance of her body. He pushed harder, slipped through the gap, and stood for a moment, taking in the slumped body and pooling blood.

He'd been clenching himself. Relief flooded in. 'Tyler,' he said. 'You dumb shit.'

Lydia had got out, Wyatt knew that now. He swept through the apartment to make sure, and returned to the body. 'Dumb shit,' he said again, looking down on the sulky mouth of Ma Gadd's nephew.

Even dead, the guy was a problem. Late that evening Wyatt drove to a costly corner of Brighton, a quiet, leafy street by the water. He guessed Ma Gadd was an embarrassment to her neighbours with her pudding shape, worn-out slippers on swollen feet, whiskery moles, permanent cigarette haze and working-class voice. They'd hate her for lowering the tone, for being richer and cannier than they were. They couldn't even accuse her of nouveau vulgarity because that described them, behind their personal trainers, grammar-school children and BMWs.

It was almost midnight when he knocked on her door. He wasn't surprised when his answer was a gun barrel grinding at the base of his spine.

'Hello, Ma.'

'You're losing your touch, son.'

'I knew you were behind me, Ma.'

'Sure you did,' Ma said, letting her gun arm drop.

Wyatt turned to face her. 'You've got a leaf in your hair.'

'Shut up. I'm assuming this isn't good news?'

'Correct.'

Ma sighed. 'Let's go inside.'

No one could see them on the shadowy front step, for Brighton was a forest of dense hedges, but voices carry at night. 'Around the back,' Ma said.

Wyatt followed her to a deep, broad yard landscaped with roses: roses on trellises, in clumps or meandering along white pebble paths around goldfish ponds and beds of herbs and English flowers. The air was fecund, not unpleasant, and Wyatt breathed it in as Ma opened a glass door in a glass wall and ushered him to a honey-coloured cane chair beside a glass-and-cane table.

'Drink?'

'No.'

'I think I'm going to need one,' Ma Gadd said, leaving the sunroom.

Wyatt tensed a little, but when she came back she was alone and carrying a glass and a bottle of Glenfiddich. She poured, drained the glass, poured again.

'Where is he?'

'Lying inside my front door.'

'You put him there?'

'He put himself there, Ma.'

'You put him on the floor, I mean.'

Wyatt shook his head. 'He was waiting to kill me. Someone knocked on the door. When he put his eye to the peephole, that someone shot him.'

Ma gave a bleak smile and drank again. 'Hadn't the sense he was born with.'

Wyatt said nothing.

'He must have followed you home sometime,' said Ma, as if butter wouldn't melt in her mouth.

'That must be it,' said Wyatt.

They were silent, Ma apparently looking back down the years. She said, 'You pissed some people off and my nephew suffered for it.'

Wyatt didn't want her to read it like that. That's why he was here. He told her what had happened.

'You fixed this shooter?'

'Yes.'

Ma smiled without much warmth, accepting that Wyatt hadn't done it to please her. 'I hear there's a Frenchman.'

Wyatt stared at her. Ma had another hit of scotch and apparently slumbered for a while. Without opening her eyes she said, 'You don't want me for an enemy. That's why you came here tonight.'

'You've got a long reach and a longer memory,' Wyatt agreed. 'You know a lot of people. A lot of favours are owed to you.'

'Better believe it,' Ma said.

They were silent again.

'I suppose you could have dumped him at sea,' Ma said.

'If I had been the one who'd killed him, then yes.'

'Even so, you could have hidden him where he'd never be found.'

'If I did that,' Wyatt said, 'if he disappeared without explanation, you'd eventually come after me.'

Ma nodded. 'He was obsessed with you. He knew you had a job in the pipeline.'

'I'd never have cut him in,' Wyatt said. 'Not in a million years.'

There was a flash of something like anger in Ma, but then she sighed. 'True.'

'You have the resources to collect his body and give him a proper burial, no questions asked,' Wyatt said. He fished in his pockets, Ma watching like a hawk, and located the apartment key. He placed it on the glass top.

Ma nodded her thanks. At the same time, she was a businesswoman; making money was as important as familial rights and responsibilities. 'You get your apartment cleaned up. What do I get?'

'Apart from being reunited with your nephew?' Wyatt said, raising an eyebrow.

This counted as humour in Wyatt. Ma scowled and it was like a storm cloud gathering. 'You think that's enough? Tyler was a loser. His mother—my sister—was a loser. I'm owed something for the years of strife *and* for cleaning up your mess.'

Wyatt gave her his cold smile to show that he'd only been needling her. 'I'm selling the apartment. I've wiped it down and removed all of the paperwork. The furnishings are yours.'

'Terrific. A couple of Ikea chairs and a microwave.'

'Paintings,' Wyatt said, 'worth a quarter of a million dollars.'

'Paintings?'

Wyatt looked around at the open door to the main part of the house, the bare walls of the hallway beyond. 'Look good in there, Ma.'

He could tell she was intrigued. Her idea of decorating a house was to hang the walls with Collingwood Football Club posters and pennants. He wrote her out a receipt and handed over the provenance papers. 'They're now officially yours. They're clean, I bought them legally.'

'Warner?' said Ma, screwing her eyes up, the papers a centimetre from her fleshy nose.

'It's a name I can't use any more.'

'So where'll you go now?'

'Where the money is,' Wyatt said.

48

Le Page's corner of the world was at its best in autumn. Many
people preferred spring, but spring was too rampant for Le
Page's tastes, the blackberry bushes reaching out their ensnaring
canes, the trees overloaded with immature leaves, the bracken
too glossy, the rivers and hillside streams flowing unchecked
with the snowmelt, the roads, hiking tracks and villages already
choked with tourists. Le Page had never met a tourist who was
not vulgar and over-equipped. There was a factory, somewhere,
churning out tourist clones.

Give him autumn.

He liked to walk in the afternoons, and most days he took
a set route. His dirt-and-gravel access track wound for a
kilometre through a beech forest, under a small-leaf canopy so
dense that light and sound were diminished and his footsteps
were almost silent on the leaves that freckled the moist ground.
At a couple of places he was obliged to watch his feet over
washaways and patches of black mud where ever-running

streams cut across the road. In fact, the sound of water flowing over mossy stones and down the grooved runnels of the mountainsides was constant.

In recent days, Le Page had been listening for the sounds that didn't belong. He did it again today, but heard only the water, then the buzz and snap of insects and blowsy blowflies, and the distant tock and tinkle that marked the motions of the sheep in the meadows above, below and across from his mountain slope. The old ways still persisted here. The Toulouse bourgeoisie converted the old fieldstone barns and farmhouses into weekenders, homes away from home, and found themselves alongside shepherds who had never married, never left the mountain valleys but tended their little flocks, ruled by the seasons and the ways of their forefathers.

Le Page waved away a butterfly and stepped over a couple of jet-black slugs. He'd reached the head of his access track. To the right a dirt road wound upwards to a couple of summit farms and the steeper slopes above the snowline. He was rarely inclined to go that way, for it took him away from civilisation. He had little regard for civilisation, but it did exercise his mind and senses, and so he took the left fork, which wound down to one of the narrow sealed roads that stitched together the farms and villages. The trees cleared to sparser clumps of ash and silver birch, while the road itself was lined on either side by grass, nettles and blackberry bushes. Late berries hung from the snarling canes and he stopped for a while to pick and eat them. No one came for these berries; the locals and the tourists came for those on the walking track beyond the crossroad ahead of him. The track drew a winding inscription across the glossy green meadowland above the valley villages and farming compounds. Here you'd meet jolly, striding hikers, old men out walking and middle-aged couples picking berries, their little Renaults and Citroens parked below somewhere. You might meet sheep, too, and silent old shepherds. Once upon a time you'd have met smugglers passing to and from Spain, and during World War II you'd have encountered members of the Resistance guiding downed Allied pilots over the Pyrenees.

Le Page stopped at the crossroad to catch his breath. He could see the smudge of his house on a distant ridge, the roof catching the autumn sun. Before long—within weeks—it would be dusted in snow. The snow would accumulate until the steep pitch encouraged gravity to do its job. He glanced the other way, down along the road that plunged into a little valley, with a village at the bottom that served the clusters of nearby farm buildings, where farmhands turned silage and fed stock. He had no interest in knowing them or their old ways.

He started off again, pausing to check his letterbox, which was the second on the right in a line of boxes belonging to the householders who lived along the back lanes, where the postman was not obliged to call. There was one item, a business letter. He tore it open. His services as a courier for Levine & Levine, of Geneva, London and New York, were no longer required. There had been other letters like it, from other sleek firms, and Le Page knew that word of his association with Aleksandr had got around. But he had the bonds; he didn't need Levine & Levine. His life would move to a new phase—once he'd finished with the man named Wyatt.

It was a matter of honour. Wyatt tried to rob him. Wyatt ruined his Australian operation. Henri and Joseph were dead because of Wyatt.

Le Page was patient. He'd kept an eye on the unfolding story in the on-line editions of the Melbourne dailies, the *Age* and the *Herald Sun*: Eddie Oberin shot dead in a courthouse building, the body of a female gunshot victim found in a burnt-out car on the banks of the Yarra River, police appeals for the woman seen at Henri Furneaux's house to come forward.

The courthouse shooter was a man, according to witnesses. No doubt Eddie Oberin had made many enemies in the course of his undistinguished life, but Le Page saw the shadowy partner, Wyatt. Wyatt had succeeded in killing a man who was in a public place and escorted by armed police.

Just then, Le Page shivered involuntarily on the side of the mountain. He folded the letter from Levine & Levine into his pocket and stepped into the road again, heading for the valley. He passed a weathered stone cross. A testament to futility and madness, the cross had been erected by a grieving and guilt-ridden eighteenth-century farmer, who had tied his small son to a cow as punishment for being naughty, only to witness the animal trample the child to death.

Le Page walked for two hours. When he returned there was a message on his answering machine. He'd been expecting it. Knowing someone would come for him one day, he'd alerted the stationmaster, ticket collectors, village gendarme, shopkeepers and restless children to keep an eye on strangers entering the valley. Now Jeanne, a waitress in the station café, had called. Would monsieur care to call her back? She saw many strangers every week, but this afternoon one man in particular had caught her attention.

Le Page did not call but slipped out his back door and began a search of the little meadows and bracken thickets below his house, and the beech forest and glades behind it. The setting sun was at a shallow angle now and therefore perfect for tracking quarry or prey. Kicked-up soil, broken twigs, bruised grass stems and bent stalks, the moist undersides of disturbed pebbles, scrape-marks in licheny rocks or tree trunks, are best viewed in slanting light. He was also looking for footprints and the circular indentation of a resting knee, and listening for the wing beats, flurries and cries of disturbed birds and animals. Le Page read the natural world and moved in it like a creature himself. But there were no signs apart from those that he himself had left: no footprints, broken twigs, bruised leaf mould, snagged clothing or foliage bent away from the sun.

Which meant that Wyatt was too good for him, or would come in darkness.

49

Wyatt reached Le Page's house at dusk, and saw that it would be a mistake to go in until he knew more.

The light was tricky, he didn't know the terrain, and he'd lose if Le Page sensed him out on this mountain slope and came after him. He didn't know the internal layout of Le Page's house, either. He knew the position of the house in relation to the woodheap, well, generator, sheds and garden beds, but long grass and longer shadows blurred their precise configurations. A mess of shapes conspired against him. He might injure himself on a piece of machinery before reaching the house, and if he survived crossing the yard, he might set off alarms, sensor lights, guard dogs or a squad of armed muscle.

He tried to read the light again. It was throwing up stripes, tangles and dead spots as the sun settled. Then, as the moon rose, the light grew trickier.

Wyatt retreated to a shallow depression within an outcrop of rocks, where he stretched out on a mat of fallen leaves and rested, almost immobile, almost silent, as the long night passed. He'd done everything in his power to escape notice. For a start, he wasn't easy to see. His spot was hidden, he'd blackened his face and hands against torchlight and moonlight, he wore dark clothing and he'd tucked bracken fronds into his belt, pockets and collar. There would be no moon gleam from his knife, which was in a sheath, or his pistol, which was matt black and stuck in his belt. For hydration and energy he was carrying small amounts of food and water, which he took sparingly, keeping his movements to a minimum. The water was in a non-reflective plastic bottle, and he sipped to avoid sloshing the liquid. The food was dry and odourless—raw nuts and dried fruit in a small cotton sack that emitted no sound when he rummaged around in it.

And there were no telltale odours to betray him. He'd washed without soap or shampoo and wore no deodorant or aftershave. He'd thrown away his travelling clothes, for they'd become impregnated with cigarette smoke, exhaust gases and urban toxins, and he wore new clothing that he'd laundered in plain water.

Finally, Wyatt shut down his thoughts and feelings. No matter how well a man conceals his physical presence, he's also a mental presence. If Wyatt waited the night away in a state of heightened nerves or anticipation, Le Page's antennae would pick up the signals, for surely Le Page was a receptive man. There was a downside, however. If Le Page was as silent, odourless and barely human as Wyatt, then Wyatt wouldn't know he was there until the last second.

And so Wyatt rested. It was not sleep, exactly—twice he stiffened when foxes, somehow sharper-looking than Australian foxes, trotted past—but a kind of alert relaxation. And these hours until dawn were like a gift, allowing him to reflect. Curiously, the foxes reminded him of Lydia Stark: their russet coats, lean shapes and intent faces. He could have been looking for her right now, but moving against Le Page mattered more. Retrieving the bonds, or the money Le Page had realised on them. Then the sun crept between the mountains, lighting the meadows and trees, and he was ready.

The temperature was low; his breath fogged the air, a dead giveaway. Tying a scarf around his mouth and nose, Wyatt left his nest of leaves and headed towards the rim of the bank behind Le Page's house. He had two hundred metres of sloping land to cover, heavily treed, with many intervening traps: massive fallen trunks, rocks, animal burrows, open ground and the remains of a wire fence. He could not be completely silent, not when the autumn leaves swished around his boots and low branches brushed his head and shoulders. And the sounds of his progress would obscure the sounds of any potential pursuer. So Wyatt used an old technique: he took three slow steps, then stopped to listen, five quick steps, stop and listen. In this way he covered ground while giving himself a chance to hear Le Page or the man's dogs or hired guns. He decided that if more than one gun was after him, he'd shoot to wound rather than kill. A wounded man's cries of pain might unsettle the others' resolve and oblige Le Page to remove the victim, split up the team, restructure and re-plan.

By now Wyatt was halfway there, moving down-slope in a skirting, zigzag pattern that used up time but gave him a chance to learn the lie of the land and spot mantraps and ambush sites. He scanned constantly, not letting his gaze settle for too long or he'd miss the movement, object or person that might bring death. He was also listening, and whenever a sound troubled him he swung his whole body around, tracked with his whole being: eyes, ears, nose, gun hand. He knew that the one-second delay between finding his target and bringing his gun to bear on it could be the one second that killed him.

Even so, Le Page had most of the advantages. By moving, Wyatt was breaking cover, when his rule of thumb was to let the enemy make the first move, the first mistake. If he remained in hiding there was a chance that Le Page would feel the pressure, break cover and approach across ground that offered little or no protection, but what if Le Page was a man like himself, prepared to wait forever? Wyatt saw that it was better to go on the offensive this time. It was better to flush Le Page out than wait or go in so cautiously that Le Page had time to anticipate, outflank, backtrack or come in from behind.

The pistol was in Wyatt's hand, the knife strapped above his ankle. Twenty metres short of the bank above Le Page's house he saw a natural track. It took the path of least resistance between rocks and trees and disappeared down towards the house and sheds. The track was inviting: an innocent person would take it without a second thought. Wyatt didn't. He began to skirt around it and everything happened at once, good and bad.

Something, a shift in the atmosphere, made him twist and duck. That saved his life, for the lightweight crossbow bolt plucked through his shirt sleeve, through his sinewy upper arm, instead of his chest. He lost balance and toppled to the ground, involuntarily firing the pistol. The pain was acute and, stunned, he found his arm pinned by Le Page's boot.

Le Page said nothing but wrenched the pistol from Wyatt's grasp and took several steps back. He cocked his head at Wyatt, amused, the crossbow in one hand, the pistol in the other. 'I shall use your own weapon on you, I think.'

He pointed and fired.

All he got was trigger movement.

Wyatt had already fired the only bullet. The others were in a spare clip in his pocket. He'd been working on the principle that he'd only need one kill shot. If that failed, and his weapon was seized, then it couldn't be used against him, yet if he walked into a firefight then it was either too late or he'd have a couple of seconds in which to substitute the empty clip for the full.

Le Page blinked. That was a mistake, for it cost him a moment of time. He even turned the gun toward himself and examined it, and that cost him another moment of time.

Time for Wyatt to unsheathe and throw his knife.